ONE DOG
TOO MANY

D0817241

ONE DOG TOO MANY

A MAE DECEMBER MYSTERY

LIA FARRELL

CAMEL PRESS

Seattle, WA

CAMEL PRESS

Camel Press
PO Box 70515
Seattle, WA 98127

For more information go to: www.camelpress.com
www.liafarrell.net.

Cover design by Sabrina Sun

One Dog Too Many
Copyright © 2014 by Lia Farrell

ISBN: 978-1-60381-967-1 (Trade Paper)
ISBN: 978-1-60381-968-8 (eBook)

Library of Congress Control Number: 2013947719

Printed in the United States of America

Acknowledgments

———

We would both like to acknowledge and thank:

Our agent Dawn Dowdle, Jennifer McCord, Catherine Treadgold and their team at Camel Press, and Bob Pfannes, of the Ann Arbor, Michigan Police Force, for sharing his knowledge about how rural murder investigations are handled by local sheriffs.

Lyn's acknowledgements:

I want to first and foremost acknowledge the immense contribution of my daughter and co-author Lisa Fitzsimmons to this book. Her precise writing style coupled with her ability to see the humor in life have brought our protagonist to life. My younger daughter, Shauna, and my husband's daughters Lin and Jacquie have all been bulwarks of support during this process. My son Mark Farquhar has always believed in me. The support of all my children and grandchildren has been unfailing. Lastly, I would like to express my gratitude to my dear friend Jo Grandstaff, a fellow dog lover, who served as First Reader for this book.

Lisa's acknowledgements:

I'd like to start by thanking my mother and co-author Lyn Farquhar, who has been both the instigator and the driving force behind this project. Were it not for her energy, persistence and creativity, this book, (and the series) would not exist. Thanks also to my husband Jim—the love of my life and a very patient man—for his suggestions and perspective. My kids— sweet, smart, good looking, great dancers, good spellers, and downright hilarious, both of them. They inspire me in myriad ways. To Colton, Vivien and Kelly Lyn, for reminding me of what really matters in life. I'd like to thank my friends for listening patiently, and for their encouragement. My little sister is the best. She and M. always have my back. Thank you all.

Chapter One

———

March 18
Mae December

MAE DECEMBER RAISED her head from the pillow with great reluctance. She opened one eye and squinted blearily at her bedside clock. Six thirty a.m. What could have woken her at this hour? Then she heard it again. That blasted dog yapping out in the kennel. If only she could stay in bed a while longer, curled under her old quilt. The spring sunshine slanted through her window and warmed the bedding. The wood floor would be cold on her toes, but she had to get up. Her own dogs had the decency to wait until at least eight in the morning to begin whining for food, but Elvis—a pharmacologically challenged Pomeranian she was boarding—was up early.

Elvis was supposed to spend two weeks with her while his owner, Ruby, vacationed in Hawaii. It was now two days past her alleged return date and, despite Mae's repeated phone calls, Ruby was a no-show. Mae reluctantly pushed back her faded yellow-star quilt. Putting her bare feet on the floor, she stretched and rubbed the sore spot on her forehead.

Elvis continued his sharp and insistent yapping. Couldn't he at least be quiet the morning after St. Patrick's Day? Sighing, Mae put on a red sweater with her jeans and hurried downstairs into the kitchen of her 1912 farmhouse. There were older historic houses in Rosedale, Tennessee, and she was glad she didn't live in one of them. This house had been work enough. She had been remodeling for nearly three years, and in that time she'd gotten used to stepping over piles of sawdust and debris. At this point in the remodel, her kitchen only had one small piece of countertop left, but the coffeemaker was on and the smell of hot coffee mingled with that of fresh plaster in the morning air. Mae poured herself a generous cup. Thanking God for coffeepots with timers, she straightened her shoulders and slipped on her barn jacket.

As she walked by, the dogs squinted up at her from their beds. There were her two dogs, a black Pug named Tallulah and a Welsh corgi named Titan, as well as Thoreau, her former fiancé's elderly Rottweiler.

"C'mon, guys. Up and at 'em."

They followed her sleepily as she stepped out into the cool spring morning. Tallulah waddled along very slowly. Almost too pregnant to walk, she still managed a jaunty head tilt. Titan, on the other hand, plodded along with his head down. He was not a morning dog. Mae led the little procession out to the barn, where she got fresh water and food for her good, quiet, doggie boarders as well as the vociferous Elvis.

Returning to the house, she turned on her small kitchen TV and listened to the local meteorologist talk about the unusually warm weather. When the news came on, she could only stand a few minutes of details about the calamities around the world, so she turned it off and placed another call to Elvis' owner, Ruby Mead-Allison. No answer. The sore spot on her forehead was trying to become a migraine, which wouldn't go away by itself. She mixed a Goody's Headache Powder into a glass of orange juice and downed it quickly.

Several years ago her best friend Tammy had decided

that they were too mature for green beer and had declared Margaritas to be their official St. Patrick's Day libation. Mae hadn't wanted to go out at all this year but had conceded defeat after Tammy described her social life as "obscenely" boring. Making a mental note to limit herself to two Margaritas next time, Mae took her sore head back upstairs where she took a long, extra-hot shower. Swiping at the mirror with her towel, she gave her almost thirty-year-old naked self the once-over. She was a little pale this morning and her brown eyes looked almost black. Her soaking wet hair hung in dark blonde corkscrews over her shoulders. Mae turned sideways, tightening her abs—not bad at all. Then she turned to face the mirror and her rounded hips. She narrowed her eyes at their curviness. Well, Noah had appreciated all of her, even the extra ten pounds. Although she'd lost him in a car accident last February, memories of the man she would have married always brought a bittersweet smile to her face.

Foregoing makeup and leaving her unruly hair to air-dry, she put her clothes back on and went into her bedroom. The sun pooled temptingly on the four-poster bed. Resisting the impulse to climb back in, she smoothed out the sheets and fluffed her quilt, looking out the window at the barn. The feisty little Pomeranian's yaps continued unabated. There was no reason to call Ruby again. It was time to take action.

Mae hurried downstairs, grabbed her car keys and a tote bag and walked out to the barn. The other dogs glared at the noisy Elvis as she opened his kennel and seized him, swiftly popping him into her tote. Blessed silence reigned. Mae slung the bag over her shoulder and went out to her car. She hopped in and drove down the street to Ruby's house. With any luck, she could return Elvis and collect the rest of her fee.

Several soggy newspapers were strewn across the drive, and Ruby's mailbox lay on its side in the ditch. The existence of a mailbox on Little Chapel Road was precarious, to say the least. Mae had replaced hers five or six times in the last few years, thanks to wayward drivers. Picking up the mailbox, she set it back on top of its post, then walked to the front door with Elvis in her bag and rang the bell. No one answered. On her way around to the back, she tried peering through the garage window, but it was too grimy to see much. Finding the side door unlocked, she pushed it open and glanced around. Ruby's car was parked inside. She had driven herself to the airport, so she must be back in town. Irritated, Mae walked to the back door and knocked loudly. Still no answer. One of Ruby's red cowboy boots lay on its side beside the walkway so Mae picked it up and took it out to the car with her. Ruby had bragged about these boots the day she dropped off Elvis. She wouldn't have left one of her "high-dollar" boots lying on the ground. Where could Ruby be?

Feeling increasingly apprehensive about her neighbor, Mae drove Elvis and the boot to the sheriff's office in Rosedale. She'd been there countless times as a child, waiting while her freelance photographer father turned in photos to the sheriff or her journalist mother picked up tidbits for her column. The building was a time capsule from the fifties. Fluorescent lights flickered overhead and the whole place smelled stale and old.

Dory, the office manager, raised her eyes warily from her computer screen at the sound of the door opening, but her face lit up when she saw Mae. "My Goodness, child, I haven't seen you in ages."

Dory had been a close friend of Mae's mother for as long as she could remember. She'd outlasted several sheriffs in her forty-year tenure. Showing no signs of slowing down, she ran the office like a well-oiled machine. Her smooth, dark-brown complexion—she was Afro-American—and youthfully stylish attire belied her sixty-something years. Smiling broadly, she jumped up and enveloped Mae in a warm hug. Elvis gave a little chirp as the tote bag was squeezed between the two women. Dory opened the bag and laughed.

"You aren't bringing me that little critter, are you?"

Mae shook her head. "Don't worry. I wouldn't do that to you. I need to see the sheriff and get this dog back to his owner as fast as I can. How've you been?"

"I'm just fine, honey. You look good. Is everyone okay?"

"Everybody's doing well. Is the sheriff around this morning?"

"Between you and me, he's around here a little too much these days. When he doesn't have active cases he paces around and pesters me." Dory rolled her eyes. "Please entertain him for a bit, will you? Haven't seen very many good looking women around here lately. He always perks up when one comes in."

That was hard for Mae to imagine. She had seen pictures of the sheriff on his election posters. Such a good-looking man in a public position would have many women interested in him, wouldn't he?

"I'll buzz his office and you can go on back."

Sheriff Bradley sat at his battered desk, facing the door, which stood open. He was far better looking in person than in pictures, with blue eyes and light brown hair that curled back from his forehead. He stood up and walked around his desk, holding out his hand.

"I'm Ben Bradley, I mean Sheriff Bradley. Have a seat. What can I do for you?"

"I'm Mae, nice to meet you."

In addition to his handsome face, Ben Bradley was tall. At five foot ten, Mae had to tip her head back to meet his eyes. She sat down in the chair he indicated and adjusted the wiggling tote bag on her lap.

"I want to report that my neighbor, Ruby Mead-Allison, is missing. She's two days late getting back from her vacation in Hawaii and I found her favorite red boot lying in the backyard when I went over to her place this morning."

The sheriff sat back down behind his desk. Leaning forward, he rested his chin in his ring-less left hand. "I'm not following you. Why is this red boot so important?"

"When Ruby dropped Elvis off, those boots were on her feet.

She told me she got them to wear on her trip and that she was driving straight to the airport from my place."

"And Elvis would be?"

Mae rolled her eyes. "The King of Rock-n-Roll. As well as her neurotic, drug-addicted Pomeranian."

"Why do you have her dog? Are you a friend of hers?"

"Good heavens, no. I board dogs. Mae's Place is the kennel business I run out of my home on Little Chapel Road." Mae smiled at him. It certainly wasn't his fault she still had Elvis. She couldn't blame the headache on him either.

"You must be Mae December." A grin tugged at one corner of his mouth.

"Yes. How did you know my last name?"

"My nephew told me about you. He calls you the Puppy Lady. Apparently, you take your dogs up to the elementary school. He says the first graders read to your dogs and your name has two months in it."

"Yes, that's me. My real name is Maeve, but my older sister couldn't pronounce it when she was little. She called me Mae and the name just stuck."

"What's your sister's name?"

"Julia Grace. But I was born in May and she was born in July so my parents started calling her July after she changed my name to Mae." She shook her head. "Anyway, could we get back to Ruby? I've been keeping her little nightmare of a dog for over sixteen days now. She only paid for fourteen. I've been trying to reach her for the last two days with no answer. This morning I went over to her house to look for her and found this boot in the flowerbed by her back door. Her car was in the garage too, so she must be back in town."

"You seem pretty anxious to give her dog back."

"Oh, Lord, yes. He had the last of his tranquilizers the day before yesterday, and now he's running me ragged and terrorizing the other dogs."

"How many canines are we talking about?" An official look

clouded his handsome features. "There are ordinances, you know."

"I'm well aware of the regulations. I'm allowed to board up to ten dogs." Her cellphone rang. "I'm sorry, Sheriff, I need to take this. Excuse me a moment. It's my contractor." She turned her face away and flipped open her phone. "Joe, is everything all right?"

"Not really. Tallulah's in labor in the living room."

"Has the floor been sealed yet?" she asked.

Hearing a sigh from across the desk, Mae quickly ended the call and turned her attention back to the sheriff.

"I'm sorry. I need to get back home. My pug, Tallulah, is in labor. Apparently, I don't pay my contractor enough to be a dog midwife as well."

She reached into the capacious bag at her feet and pulled out the boot, using her other hand to keep Elvis inside. "Stay there, Elvis." Mae turned her brightest smile on the sheriff. He wasn't smiling back.

"Is that a service animal?"

"Please. He's no help to anyone and I really have to go. I think you should have this." She handed him Ruby's boot. When Sheriff Bradley reached out to take the boot, their fingers touched briefly.

"All right. I'll look into it," he said. "She'll probably turn up, but you be sure to give me a holler if you hear from Ms. Mead-Allison, okay?"

"I'll do that." Mae stuffed the grouchy little dog farther into her bag. "Right after I wring her neck."

MAE SPENT THE rest of the morning helping Tallulah deliver her five precious little Porgis. This new breed had become her specialty, a combination of a black Pug mother and a Pembroke Welsh Corgi father. Usually they were born black with a white ruff. They had the barrel-shaped bodies and short legs of their father and the shiny black coats, curly tails and flat faces of their mother. They were adorable. She was building quite a reputation for herself as a breeder. Mae's Porgis sold all over the country.

Dog pregnancies were approximately nine weeks long and Mae always had her vet x-ray Tallulah at seven weeks. Luckily, the dog could deliver without a C-section. The vet had state-of-the-art imaging equipment, so they had known that she would deliver five puppies for this, her fourth, and probably last litter. Pregnancy was hard on small dogs, and other breeders had told Mae that more than four litters could be unhealthy for the mother.

By the time all five pups were clean, dry, and nursing greedily, Mae's headache had vanished. She spent some time talking with Joe, her contractor, about the kitchen cabinets and the new granite countertops. He was a very cute and hardworking MOC (married, of course) with four little kids. Thin and wiry with sandy hair and green eyes, he sported a perpetual tan from his outdoor work and was a little shorter than Mae. He grew up down the street and had done most of the home remodels and repairs in the area. When she and Noah bought the house three years ago, several neighbors had recommended him. Joe impressed her with his careful work and they had since become good friends. He was leaving when the phone rang. The caller ID showed Suzanne December.

"Hi, Mama, how are you?" Mae said.

"I'm fine, honey, and you?"

"Well, I've had quite the morning. You remember Ruby Mead-Allison's dog, Elvis?"

"Um hum, is the little wretch still with you?"

"Yes, and it's been sixteen days. This morning I ran over to Ruby's to try to drop him off. She still wasn't home and I found the strangest thing. One of her fancy red boots was in the flowerbed by the back door. I took the boot to the sheriff's office."

"Whatever for?"

"I started to worry that something might have happened to her. She was wearing those boots when she dropped Elvis off. They're custom made, probably cost her a fortune, and she was headed to the airport when she left my place."

"Wasn't she going to Hawaii? She could have been rerouted because of that terrible storm. Or maybe she's hiding out because she doesn't want the miserable little beast back."

Mae laughed. "I don't think she'd pay for more boarding than she has to, and the woman plainly loves Elvis. The sheriff said the same thing about the storm. She probably ran into delays on her way back. If that's the case though, why was her car in the garage?"

"That is kind of odd. But on another note, I'm sure you know the conflict about your road is really heating up. Ruby will definitely be back in time for the meeting of the Road Commission tomorrow night. I think there's another protest scheduled in your neighborhood. She wouldn't miss it for anything."

"I can't think of a single reason why the road shouldn't be widened," Mae said. "I know Ruby doesn't want it, but even she'll have to see reason eventually."

Suzanne snorted inelegantly. "I doubt it. See if you can fish the newspaper out of the recycling and read my column. You'll get the picture. Ruby is really stirring things up. Anyway, do you want to come over for dinner tonight? Dad and I are having steak and there's plenty. Your sister and Fred are coming with the kids."

"I'll pass. Thanks. Tallulah had her puppies this morning. I shouldn't leave her alone yet."

"She did? That's wonderful! Is Tallulah okay? How many puppies did she have?"

Mae laughed at her mother's enthusiastic response. "She's fine. There are five healthy puppies. It's all good."

They said their goodbyes and Mae spent a few minutes imagining Ruby in an airport somewhere, pacing impatiently, demanding to know why the bar didn't stock Grey Goose with bleu cheese stuffed olives and making everyone around her miserable. The old saying about dogs and owners being alike was definitely true about Elvis and Ruby—both feisty redheads. No doubt, she'd be back soon. Ruby could be fun when she felt like making the effort. She was a manager for country music artists and sometimes shared salacious anecdotes about her clients at parties. Despite her stiff-necked prickliness, everyone would welcome Ruby home.

Sometimes when Mae drove down River Road to turn onto Little Chapel, she remembered finding the area for the first time with Noah, the man she had loved passionately and planned to marry. The disastrous car wreck that took his life had been a little over a year ago. According to the police, he took a turn too fast and careened down the hill to crash against a tree. She still felt a wave of sorrow whenever she thought of him.

When she and Noah discovered Little Chapel Valley, they felt they had stumbled into a secret place, one much farther than thirty miles away from Nashville. The road wound through a valley, protected by high hills on either side. The landscape was green and leafy. The day she and Noah first came here he had said, "I think we're in Narnia." Mae had felt the same. They had wondered if the road was an old Indian trail and, perhaps even earlier, a track made by the local deer population. In the spring she often saw deer with their fawns, moving silently through the valley and raising their white-flag tails. They seemed almost magical to her.

But now her Noah was gone. It still didn't seem real. A tear slid down Mae's cheek. Although she still grieved for him and missed him every day, Mae had found a home on Little Chapel road. She always felt safe here.

At first she worried that her neighbors would object to a kennel on their street, but everyone had been great about her business. She'd been careful to maintain the historic appearance of her sprawling old farmhouse. The old barn had to be replaced, but she tucked the new one for the dogs she boarded in the exact location of the original behind the house. Other than some repairs and a coat of fresh paint, the big white house with its wraparound porch and the little red barn looked identical to the old black and white photos Mae had found in the attic. The small "Mae's Place" sign that she'd put up by her mailbox was the only change visible to her neighbors. A close-knit group, they even treated Ruby well, despite the nearly constant trouble she tended to stir up.

THAT NIGHT MAE dreamed she was walking through an endless house, a long skirt of blue velvet swirling around her ankles. She entered room after room, crowded with puppies of different sizes and breeds. In the dim light, she tried to sort them by age and color, getting them ready for their owners to pick up. A chocolate lab pup followed her everywhere, holding the hem of her skirt in his mouth. She gazed down into his green eyes and he looked back steadily, wagging his tail.

"You have to let go now. I hear the doorbell."

Bending down, she pulled her skirt hem out of his mouth and turned away. She woke up with the phone ringing in her hand and the sheets twisted tightly around her legs.

"Hello."

There was no response. Just breathing.

She was fully awake now. "Who is this?"

A man's voice on the other end let out a laugh.

Sweat ran down between her breasts in the cool night air. "Tell me who you are. What do you want?"

"Good night, Miss December." There was a click, followed by a dial tone.

Chapter Two

———

March 19
Mae December

Elvis permitted Mae and the other dogs to sleep until almost eight the next morning, possibly the result of the warm milk she had given him at bedtime—laced with a few drops of brandy. The spring sunshine warmed the grass outside. Mae took her coffee to the front porch and sat there petting Titan, who gazed soulfully into her eyes, glad to have some attention. The forsythias were blooming and the front yard spread out below her, green and peaceful. The new kitchen countertops would arrive today. Mae took the opportunity, as she did almost every morning, to call Tammy, her best friend since the sixth grade. They had both gone to Rosedale Middle School and then high school together.

Tammy, an inveterate morning person, sounded happy to talk, even at this hour. That is, until Mae told her about her dream and the call that woke her from her restless sleep.

"That's a little scary, Mae-Mae. Are you sure you didn't dream the whole thing?"

"Yes, I'm sure. I almost recognized his voice when he called me Miss December."

"Did you try star sixty-nine?"

"I tried to do that once and was told it wasn't part of my package. It was probably just some weirdo. If he calls again, I might get rid of the house phone and keep only my cell and the landline for the kennel."

"That's a good idea."

Mae felt better. Tammy always lifted her mood. She wouldn't waste any more time on some mouth-breather with nothing better to do than call her in the middle of the night.

"It'll be fine. I should get on with my morning and let you go. Have a good day, Tammy. Bye."

Mae busied herself feeding all the dogs, except Tallulah, who hadn't eaten since delivering her pups and would only drink water. Next, she cleaned out the kennels. Back in her kitchen, she fed her bread starter and checked the calendar for the next time she needed to make bread. Her friend Cindy had given her the starter for Amish Friendship bread last year. It required some babysitting to cultivate, but the bread was delicious. She planned to make a batch of apricot walnut bread soon and made sure she had all the ingredients.

Cindy had given the starter to Mae after Noah's death. At the time, she had protested, saying the last thing she needed was something else to take care of. She could barely care for herself, let alone the dogs. But Cindy made her promise to try it out and pass along the starter when she had extra. In return, she helped Mae with the dogs. She learned a lot about dog training from Cindy and to Mae's surprise, she had enjoyed making the bread. Cindy lived in L.A. now but she emailed Mae often about her career as a trainer and dog walker for the stars.

Mae went out to the barn and put leashes on the two largest dogs in her boarding kennel, a Great Dane and a Rhodesian Ridgeback. After walking for about a mile, they came upon her neighbor, Mr. Ryan, walking alone. It was strange to see him without his dog, as the two of them were always together. His dog's name was Tószt (Hungarian for toast) but since no one could pronounce the word properly, everyone just called her Toast. Mr. Ryan was limping.

"Good morning. Are you all right?" Mae asked.

He was breathing hard and his face was pale. "Good morning, Mae. I'm fine, I just slipped and one of my feet went down into a pothole. How I wish they'd fix this road! I think I sprained my ankle. Tószt has run off. When I tripped, she pulled the leash right out of my hands. Who are these big guys?" He indicated her two boarding dogs, sitting quietly at her feet.

"This is Rusty." The Ridgeback wagged his swooping tail. "And the Dane is Christiansen. We'll walk you home. Then I'll see if I can find Toast."

They walked slowly to his house and Mae saw him safely inside, where Mrs. Ryan grabbed him some aspirin, a bag of ice, and a stretch bandage, before leaving to look for his dog—a Hungarian Viszla pointer. It didn't take Mae long to locate her. Toast was standing at the eastern end of Ruby's property, near the road. With her beautiful strawberry blond coloring and strong but slender build, she exemplified the breed standard. Mae had loved Toast since the Ryans brought her home two years ago as a puppy.

"Toast, come here." Mae walked closer. Toast's slender nose was pointed toward a little copse of trees and brush. Three black vultures were perched in one of the trees. Rusty whined, straining forward against his leash and a low growl rumbled from Christiansen. When Mae directed her gaze toward the area beneath the tree, she saw a flash of red. There was a sickly sweet smell and a sudden sense of dread made her stop in her tracks. She took a deep breath and made herself start walking again. As she neared the grove, one of the vultures flew down and landed on a red boot. The boot was on a foot. Her eyes travelled up the leg, then the torso. Below the head, a rubber-coated metal cord was curled around a long white neck that lay at an awkward angle. Mae was horrified to see that the woman's eyes were open and that there were flies in her open mouth. Mae gagged. It was her neighbor, Ruby. She was dead.

Mae staggered back and grabbed Toast's leash. With all three dogs in tow, she ran as fast as she could. She had to get home. She'd be safe there. That was the only thought in her head. When she got to the house, she put the dogs in the front fenced pasture and closed the gate. Her stomach heaved, and she pushed the door open, tumbling into the kitchen. She leaned against the wall for a minute and then slid down to the floor. After catching her breath, she stood up, grabbed the phone and called Noah's younger brother, Patrick. He was always helpful in a crisis.

"Hello." Patrick's voice issued sleepily from the receiver.

She couldn't speak for a moment.

"Mae, are you there?"

"Patrick, you have to come over here right now."

"Are you all right?"

She drew a ragged breath. "No, not really. Can you please come?"

"Okay. I'll be right there. Hang on."

She managed to say "thank you" before pushing the off button. Ruby's one bare foot flashed in front of her mind's eye—bluish-white, with dark red polish on her toes. Mae shook her head to clear it. She didn't want to picture Ruby's violent death. She took a deep breath to steady herself and called the Ryans to let them know she'd found Toast.

Patrick arrived shortly. He came through the door, shirt buttons askew and black hair standing on end, a frown of concern clouding his features. "What's wrong?"

Mae's voice shook. "I found my neighbor… I found Ruby's… Oh Patrick, I found her body."

"What do you mean 'her body'? Is she dead?"

Mae nodded wordlessly, staring into Patrick's pale blue eyes. There was a moment of pin-drop silence before he gathered her into his arms. She surrendered gratefully to his hug. His tall rangy body reminded her so much of Noah's. After a moment, he pulled away, giving her a worried look.

"Where did you find her? Did you call nine-one-one?"

"No, but I should have. If you ever find a dead body, you'll know how awful I felt. I panicked."

Turning away from him, Mae realized that she was calm enough now to pick up the phone and dial the familiar number.

"Rose County Sheriff's office, Dory Clarkson speaking. How may I direct your call?"

"Dory, it's Mae. I need to talk to Sheriff Bradley."

"What do you need to talk to him about?"

"Just tell him I found Ruby. Oh, Dory, she's dead."

"I'll get him, honey. Sit tight."

While she waited for Sheriff Bradley to come to the phone, Mae distracted herself from the image of Ruby's pitiful body by thinking about the ageless Dory. Her mother's friend was single now, but she had been married to Elmer Clarkson for many years.

Mama always said that Elmer had enormous charm and charisma. He left Rosedale years ago, but he and Dory were still in touch. Elmer was a talented bass player. According to Mama, he continued to play small gigs all over the middle south.

Mae glanced over at Patrick. He was standing very still, looking out the kitchen window. With his back to her, he could have been Noah's double. Making a marriage work with a musician had proved impossible for Dory and Elmer. Would her marriage to Noah have worked out? As a songwriter and musician, he would have been on the road many months of the year.

When Sheriff Bradley's voice came on the phone, Mae quickly told him about Ruby's body.

"Go back to where you found her. I'm going to call the medical examiner and we'll meet you there." He sounded very calm, a lot calmer than she felt. Mae hung up and turned to Patrick.

"He said to go back to where I found her."

"C'mon. I better drive."

They went out to Patrick's car.

"Go right, down past Ruby's house."

He nodded wordlessly.

Patrick pulled to the side of the road at the spot she indicated and shut the car off. They sat silently near the small grove of trees where Mae had found Ruby's body.

"Where is she?" he asked.

Mae pointed to the spot where she had found Ruby earlier. She couldn't walk back to the body, but Patrick did. She watched from the car as he went quickly to the grove of trees and looked down. He froze for a second then walked back to the car with a look of horror on his face.

"Well, did you see her?"

He got back in on the driver's side and sat staring down at his hands, which were clenched tightly in his lap.

"You didn't tell me she had a cord around her neck. Mae, Ruby was murdered."

Within minutes, Sheriff Bradley arrived with several other officers. They immediately surrounded the grove of trees with yellow crime-scene tape. Mae and Patrick watched from the car as more vehicles arrived, including a van with a "Crime Scene Investigations" side panel. An elderly man in a coat and tie got out.

Mae could tell, parked on the edge of the street, that she and Patrick were making Little Chapel Road even more of a hazard than usual. Patrick walked over to the sheriff, spoke with him for a few minutes and then returned. "The sheriff said we can go, but he wants you to be available when he's ready to talk to you."

They went back to Mae's house and sat down at the kitchen table.

"So it's possible she was murdered?" Mae's hands involuntarily went to her throat.

"There's nothing possible about it," said Patrick. "She had a cord around her neck. Somebody strangled her. I wonder why?"

Mae went through the recycling bin and pulled out some of her mother's columns, entitled "Suzanne about Town."

"I have to take off, Mae. Will you be okay?"

"I think so. Thanks for coming when I needed you." She dropped into a chair cluttered with old newspapers and a blanket. Maybe reading would distract her from the awful vision of Ruby lying in the damp grass, her wet nightgown twisted around her legs, splayed out like a rag doll. Mae got queasy again just thinking about it.

The sheriff knocked on her door an hour later. After a brief greeting, he stared at her intently. "You look awful. Would you like a drink of water before we get started?"

She laughed. "Where did you learn how to talk to women? You never start by telling them how bad they look, even when it's true. Yes, thank you, I'd like some water before you interrogate me. I'll get some from the fridge."

He shook his head. "I'm not going to interrogate you. I only need you to walk me through the events of the morning. Let me get the water."

He went over to the refrigerator and opened the door.

"The bottles are on the bottom shelf."

The sheriff bent over. *He has a cute behind.* She smiled at him when he handed her the cold bottle. The corners of his blue eyes crinkled when he smiled back. What kind of inappropriate behavior was this? She hadn't felt like flirting with anyone since Noah died. Now, after finding her neighbor's dead body, she was acting as if she were back in high school. She stood up unsteadily, grasping the edge of the countertop. "I don't feel very good. I'm not sure I can do this right now."

"I'll have to get your statement at some point, Miss December, but I need to go back to the crime scene anyway, check on my team and get rid of the spectators. If you'd rather wait, I can talk to you later."

Tears welled up in her eyes. "I can't believe Ruby's not here for the protest today. I didn't agree with her, but I respected her commitment to stopping development on our road. She organized the whole thing. Now she'll never march again."

"It's not a problem to wait. I'll come back. It looks like I'll be in the area."

Mae stood in her front yard, watching him drive away. A bluebird flashed by in front of her, its back and wings a vivid streak of lapis. Everything was quiet and peaceful. For the first time in days, Elvis wasn't barking. Maybe Patrick had done something to settle him down.

Mae walked into her kitchen. She was alone in the empty house; no one was sanding, painting or caulking. Joe had installed the new granite countertops, sanded and sealed the living room floor. The dining room was still an awful mauve color, but his crew would be repainting it soon. Mae had stripped all the woodwork on the staircase. The beautiful red color of the native cherry shone. She bit her lip. *Things last longer than people do.* Mae felt on the verge of tears again. She called her mother and left her a message about Ruby.

At about eight thirty that evening, Mae's older sister July drove up her driveway. Mae walked out to meet her, enjoying the signs of spring. The early jonquils were blooming, their pale yellow trumpets radiant in the porch light. They walked into the house and July admired the new cabinets and countertops. She wanted to see the newest Porgi pups and picked them up gently, one at a time.

"There are three females and two males. Is that a good mix?" July asked.

"Most people seem to like the females, but if the puppy is a gift for a little boy, they like the males. Everything works out."

"Mae, did you know there's a press conference being covered

by Channel Four News on your street? The reporters are down by the ditch near Ruby's house. That's where you found the body, right? Mama called and told me. I want to see if the news is on TV."

A perky brunette reporter interviewed Sheriff Ben Bradley, who said the deceased's name was Ruby Mead-Allison, that she was a manager for country music artists, and that his department was treating her death as suspicious. The reporter pressed him to say whether Ruby had been murdered, but he declined to comment. An older man stood beside the sheriff. He had salt-and-pepper hair brushed back from a receding hairline and a powerful build with a slight paunch. The sheriff identified him as Detective Wayne Nichols. They would both be talking with anyone who might have information about Ms. Mead-Allison's death. They urged people in Rosedale, or the middle Tennessee viewing area, to call the tip line if they knew any relevant details. The TV flashed the phone number over and over on a continuous loop.

Chapter Three

——

March 20
Mae December

MAE WOKE WITH a start. She lay on the couch with the television still on. July had gone home, leaving Mae two sleeping pills next to a glass of water. Mae picked them up and swallowed them with a big gulp of room-temperature water. After turning off the TV, she forced herself to walk upstairs and climb into bed. Her sleep was restless and troubled by terrible dreams.

When she went back downstairs in the morning, she found a note Patrick had left on top of the tarp covering her kitchen table. His note said Tallulah had eaten a grilled cheese sandwich and he'd be back later to help her look for Elvis. Mae remembered Patrick's frowning face in the middle of the night. Oh, God, did he say he couldn't find Elvis? Her stomach contracted with worry.

She flew out to the kennels with her cellphone in hand, praying Patrick had found Elvis before he left, but his dog run was empty. Patrick was often a source of mixed feelings. On the plus side, he had fixed Tallulah a grilled cheese sandwich, which she ate. One worry was off her mind. Tallulah would be able to nurse her puppies. Tube feeding them would have been an around-the-clock challenge. However, Patrick must have released Elvis for a quick run and the Pomeranian had never been trained to come when called. He certainly didn't need to be running loose with a crime scene down the street. She called Patrick and thanked him for getting Tallulah to eat.

"What happened to Elvis?" she asked.

"I stopped back about eleven last night, but you were crashed, so I let Elvis out for a minute. He ran into the kitchen and barked so loud I thought he was upsetting Tallulah. I grabbed him and tried to put him back in the kennel, but he got away. I'm so sorry, Mae. I tried to wake you. You were pretty out of it."

"It's okay. July left me two sleeping pills last night. That must be why I slept as hard as I did. That little demon probably did upset Tallulah, but now we have a free-range Elvis situation on our hands. Did you see which way he went?"

"He darted straight up the hill and into the woods. I tried to find him, but I couldn't see a thing in the dark. I knew I'd be too tired to play in my tournament today if I didn't get some sleep, so I had to go."

Patrick worked constantly on his standings in disc golf, hoping to go pro by the summer. Apparently, it was of vital importance for him to participate in all the tournaments possible. She sighed, wished him luck and got off the phone.

Mae stood in her unfinished kitchen and considered her options. She could drive around and look for Elvis, but he wouldn't surrender easily. However, she had seen several good-sized coyotes in the valley recently and he'd be no match for them. Mae grabbed her granddad's old walking stick out of the hall closet and was on her way out the back door when the unmistakable sound of Joe's decrepit work truck chugged up the drive. She ran out with the walking stick clutched in her hand.

"Whoa there, Hon. Where're you going with that weapon?"

"I'm trying to find Elvis. He's been missing since late last night."

"Now, darlin', it's time you realized the King is dead." Joe grinned. He must not have heard about Ruby yet, Mae thought or he wouldn't be so lighthearted. Joe and Ruby, although they had clashed in recent times, had a history. He had been crazy about her back in their younger days.

"Joe, I'm looking for Ruby's dog. Patrick let him out late last night. Ruby's ... Oh, I can hardly tell you what's happened. I found a body yesterday." Her voice broke. "It was Ruby's body. Someone killed her."

The grin slid off his face, and she reached out to hold him. A shudder passed through his body as he grabbed Mae's shoulders.

"Why wouldn't she listen to me?" He sounded angry. "I told her to watch out for that guy. She always did everything the hard way."

Who was he talking about? Before she could ask, the sheriff's car pulled in behind Joe's truck. Sheriff Bradley and an overweight, red-headed deputy got out of the car. Joe released his grip on her shoulders and turned to face the sheriff.

"Hey, I hope I'm not interrupting anything here." The sheriff grinned.

"Don't be an ass," Mae said.

The pudgy deputy put a hand to his mouth, partially stifling a laugh.

Then she shook her head. "Sorry, that was rude. Let's start over. Good morning, Sheriff, I just told my contractor, Joe Dennis, about Ruby's death. He's a friend of mine. He's also an old friend of Ruby's. Naturally, he's upset."

Ben's eyes narrowed a bit. "Are you an old friend or an old boyfriend?"

Joe took a deep breath and made a visible effort to control himself. "We dated a long time ago. Since then I've tried to be a friend to her. She didn't have many."

"I guess I'm going to need a statement from you too, Joe. This is Deputy George Phelps. We'll get your statement now, if that's okay."

"Sure." Joe turned to Mae. "Could we do this inside?" he asked.

"Of course. Feel free to use the house and get yourselves some coffee. I'll be back later. Right now I've got to go look for that dog."

"Take your cellphone with you," Sheriff Bradley called. "It's not as safe as you might think around here."

She took her phone out of her coat pocket, waved it at him and holding the walking stick, started up the hill. The minute she was out of sight she would call Tammy. She'd tried to reach her several times the previous day with no luck. By now, Tammy would have heard the news about Ruby's death, but she wouldn't know that it had been Mae who found the body.

She stepped into the trees and pressed three on speed dial. Tammy didn't answer. Mae left her a one-word message "Avalanche," their code for a bad situation requiring help and/ or chocolate. She'd know what to do when she got it.

After spending a fruitless twenty minutes looking for Elvis, Mae headed back down the hill and walked through her back door. Joe sat across from Ben at the kitchen table. Deputy Phelps stood by the back wall. He was operating a small digital recorder.

Tammy was leaning against the wall behind Joe. Her short, silver-blond hair was artfully tousled and her makeup was flawless, as usual. With her diminutive size, heart-shaped face and huge brown eyes, she looked like a waif in need of rescue. Men responded instantly. In her hand was a bakery bag. On her face was an expression Mae knew very well. She was up to something. Mae could only hope she'd gotten home in time.

"Would it kill you to put on some lipstick?" Tammy hissed.

Mae pried the bakery bag from Tammy's hand.

"Don't eat both of those brownies." She gave Mae a grin. "The smaller one is for me."

None of the men said a word. Ben was reading a piece of paper on the table in front of him. Mae took her brownie out and handed the bag back to Tammy. After taking a few bites, she casually leaned over to see Ben's reading material. He deftly slid the page under a newspaper, but not before she recognized the distinctive interlocked cherub logo at the top.

"When did you start using this new paper color, Tammy?" Mae kept her tone as mild as she could manage.

"Do you like it? I got tired of the pink, and I got a good deal on the copper color, so ..." She let her voice trail off, having intercepted Mae's evil glare. Tammy ran a dating service in Rosedale called Local Love. Mae had forbidden Tammy to put her information into her database. However, she could have sworn the sheriff was reading her profile.

Joe stood and picked up his keys. "I need to go. I'll be in touch. You girls try not to fight."

The men exchanged business cards. Ben kept his eyes on Mae the whole time. The sheriff was cute, but he was starting to get on her nerves.

"Is that my profile you're reading? I'm sure it's very boring."

"Actually, I'm reading this article in the newspaper called the 'Battle of Little Chapel Road.' It's very interesting. The article mentions Ruby several times. She and Aubrey Stillwell had quite the feud going. Don't be mad at your friend. She only gave me your profile to bring me up to speed."

"Up to speed on what? Never mind, I'll deal with my friend later. Who's Aubrey Stillwell?"

"Honestly, Mae," Tammy said, "don't you read your mother's column? He's the road commissioner for Rose County." She shrugged. "Don't worry. It's not like I run around town passing out your profile to random men."

The sheriff snorted faintly.

Tammy tossed her head. "I wrote down a few salient details

a few weeks ago. I was going to show it to you. It's been more than a year. I was hoping you might be ready to start dating again."

Mae closed her eyes. When she opened them, Tammy and Ben were both gazing at her with similar expressions of concern.

"It's all right. I'll tell you when I'm ready. I usually do read Mama's columns."

"Your mother writes the 'Suzanne about Town' column?"

Mae nodded.

"I'd like to ask her for some background. And I still need to get a statement from you."

"I'll give you my statement. Mama usually comes by around mid-morning to say hello to her dogs. I'm keeping them here during her landscaping project. She's putting in a big water fountain and it's impossible to keep Kudzu and Lil'bit from digging everything up. I'm sure she'd love to talk to you."

Tammy left shortly thereafter, saying she'd be happy for the sheriff to interrogate her at any time, but she'd let Mae go first. When Mae looked at her in exasperation, Tammy merely smiled and took her leave.

"Miss December, I'd like to take your statement now, if that's okay."

"Of course, that's fine. Won't you please call me Mae?"

He shook his head. "Not while you're part of a murder investigation."

"So, Ruby was murdered?"

He nodded. "Yes, but we're not making it public yet. Please keep it to yourself."

"Am I a part of this?" She tried to control the quaver in her voice.

"Well, you reported Ruby missing, saying you wanted to wring her neck, and then the next day you reported finding her body. Your fingerprints are all over her red boot. Yes, I'd say you're definitely a part of this."

"Sheriff, I'm not considered a suspect, am I? I'd be the last person to wish Ruby dead. You know I only wanted to get Elvis out of here and back to her."

"So you said. Elvis isn't much of an alibi, though. I'd like to see him, by the way. Is he in the kennel?"

"Actually, Patrick let him out last night and he didn't come back. He's the dog I was out looking for earlier."

"Elvis is missing?"

"Yes, he's missing, but hopefully not for long. He's a tough little dog and he's fast. I'm sure he'll be back soon. Patrick will tell you the same thing."

The sheriff looked frustrated. Mae quietly added some fresh coffee to his cup and glanced enquiringly at Deputy Phelps, who shook his head. Mae turned her attention back to the sheriff.

"Miss December, let me read this to you, please. It's what I have in my notes from our conversations. 'On March eighteenth, Mae December (of fifteen oh nine Little Chapel Road) went to Ruby Mead-Allison's house in hopes of finding her at home. She planned to return Ms. Mead-Allison's dog that she was boarding. She noted a red boot in the flowerbed by the rear of the house, put the boot in her tote bag and brought it to the sheriff's office.' Did you do anything else while you were there?"

"Well, I set her mailbox back up on the post—it was down in the ditch. Oh, and it was empty. Ruby must have gotten home before yesterday and picked up her mail. I also peeked in the garage window and opened the side door. Her car was there. Did I mention that she drove herself to the airport? When I saw her car, I knew she'd returned from her vacation."

"All right, I'll add that. 'On March nineteenth, Mae December walked her dogs around eight fifteen a.m. when Mr. Jack Ryan approached, without his dog.'" He paused. "Tell me what happened then."

"I spoke to him about his ankle, which he thought might be

sprained, and I walked him home. Then I went past the place where I saw him originally and started calling his dog, Toast."

He smiled. "There are an awful lot of dogs in this case."

She nodded absently, still upset at recounting her discovery of Ruby's body.

"What happened next?"

"I kept calling Toast. I found her near a small grove of trees. When I got close enough, I noticed she was in a full point position."

"Okay, and this grove of trees that the dog was pointing to is near the road you live on, but about thirty yards off the road, correct? It was actually on Ruby's property?"

"Yes, right. I went to see what she was pointing at and noticed something red at the base of one of the trees." She stopped, overcome with nausea.

"Go on. What happened then?"

"Just a minute." Mae went to the refrigerator and took out a pitcher of fruit tea. She poured a glass and added ice. She stood and looked out her window for a moment, seeing the lush spring morning that contrasted starkly with Ruby's demise. She took a few deep breaths to compose herself before she turned back to the sheriff.

"When I got over to the trees, I saw a red boot. The boot was on a foot. Ruby's foot."

"Then what happened?"

"I had three dogs with me. Somehow, I got all the dogs back to my house and put them in the pasture. I ran inside and practically fell on the kitchen floor."

"What did you do next?"

"After taking a couple of minutes to calm myself down, I called Patrick."

"Could you tell me Patrick's last name and his relationship to you?"

"It's West. Patrick is Noah's brother. I used to be engaged to Noah." She felt calmer, but still upset, as flashes of Ruby's cold, bedraggled body came back to her.

The sheriff's eyes widened. "Noah West? Is that why you broke off the engagement? Because you didn't want to change your name to Mae West?"

There was a faint snicker from Deputy Phelps.

Mae shot him a withering glare before turning her attention back to the sheriff. Clearly, she'd been right to call him an ass.

"Noah died in a car accident last February."

She had awakened to the sound of her doorbell late one night. Nashville police officers stood on her porch. Moths circled under her porch light. As soon as she saw the men standing there, she knew Noah was gone.

The sheriff's face flushed brick red. "I apologize, that was out of line."

He checked his notes and cleared his throat. "So, you called Patrick and he came to your house? How long before he got here?"

"He came right over. It took maybe ten minutes."

"What did you do while you waited for him?"

"I called Mr. Ryan to tell him I had found Toast. I didn't want them to be out looking for her."

"So I assume you told Mr. Ryan about finding Ruby's body."

He sounded irritated now.

"Yes, of course I did. I also told him his dog was fine. She hadn't touched the body."

He gave her a sharp look. "Are you sure the dog didn't touch the body?"

"Yes, I'm sure. Viszlas hold the point until given the command to proceed. She's very well trained. I worked on her training with both the Ryans. She would have held her point perfectly."

"When did you call my office?"

"When Patrick got to the house, I told him what I'd found. He said I should have called nine-one-one immediately, but since I hadn't, I called your office."

"Why didn't you call nine-one-one?"

What was it with these men? They acted as if they'd be perfectly calm in the same situation, but she highly doubted it. Well, maybe the sheriff would. It was his job, after all.

"I was totally rattled. I'd never seen a dead body before. I wasn't thinking."

"Okay, we're almost finished. Do you have any more coffee?"

"Yes, of course. Do you like it?"

"The coffee? Yes, it's good. Much better than what Dory makes at the station."

Mae's peripheral vision caught a glimpse of something moving quickly. Mama's car flew up the drive. "My mother's here," Mae said with a feeling of relief.

Chapter Four

—

March 20
Sheriff Ben Bradley

Raised by a good Southern mother, Sheriff Ben Bradley immediately stood up when Mrs. December came in the room. She was slim and striking with short dark hair, in contrast to her daughter, who was blonde and curvier. She tsk'd as she walked past a pile of wood shavings swept into a corner of the room. Mae closed her eyes briefly but didn't move to sweep it up. Ben wondered whether Mae resented her mother's efforts to improve her housekeeping, but then noticed Mae was unfazed by the implied criticism. In fact, Mae seemed calmer with her mother present.

"I'm Suzanne December and it's a pleasure to finally meet you, Sheriff. I know your parents. They're lovely people." She smiled and took his hand in a surprisingly firm grip.

"Thank you, Ma'am. This is Deputy Phelps. He's helping me out today."

George Phelps nodded at Mrs. December but didn't offer his hand in greeting. Instead he stayed near the digital recorder. Ben sighed inwardly at George's lack of social graces. To his dismay, George displayed a pretty lackadaisical approach to his job in general. His shirt was buttoned wrong over his pudgy stomach. He had inherited Phelps from the previous sheriff so he tried to be philosophical about his deputy. Due to his length of service, removing him from his position would be a nightmare and, once in a great while, George found out something useful.

"I'm here in connection with the death of Ruby Mead-Allison. Her death may tie in with the controversy surrounding the widening of Little Chapel Road. I was hoping that you could give me some background on the issue."

"I'm happy to do anything to help the law, and especially such a handsome young man in uniform." She smiled flirtatiously at Ben.

"Mother, would you like some coffee?" Mae stood at the sink with her back to them. "No thank you, dear. Let's see … The effort to widen Little Chapel Road began about five years ago when the road commissioner, Aubrey Stillwell, proposed an extensive widening project. Mae, there are nine houses on this street, correct?"

Mae nodded.

"All nine families rejected Mr. Stillwell's original proposal to make Little Chapel Road a four lane boulevard. Then there was the regrettable incident involving the Jensen boy. Do you remember that, Sheriff?"

"I think so, but I was new on the job then. Could you refresh my memory?"

"The boy was waiting for the school bus, standing ankle-deep in water with shrubs all around him. This road has no shoulders and no true bus stop. When the bus came, the driver didn't see him. The school secretary called the parents because he wasn't at school. Since his parents knew he had gone down to the bus stop, they were in a panic. Before the whole incident was over, the police were on site and divers were prepared to search the river. Luckily, someone spotted the little boy walking near the school and called his parents."

"What is the current plan for the road?"

"Mama, I can tell him about the current plan," Mae said. The road will still have two lanes, but they'll be much wider. There will be shoulders and a bus stop. They can do all that without impacting the slave wall."

Ben Bradley cocked his head. "Tell me about the slave wall." When he first saw the traffic counting cord around Ruby's neck, he sensed that her opposition to widening the road might be the motive for her murder. He adjusted his posture to a more alert stance and listened intently.

Mae walked away from the sink to stand in front of a huge painting—an abstract landscape in vivid colors—hanging on the only wall in the kitchen that seemed totally finished. "Malone" was painted across the bottom right corner of the canvas in bold red letters.

"Excuse me, Mrs. December, but I just noticed the painting. I have one of his works, too." Ben walked over to the artwork.

He caught the look Mae exchanged with her mother. *What was that about?*

"Sorry to interrupt you, Ma'am."

Suzanne cleared her throat, "Please have a seat at the table with me, Sheriff. As I was saying, slave walls are those old dry stacked rock walls that line roads and divide pasture land throughout Tennessee. They go back to the seventeen hundreds and slaves built most of them. Many people feel that if the walls are allowed to disappear, much of the area's charm will go with them."

"Thank you. Now, can either of you tell me how Ruby fits into this picture?"

Suzanne continued. "Ruby Mead-Allison was totally opposed to widening the road. She filed a lawsuit to prevent the action. I thought the suit was frivolous and was surprised when James Connolly, her attorney, took on the case. Ruby always was a spoiled child. She insisted on getting her way and was a little too free with her person in high school and college. Are you getting all this, Sheriff?"

Ben stifled a grin. "Free with her person" was an awfully refined way of saying the girl slept around.

"Yes, Ma'am. Thank you. This is very helpful."

Suzanne smiled. "Before the judge ruled on the action, he asked to have the traffic volume measured. Aubrey Stillwell did that, using a laser light system, and the results favored the need to widen the road. Then Ruby dug up some information about the laser light equipment being unreliable. She purchased one of those cords that lie across the road and count vehicles. Her testing showed slightly different results. Mae, I think I'll have that coffee after all."

Mae was standing by the large window over the sink, looking out toward the barn and the trees behind the house. As she brought over the coffee pot and a cup for her mother, Ben took a moment to look around. Although the house was in the process of being remodeled, he could see that the wall between the old kitchen and the dining area had been removed. Light flooded both spaces. The cabinets were white and a period after Shaker style. There was a pot of red geraniums on the windowsill. It was a pleasant space.

"The road commission hearings degenerated into free-for-alls. Two weeks ago, poor Mr. Stillwell announced that he'd delayed his retirement. He said he'd do so again if necessary, just so we could have Little Chapel Road meet the standards of the county. He just hoped he'd live long enough to see it happen. Is this what you needed?"

"Yes. This information has been extremely helpful. As you probably already know, Ruby didn't die a natural death. Do you have any ideas about who might have had problems with her?"

"I've already heard several theories," Suzanne said. "Some say Mr. Stillwell snapped and killed her. I don't believe it for a moment. I've known Aubrey since we were in high school. I've also heard people say David Allison might have done it. They were in the middle of a contentious divorce. David is staying down the street with his business partner Steven Fanning. I assume David would inherit Ruby's property if she died before their divorce was final."

"Provided he wasn't involved in her murder," Ben said, coolly.

"Quite so," Suzanne said. There was a short silence. "I've heard rumors that Ruby's attorney, James Connolly, once tried to ditch her frivolous lawsuit, but she forced him to pursue it. His aunt and uncle live at the end of Little Chapel Road, down by the river, and they signed the petition to support the widening, but people say Ruby utterly refused to allow Connolly to drop it."

Ben stood up from the table. Mae was picking up cups and carrying them to the sink. His eyes lingered on her graceful movements and curvaceous figure. "Thank you both again. We'll definitely check all these folks out. Right now, I think I'll pay a visit to David Allison." Ben knew that, other than the person who found the body, the most likely killer was a spouse or ex-spouse.

Mrs. December stopped him as he and Deputy Phelps were leaving.

"Since there's been a murder here on the street, I expect you and your force will keep a particular eye on Mae. She lives here all by herself, you know. I need your assurance that you'll protect her."

Ben tried unsuccessfully to suppress an image of Mae clinging to him, begging for protection. He really needed to get a life.

"You don't need to worry. We'll be patrolling the street."

He paused on the porch and heard Mae's voice. "Mama, I can take care of myself."

"Of course you can, sweetie, but it doesn't hurt for the sheriff to be reminded that you're here alone. He certainly is a handsome man, isn't he? Good taste in art too."

Both women laughed. George looked at Ben with his eyebrows raised. Ben stopped eavesdropping and hurried out to his car. He wasn't sure that he wanted to hear Mae's answer to her mother's question and he definitely didn't need his deputy to hear it.

Ben drove back into Rosedale and dropped Phelps at the office. As his deputy was getting out of the car, Ben said, "George, I need information on Ruby's financial situation. Can you handle that?"

"Me, boss?" George asked, sounding astonished. "Doesn't Dory usually do that sort of thing?"

"You two can work together on the money angle," he said firmly. If he didn't give George a job, he knew the deputy would while the day away on the Internet. Driving away, he mentally reviewed the most likely suspects in Ruby's killing, coming up with the husband, road commissioner, attorney, unknown lover, and old boyfriend.

He called Wayne Nichols' cell and they agreed to meet for lunch. He wanted the older detective with him for David Allison's interrogation. Ben respected Wayne as a detective. At fifty-eight years of age, he had the experience and skills that allowed him to pry deeply held information out of suspects and had a very high "solve" rate. However, Wayne tended to treat him as the new kid on the block, and Dory was no help, often laughing at his naïveté. He knew he was still earning their respect. Between Wayne and Dory, he had an uphill climb to be seen as the boss at only thirty-two years of age.

Driving to the restaurant, Ben reluctantly acknowledged his shortcomings when it came to investigating such a high profile murder. Detective Wayne Nichols had worked fifty murders or more. Ben had only worked two previous murders and each one had ended with a spontaneous confession. This victim wasn't some lowlife druggie or hired thug. This was the murder of the only daughter of the most prominent family in Rosedale. Unlike his detective, who seemed to relish the idea of hunting for a killer, Ben feared he was out of his depth.

Chapter Five

—

March 20
Detective Wayne Nichols

While Sheriff Bradley was meeting with Mae, Detective Wayne Nichols and Deputy Robert Fuller began "house to house" interviews with Ruby's neighbors on Little Chapel Road. They arrived at the Ingram residence by 7:15 a.m. The houses were all located on large parcels of five acres or more. The Ryans on the north side and the Ingrams across the street had been Ruby Mead-Allison's closest neighbors.

Wayne Nichols served as Chief Detective for Rose County and the neighboring counties on an as-needed basis. Deputy Robert Fuller aspired to be a homicide detective. He was of average height and weight, wore his scruffy golden-brown hair short and had gray eyes that could be piercing. His smooth skin and owlish glasses made him look even younger than his actual age of twenty-six. Wayne would have preferred to work alone, but Ben insisted two people had to be present for all interviews. If he had to have a partner, Robert was certainly better than the laid-back Phelps. Fuller paid close attention to what was happening and often had astute observations to offer.

Wayne rang the doorbell.

Lucy Ingram answered the door looking more washed out than when he had seen her last. She wore pajamas and her feet were bare. Her light brown hair was wildly tangled. "Good grief, Wayne. You know I pulled a long shift last night. I didn't even start work until nine and the ER was ridiculously busy. The ambulances were playing my song all night."

Wayne knew Lucy's job as an ER physician was extremely stressful. He admired how effectively she dealt with life and death situations day after day. They had been dating until a few months ago. A stab of remorse hit him as he remembered how they had ended things.

"Sorry. I'm not here to ask you about the hit and run from last night. This is about your neighbor, Ruby Mead-Allison. I'm sure you've noticed the yellow crime scene tape we put up near her driveway."

"Yes, I did. I wondered about it, but I haven't heard anything yet."

"I'm sorry to tell you this, but Ruby was murdered. Her body wasn't found until yesterday. I knew you'd be sleep-deprived, but we needed to talk to her neighbors as soon as possible."

Lucy's hazel eyes widened and she swayed where she stood. Wayne put a gentle hand on her shoulder and anchored her in place. The skin under her light pajama top was warm.

"How awful." Her voice was quiet. "You two better come in. It's cold out this morning. I'll have the coffee going in a couple of minutes."

They trailed Lucy's slight form into her spacious home. The slate tiled entryway led into a gleaming new kitchen with stainless steel appliances, soapstone countertops, and a gray and silver tiled backsplash. Light streamed pitilessly through the oversized windows, highlighting the faint scars on Lucy's intelligent face. She had never explained their origin. A lab accident? A fire? Maybe if they had managed to share such details, they would still be together, Wayne thought regretfully. But then he remembered Lucy's words, accusing him of wanting to know everything about her while sharing none of his own background. She had been right. His past was sealed.

"This is the first time I've been in this room since you remodeled. The kitchen looks like a lab."

"You're right," Lucy said with a half-smile. "I am what I am." As a doctor, Lucy had once mentioned she preferred a simple, sterile environment at home as well as at the hospital.

They each took a chair around the clear Lucite kitchen table. A small crystal vase in the center held a few wilted daffodils but no water—another indication of the long hours she worked

"When was the last time you saw Ruby?" Wayne asked.

"The fifteenth, I think. Hang on. Let me get my cellphone." She left the room briefly and returned to the kitchen carrying the phone and looking calmer. "I worked until nine and was home by ten. I remember now. I didn't actually see Ruby that night, but there was a car in her driveway and her lights were on."

"All right, good. Try to go back to that evening in your mind if you can. It's been warm lately. Did you sit outside on your porch?"

"Yes. I was trying to get used to my shift change. This visit, by the way, is screwing me up again." She glanced at Nichols and narrowed her eyes but then smiled as she shook her head.

"It's not the first time my schedule has collided with yours, is it?" Wayne said with a grin.

Lucy turned to the Deputy Fuller, who had been focused intently on their conversation. "Detectives make lousy boyfriends."

"Or maybe ER physicians make lousy girlfriends," Wayne said.

Robert shook his head, looking embarrassed "Please, can we get back to business?"

Lucy and Wayne exchanged wry looks.

"I sat out on my front porch until past midnight."

"Can you see or hear much that goes on at the Mead-Allison residence from your porch?"

"Yes, I can. I often hear Ruby's music, mostly her clients' country songs. Sometimes I smell cigarettes, or something stronger," Lucy raised her eyebrows. "If the wind is blowing just right, I can hear the sound of ice tinkling in glasses. I heard two people arguing that night but couldn't make out what they said. It was Ruby and a man. She had a loud voice, so I know it was her, but the man was quieter. I didn't recognize his voice. Then, later I heard the car pull out of her driveway."

"What time was that?"

"Around eleven or eleven thirty."

"Did you hear anything else?"

"Not for a while. Ruby probably went into the house and shut off the music. The lights were all off by then. At about one a.m.—I was still trying to stay awake to get my body used to working nights again—there was a second vehicle in her driveway."

"Was it was the same car?" Wayne asked.

"No, it wasn't. The moon was full and I could see it was a truck. A pickup."

He gave her a slow, encouraging smile. "What else?"

"Shortly after the second vehicle arrived, Ruby's back door opened. That door always squeaks. After that, I didn't hear a thing. I fell into bed and slept like a stone. Nothing wakes me after a sixteen-hour shift. Sorry."

"Very helpful info. One other thing," Wayne said, "how did you get along with Ruby? Would you say you were friends?" Robert sat up a little straighter, absorbing every bit of Wayne's questioning style.

Lucy seemed to be taking her time responding and Nichols waited, watching her closely. He wanted to carry out this interview by the book, despite their former relationship. Law enforcement training repeatedly stressed the importance of never letting personal feelings get in the way of professionalism. Besides, Robert was watching his every move.

"We used to be, before she sued me."

Wayne leaned forward, listening intently.

"It happened during my kitchen remodel. I had to have an excavator dig up my septic tank. Ruby thought the digging changed the drainage from my downspouts, forcing the water across to her driveway." Lucy's voice shook and her neck and chest flushed. "Instead of talking to me about it, she had her attorney file a motion to stop construction and sued me for damages."

"How were things resolved?"

Lucy gave a short laugh. "I had to pay her off in order to finish my kitchen."

"So, she was scrappy then, like you?" Wayne teased.

"No, not like me. I'll only fight if I have to. If Ruby thought that someone had hurt her or her property, she would go after them with everything she had. She pestered me about wanting to buy the lot next door for a while. When I told her I wasn't interested in selling, she was furious. I don't know why she even wanted it. Poor David was completely under her thumb, and once she had dominated him she lost all interest in the marriage. Everything was a battle with that woman."

"This is really helpful. Thanks for the coffee. If you remember anything else about the evening of the fifteenth, please call me," Wayne said. "I hope you can get back to sleep. Sorry to have disturbed your schedule." He hated seeing her look so exhausted.

ROBERT DROVE THE patrol car down Little Chapel Road and into the Ryans' driveway. A pickup truck was parked in front of them. Robert jotted down the license plate number of the pick-up, remembering Lucy saying that she had seen a truck in Ruby's driveway the night she died. An attractive blond woman came out of the house and walked over to the driveway.

"I'm just leaving. I'll get out of your way," she said.

Detective Nichols and Deputy Fuller introduced themselves.

"Nice to meet you. I'm Beth Jensen. I was just bringing some soup and homemade bread to the Ryans. Mrs. Ryan is down with the flu. Mr. Ryan is still limping from his fall on the road yesterday."

"Mrs. Jensen, we're going to be dropping by later today to talk with you. I'm sure you know by now that your neighbor, Ruby Mead-Allison, is dead. We need to talk with everyone who lives on the street to see what they remember from the night Ruby died."

"I know. It's horrible," she shuddered. "I'll be home the rest of the morning." Beth left hurriedly, getting into her truck and pulling up into the grass to turn around. She sped around the patrol car and out of the driveway, pieces of gravel spraying from under her tires.

The two men walked to the door. Wayne couldn't stop thinking about Lucy and the night they had broken up. They had been talking about Lucy's decision to go to medical school when he sensed her starting to pull back. They sat on her living room couch, close together. Her body stiffened, and she edged away. The room was warm and the fire glowed with embers, but their conversation had moved them into new territory, dark and cold as a stream in winter.

"You don't have to tell me if you're not ready." He touched her cheek gently.

The side of her face shone in the firelight. She appeared upset. Suddenly, she glared at him. He was stunned to see that she was furious. "It's always one way with you, isn't it, Wayne?"

He hadn't responded in his momentary confusion.

She went on in an angry voice he'd never heard from her before. "You really want to get to know me? You want my whole life story? Well, this is a two-way street, my friend. I'm not going to tell you one more damn thing unless you tell me your stories—all of them. This is supposed to be a relationship, you idiot, not an interrogation."

The icy stream tugged hard on his feet. He couldn't step into the water, knowing he'd slip and fall. Then the darkness would cover him.

"What do you mean?" He was angry, too. "I told you I was raised in foster care. You know a police captain befriended me and helped me get into the police academy. I've told you everything."

She threw up her hands, exasperated. "No, you haven't. What you've told me is only the script, the goddamned script! It's what you tell everyone. It's your cover story. Everybody knows that much. It's not enough anymore, Wayne. I want you to trust me enough to let me in."

The darkness rose. He clenched his fists. They argued for a while longer, but he couldn't tell her anything more. His past lay like an oil reservoir, dark and untapped beneath the layers of his well-rehearsed life story.

"So, I'm just not worth it?"

God, he didn't want to end the relationship with her. Lucy was the smartest, sexiest woman he'd ever known. "Give me some more time, won't you?"

She shook her head sadly. "No way. You have to show me yours before you get to see mine, my friend. When you're ready, you can come back."

It wasn't that he didn't want to come back. He wished he had the guts, but he couldn't bring himself to do it.

Chapter Six

———

March 20
Detective Wayne Nichols

DETECTIVE NICHOLS AND Deputy Fuller were approaching the front door to the Ryans' house. Wayne needed to concentrate. Thinking about Lucy and his past wouldn't help the investigation. A woman had been killed. He wanted to find the bastard who had done it. Catching Ruby's killer was the only thing that mattered right now.

Detective Nichols rang the doorbell. When Mr. Ryan opened the door, his thick, white hair was damp and still bore the tracks of a comb. He was casually dressed, but his posture was almost military, his manner quite formal. His beautiful pointer, growling quietly, stood at his feet.

"Can I help you gentlemen with something?" The man's eyes were wary.

"Good morning, Mr. Ryan. I'm Detective Nichols and this is Deputy Fuller. I wonder if we might talk to you. I know you're aware that your neighbor Ruby Mead-Allison is dead. We need to talk to everyone on the road to help us discover what happened."

"Come in." He turned to the dog. "Go on, Tószt, get into your bed." He held the door open for the men and led them back to the kitchen while the dog went to lie down. The room was tidy but crowded with knickknacks and heavy oak furniture. Dark oriental rugs covered most of the linoleum floor. The scent of menthol mixed with that of a lemony furniture polish in the air.

They stood at the kitchen counter until Mr. Ryan got situated at the table, and then they sat down with him. Mr. Ryan looked at Wayne and gave a sharp shake of his head. "Her death wasn't an accident, was it?"

Wayne shook his head.

"I figured as much. Ruby lived a life filled with conflict. She was a strong-willed person, very opinionated. Well, you probably aren't here to ask me what I thought of her. What can I help you with?"

"Can you remember what you were doing the night of March fifteenth? Four days before your dog discovered the body."

Jack Ryan nodded. "I remember that night because it was quite warm, for March anyway, nearly seventy until late evening. The dog wanted to go out but I didn't let her. I finally got her to lie down by taking her into our room. By the way, my wife Eveline has a bad case of the flu that's going around. I took her to the doctor late yesterday because she was having trouble with a cough. She's resting now." He gave the two men a stern look.

"We'll try to be quick, sir." Wayne's tone was conciliatory. "Please go on about the night of the fifteenth."

"Yes, well, I took out some trash after the dog got settled down. A car was leaving Ruby's driveway."

"Do you remember the time?"

"Around eleven."

"Anything else you can remember?"

"During the night Eveline got up to use the bathroom. When she came back to bed, she said something about Ruby having more company than any young woman ought to."

"Why would she say that?"

"She said she saw David Allison's car parked in Ruby's driveway about 9:30. Then later on that evening she saw another vehicle."

"I need to ask Mrs. Ryan if she can identify that second vehicle. Can you have her call me when she wakes up?" The detective handed Jack Ryan his card.

"Yes, I will, Detective. I hope you catch the killer soon. I know we're probably not at risk, but we're worried. This is usually such a safe place. When you get older," he smiled, "you worry about being out in the country so far from streetlights."

THE TWO MEN drove down the road to the Jensens' house, a brick ranch-style home painted a soft yellow with green shutters. Two large maple trees stood in the front yard. Beth Jensen answered the door. She quickly bent down to grab a gray kitten trying to escape.

"Good effort, Weevil." She held the kitten to her chest as she stood up. The woman's eyes matched the kitten's green ones.

"Hello again, Mrs. Jensen," Detective Nichols said. "We finished early with the Ryans and need to talk to everyone on the street. Do you have a few minutes?"

"Please, come on in." Beth opened the door wider.

Both men followed her blond ponytail toward the back of the house. Unlike the other two kitchens they had been in that day, this one looked like a place where people actually cooked. The whole house was fragrant with the smell of fresh baked bread.

For a moment, Wayne flashed back to his seventeenth summer, hitchhiking in Michigan's Upper Peninsula—the memory of the only good woman he'd known while in his formative years. He was walking down a dirt road. Dust, soft as baby powder, rose in a cloud with each step. The sun warmed his shoulders as he approached an old farmhouse with a wraparound porch. A red barn in need of fresh paint stood behind the house, next to a fenced paddock full of black and white cattle.

He walked up the porch steps, past pots of red and yellow flowers, and knocked on the front door. It was nearly threshing time. He hoped the farmer would have work for him. A large pleasant-faced woman answered, flanked by two small children, a boy and a girl. The little girl's hair was intricately braided and the boy had short red curls and freckled cheeks. The woman gave him an inquiring look.

"I'm looking for work."

"Come in then." She opened the door all the way. "The rest of the men won't be here for a day or so. You'll sleep in the barn like the rest of them. I bring food down there three times a day. It's good grub. A man can't work unless he's fed. The milking shed has a shower. You leave your dirty clothes in the basket. I wash every day. Do you have other clothes with you?" She spoke with what sounded like a Finnish accent. "You're very young. Where did you come from?"

He shrugged and turned away. She had a kind face. The aroma of bread baking awakened his hunger pangs. The woman was like the bread, warm and fragrant. He ached to have had a mother like her, to have grown up here, to be her son.

"What's your name?" She put a hand on the little girl's shoulder. "I'm Alene Hagström and these two are my grandkids—Ray and Clarice."

He thought for a minute and then gave her a name he had read in a book. "It's John, John Chisolm."

"Not from around here then. Where are your folks?"

He said nothing.

"All right then. Go down to the milking shed and take a shower. Wait a minute." She left the room and returned with underwear, dungarees and a clean, faded shirt. "Take these with you. Mr. Hagström will show you where you will be sleeping."

He worked there for four weeks and Mrs. Hagström fed them three squares a day, good food—potatoes, meatloaf, tomatoes, green beans, and gravy. He learned how to tie large sheaves of yellow straw with twine, standing them upright in the open stubble of the wheat field. He worked all day in the hot sun, throwing pitchforks of wheat into the combine harvester as it pulled the wheat straw into its whirling mouth and spit out golden wheat heads into a wagon. When he leveled off the pile of grain in the wagon, the wheat moved through his hands like solid rain.

One day Clarice, the granddaughter, came down to the barn in the middle of the afternoon, carefully balancing a tray with a tall glass pitcher of red juice and fresh cookies.

"Grandma says I should tell you it's bug juice." She put the tray down and wrinkled her freckled nose. "Really it's Kool-Aid." She giggled and ran off.

The wind in the sugar maples had begun to sing of summer's end when Mr. Hagström came to him to say he needed to move on. He was washing the milking machines when the older man walked up.

"You need to get on the road, John." The rest of the men were already gone, and the wheat rested in silos, golden as a lake at sunset. "I don't have any more work for you, and I don't feed men who aren't working."

Mrs. Hagström called to him as he walked down the driveway. She went into the house and came back out with a jar of preserves, some apples and bread. "You can keep the extra clothes, John. If you get down to Gros Cap, there's an Odawa settlement there. You're part Odawa, I think. They might take you in for the winter. Good luck."

Her kind voice still echoed in his mind. Robert bumped his shoulder, forcibly recalling him to the present. Robert and Beth Jensen were both looking at him.

"Sorry. Lost in thought."

Beth cleared her throat and offered the men hot tea. It had a clean lemon scent. The three of them sat down at the kitchen table.

"Mrs. Jensen, your neighbor Ruby Mead-Allison died on the night of March fifteenth. Do you remember what you were doing that day and evening?"

She tipped her head to the side and wrinkled her brow. "Oh, yes, I do. The kids were on spring break that week. Bob and I drove up to see my parents in Ohio. Let me double-check the calendar. Hang on a minute."

She walked over to her pantry door and ran her finger across the calendar hanging there.

"Yes, right. We didn't get home until the night of the seventeenth."

"Well, that makes my job easier." Wayne smiled. "Unfortunately, it also means you can't help us figure out what happened. One last thing, did you drive the pick-up?"

"No. It doesn't have room for the kids and all their stuff. We left it in our locked garage while we were gone."

After a few more pleasantries, the men left, but not before tasting Beth's warm bread and complimenting her on her baking skills.

Chapter Seven

—

March 20
Sheriff Ben Bradley

A T AROUND TWO o'clock that afternoon Sheriff Ben Bradley and Detective Wayne Nichols got to the Fannings' place, where David Allison was staying. The CSI Tech, Hadley Johns, waited in the driveway. He would tape the interview with Ruby's estranged husband and collect any necessary samples from the house. Tech Johns followed them to the door, and the sheriff knocked. A tall man with dark straight hair, glasses and a sad expression answered the door. He wore jeans and a sweatshirt.

"Are you David Allison?" Ben asked.

"Yes." The man sounded tired.

Ben introduced himself, as did Detective Nichols and Tech Johns.

"May we come in?" We need to get a statement from you."

David took a deep breath. He turned and led them through the living room without actually inviting them in. The four of them sat down on stools at the kitchen island. David explained that he had been temporarily living with his business partner at the architecture firm, Steven Fanning, due to complications in his marriage and that he had been working from Steven's house on the day of the murder.

"Both Detective Nichols and I will be asking some questions about your relationship with the victim, Ruby Mead-Allison. We are taping this interview."

Hadley unobtrusively started the digital recorder.

"I don't understand. I already went in and talked to someone about this."

"That was to identify your wife, sir." Wayne's low voice sounded soothing. Ben knew his detective was good at getting people to talk. Often just his voice and reassuring demeanor sufficed to calm people down. "I know that must have been very difficult, and we appreciate your help, but the sheriff and I need to interview you about any events leading up to the night of the fifteenth. I'm sure you understand."

David nodded.

A blue-eyed, brown-haired woman with a ready smile came into the room and introduced herself as Steven Fanning's wife, Robin.

"I'm sorry to intrude on you, Mrs. Fanning, but we need to ask Mr. Allison some questions." Ben tipped his head at Detective Nichols, their nonverbal signal for him to continue the interview.

"Mr. Allison, I'd like to confirm some things. You're married to Ruby Mead-Allison, correct?"

David nodded. "We were getting a divorce."

"I understand. However, the two of you were still married at the time of her death, right?"

"Yes." His eyes were fixed on his lap and he fiddled with a hangnail on his thumb.

"The M.E. informed us that Ruby died on the evening of the fifteenth. We'd like your clothes from that day and evening. Do you send your shirts out to be laundered professionally?"

"I do." He smoothed his hair back, apparently a nervous

habit. His forehead was shiny with sweat.

"Is there a hamper or basket where you keep them until they're ready to go?"

"I can help," Robin Fanning said, "I have David's shirts. I planned to take them to the laundry today. They're in my car." She and Tech Johns left to collect the clothing.

"Can you tell us where you were on March fifteenth?"

"Just a moment, let me get my planner." David left the room and returned carrying a pocket calendar.

"March fifteenth was the day some V.I.P.s were here from Memphis. We had meetings at the office and then all of us went to dinner."

A small dog came into the room, nails clicking on the polished wood floor. The dog growled at the big detective and snapped in the air as he reached to pet him. Ben recognized the little red fluff from Mae December's tote bag at the office.

"That's enough, Elvis," Ben said. The little dog settled down. Ben looked back at David Allison. "I see you have Ruby's dog. Where did you find him?"

"Roaming around early this morning when I went out for a walk. Given the situation, I thought I should bring him here."

"Did you know Ruby was boarding him at Mae December's kennel?"

David swallowed, shaking his head. "No, I guess I should have."

"Please call Miss December when we're finished here. She's been looking for him."

As Wayne continued to ask David questions about his relationship with Ruby, Ben carefully observed the room. It was large and well lit with contemporary furniture and a series of canvases hanging on the walls. Each one was a splash of color. This was one of the few houses on Little Chapel Road that had been torn down and replaced with a new house of modern design. It was obviously the home of a person with taste and wealth. He wondered if the Allison & Fanning Architectural firm generated enough income to pay for a house like this. He made a mental note to check on the background of both men—David's financial situation in particular.

They finished up and prepared to leave. Wayne cautioned David Allison to remain available, since they'd be speaking with him again. Tech Johns walked out to the CSI van with David's laundry.

David picked up his phone as they walked out. Ben heard him say "Yes, that's right. I have Elvis."

WAYNE DROVE THEM back to the office, which gave Ben the opportunity to call Dory and ask her to get the deputies and the CSI Team scheduled for a staff meeting in the morning. He wanted to hear what the lab tests showed about David Allison's clothes. If he was their killer, there should be blood or perhaps dirt on what he had been wearing. He was relying more and more on the Lab's astonishing findings.

"Good thing David Allison's shirts hadn't already gone to the laundry," Ben remarked.

"Sure was," said Wayne replied. "I'm going to call Ruby's attorney's office to get an appointment for tomorrow."

Ben felt a flicker of annoyance. Wayne seemed to be setting his own agenda, rather than waiting for his lead. He paused briefly before proceeding, deciding not to make an issue of it.

"Okay. I'm going to look at the body in the morgue and talk with the M.E. about the time of death. I also want another look at the traffic measurement equipment that was laid across the vic's neck. I don't think the cord was used to kill her, but I'll double check with the doc."

They agreed to meet the following morning at seven thirty. Ben enjoyed these early morning staff meetings. When he became sheriff, he promised his staff would live in the community. He also assured the residents that there'd be more transparency in the work of the department. Now the hunt for a killer had begun, and the sheriff wanted everyone on his staff focused on the crime.

Walking into his office, Ben jotted down a list of points to clarify and confirm at tomorrow's meeting. Creating an hour-by-hour timeline of the victim's movements on the last day of her life would be critical to solving the crime.

March 2:	Mae December sees Ruby Mead-Allison leaving for airport on vacation
March 2-14:	Ruby staying at resort. She departs one day earlier than planned
March 14:	Ruby on plane back to Nashville, arrives 3:15 p.m.
March 15/16:	Ruby dies late at night on the 15th or early morning of the 16th
March 18:	Mae December informs sheriff's office Ruby is missing
March 19:	Mae December reports finding Ruby's body

What did Ruby do between 3:15 on March 14 and later the next night? Why did she come home early from her trip? Did Ruby have a new lover? She and David Allison separated in February. She could have been seeing someone new.

Arriving back at the station behind the CSI van, Ben watched Hadley carry the laundry back to the lab. Ben and Wayne Nichols went into the reception area where Dory was waiting for them. She enjoyed enormous respect as the power behind the throne in the sheriff's office. She seemed to know everyone, having lived her whole life in Rosedale. As a black woman herself, she had many connections in the black community that had proven useful in unearthing clues Wayne and Ben couldn't have learned otherwise. Dismissing Wayne with a shooing motion, she fixed her eyes on Ben.

"Sheriff, there are twelve messages for you. None of them

are important. Do you need me to find out the value of Ruby's property? I'm also assuming you need to see her will."

These days, Ben got a kick out of Dory deciding what was important and what wasn't. When he started as sheriff, however, he had found her more than a little irritating. Now, two years later, he appreciated how she ran the office—with humor and authority. Plus, she turned out to be right most of the time about which messages he really needed to return.

"Yes. Please look into Ruby's property. I need to know if she had a mortgage, and if so, its value. If you can, find out the beneficiary of Ruby's will."

At the words, "if you can" Dory narrowed her eyes. Whoops. Ben knew Dory prided herself on her ability to ferret out information. He also knew better than to express doubts in Miss Dory's abilities.

"Sorry. I'm sorry. I know you can find out anything. I'll expect those reports tomorrow morning. I'd like everyone in the conference room by seven thirty."

"Would you like Miss December to be there also?"

Mae December at my staff meeting? No way in hell, he thought.

"Absolutely not, Dory. Why on earth would you think I'd want her here for a staff meeting?"

Dory gave Ben an icy stare. Was that a stupid question? Maybe Dory was in a "men are morons" mood. Sometimes being in charge was exhausting.

Before Mae found Ruby's body, Ben had been planning to take some time off at his cabin. That was out of the question now. At least he could visit it as often as he wanted, in his mind.

The first time Ben had gone to the cabin was with Gampy, his mom's father. He was beside himself with excitement. Ben's older brother, Mark, had been out to the cabin before, but Ben hadn't been old enough until then. He knew his mom was too worried about his asthma to let him go, but the doctor told her he was starting to outgrow it.

"Don't you lose your glasses, honey," she'd called from the porch, as he climbed into Gampy's station wagon. "Be sweet!"

He manfully ignored her. At nine years old, he was already straining at the apron strings. The hour it took to drive to the cabin flew by as he peppered his taciturn grandfather with questions about everything they'd see, eat, and do on their men's weekend.

They pulled off the county road and onto a two-track that cut across an open field and ran through woods thick with cedar and bowdock trees. They came to a stop in front of a tiny log cabin. Ben threw open the car door. Gampy's dogs boiled out behind him. Gampy hauled himself out and looked around with his commanding stare.

"Place looks like hell," he said gruffly.

Ben was delighted, both by the remote cabin and his grandfather's use of a swear word.

"Does it? I love it here. You owe me a quarter for the swear jar."

Gampy looked down at Ben and shook his head. "No swear jar out here, son. Let's leave your Mama to worry about things like that."

Better and better. No big brother or parents to tell him what to do, no swear jar and his favorite person all to himself.

"What should we do first?"

"Well, let's go on in and unpack the cooler. Leave those glasses in the car, Ben. You don't really need them. And that way you won't lose 'em."

The inside of the cabin had one large, high-ceilinged room, with a ladder leading up to a loft. Ben explored every inch in a hurry. The cabin kitchen had only a small ice chest, a sink and a stove. A fireplace took up the opposite wall, with a set of old chairs that he knew Mama would call disgusting set up beside it. A small metal table sat in the middle of the room. There were three cots in the loft. Ben unrolled his sleeping bag across the closest one and skidded back down the ladder.

"Find everything?" Gampy asked.

"Almost. Where do we pee?"

Gampy's low chuckle rasped out.

"I guess your brother never told you 'bout that, huh? We go out the back door and stand on the edge of the porch. Then we water the weeds."

He pointed to the small wooden door in the far wall, and Ben gleefully ran out on the porch and did just that. They stayed for three whole days, hiking the forty acres, fishing the creek and telling stories. After that weekend, Ben pestered his grandfather to take him out to the cabin as often as possible. He wasn't allowed to go with Gampy for hunting trips until he turned twelve, but until he turned sixteen, the cabin was his favorite place on earth.

Of course, once he smelled gasoline, bought a beater car and tasted his first girlfriend's lipstick, he lost interest in the old place for a while. Gampy died when Ben was in college. Ben's brother inherited his home in Rosedale. The cabin went to Ben. He installed a rudimentary bathroom but made no other changes. Whenever his life got too hectic, Ben ran to ground there, even if only for a mental vacation.

Chapter Eight

—

March 20
Mae December

Mae's mother departed after a short visit with her dogs. Mae called Tammy, leaving the "Avalanche" message again. Checking on the puppies, she smiled, seeing them sleepily cuddled up with Tallulah. Then she called the sheriff's office.

"Dory, it's Mae. Was Ruby's cellphone found when they searched the house?"

"No honey. Not on her or in the house. Do you know her number?"

"I do. I'm going over there to try and call it. If the phone has got any power left, maybe I'll hear it ringing."

"Good idea. Let me know if you find it."

"I will. Bye."

Mae grabbed her car keys, walked out to the car and drove down the driveway. Black cumulus clouds towered over the large hills behind her home as she headed down Little Chapel road toward Ruby's house.

If she was going to have any time to search for Ruby's

phone before the storm broke, she would need to hurry. As a successful manager for clients in the country music industry, Ruby must have kept a calendar, possibly on her cellphone. If Mae found the phone, she might get some clues about Ruby's death. She parked her car in Ruby's driveway and walked slowly across the backyard. Yellow crime scene tape was wrapped around the house and she could hear more flapping in the trees around the grove. Mae kept her distance from the tape. She knew Ruby's body was gone, but she didn't want to get close to the grove ever again. The wind blew fiercely and last year's damp leaves clung to her boots as she dialed Ruby's cellphone number.

She heard nothing until she started walking back toward the house. As she got closer to the garage, she could hear a very faint rendition of "I've got Friends in Low Places" playing. There was no crime scene tape around the garage, so she opened the side door and stepped inside. Looking through the car's windows, Mae noticed a white paper sack from the drug store on the rider's seat. Beside the bag was a pregnancy testing kit. It had already been torn open. The ring-tone sounded louder now. The phone lay on the concrete behind the left front tire. Mae always carried plastic bags for "doggie poo." Taking two out of her pocket, she used one to pick up the phone and the other to wrap it carefully. She dashed back to her car as the first drops of rain slapped her windshield.

The rain was pelting down when she drove back up her driveway. Tammy's car was parked outside. They both ran into the house, laughing.

"What now?" Tammy was out of breath.

"Look what I found." Mae held up the plastic-encased phone with a flourish normally accorded an Oscar envelope.

"Ruby's?"

"Um hum and it's just like mine, so I should be able to charge it." Mae got a pair of thin latex gloves from under the sink in order to remove the phone from the bag. She pushed buttons on the phone until she found the calendar. Ruby's date of arrival back home was listed as March fourteenth and her appointment the next morning was with the road commissioner. At one o'clock, the calendar showed a meeting with Ruby's attorney, followed by a doctor's appointment.

"Well, I think this could be your chance to get to know our handsome single sheriff," said Tammy.

"What are you talking about?"

"You need to take this to Ben. Maybe he'll even let you help with the investigation."

"Tammy, you're brilliant. I've been thinking I could help him and maybe even catch the perp. That's what they call them. I've been getting more and more upset about how Ruby died. People are acting as if she practically asked to be killed, all because she didn't want Little Chapel Road widened. She was a human being, and she didn't deserve to die like this."

Tammy smiled. "You're right, Mae-Mae. She deserved better."

"That reminds me, I'd better call Dory and tell her I found the phone. She'll probably want me to bring it in right away."

"Go ahead, Mae. I need to get back home."

Tammy waved and was out the door before Dory answered.

"Dory, I found it! Ruby's cellphone. It was in the garage. Should I bring it in?"

"Could you bring it in the morning? We have a meeting with CSI and the deputies first thing tomorrow. After that you can probably meet with Sheriff Bradley."

"That's perfect. I'll see you then."

Mae dug her charger out of the kitchen drawer and plugged it into a wall outlet. She stuck the other end into Ruby's phone and left it on the counter.

Chapter Nine

March 21
Mae December

BY 7:00 A.M. Mae was up, showered and dressed in black denim jeans, a blue sweater, and silver earrings. Putting her hair in a twist, she turned around to check her backside in the mirror. The black pants made her look five pounds slimmer. She'd even remembered lipstick. Tammy would be proud.

She ran downstairs, took her dogs outside and fed the boarding dogs; then she came inside and fed Tallulah, Titan and Thoreau. After filling her coffee mug, she poured the whole pot into a large coffee urn and sliced a loaf of apricot-walnut bread. She was headed down the driveway by twenty after seven. The sky was pale blue with high cirrus clouds. A whole cluster of crocuses lay face down in the mud by her mailbox, casualties of the heavy rain. How quickly spring storms passed by in the south. Flowers paid the price, gone before their time. Like Ruby.

Mae arrived at the donut shop by seven thirty. By seven forty-five, she had hot coffee, homemade bread, donuts and best of all, Ruby's phone, to share with the sheriff. The previous night she had placed the recharged cellphone in an envelope, carefully using her latex gloves to avoid smudging any fingerprints.

Mae struggled to open the Sheriff's office door with her hands full. "Dory, did the meeting already start?"

"Yes, honey." Dory held the door open for her.

"Could you please stick your head in there and tell the sheriff I have coffee and donuts for everyone? This bread is only for you, unless you want to share."

"Oooh, apricot-walnut?" Dory held it up to sniff. "Your mother gave me some last time I visited. It's delicious. Thank you. I'll keep this. It would be wasted on those scoundrels." She stashed the loaf in her desk drawer. "I'll go see what I can do about getting you into the meeting." She left the reception area and went down the hall into the conference room. Mae moved a little closer as Dory opened the door.

"Sheriff Bradley."

"What is it, Dory?" the sheriff asked in an exasperated tone.

"Sheriff, Miss Mae December is here with coffee and donuts for everyone. She'd like to come in."

"Tell Miss December I'll see her in an hour and not before. Dory, what's wrong with you? You know I can't let civilians into a staff meeting." The door shut firmly.

Dory turned to Mae. "Sorry, I guess he'll see you in an hour."

"Did you tell him I have Ruby's cellphone? Her calendar's on it."

Dory nodded. "Now you sound like Suzanne's child, with that persistence. I'll tell him." Dory opened the door again.

"She has Ruby's cellphone." Dory's voice was deadpan. "It has her calendar on it."

"Fine," Ben snapped.

Dory turned to Mae. "The sheriff said you can come in."

Both women walked into the conference room and sat down at the table.

"Good morning, all." Mae smiled as she set down the box of donuts and the coffee urn. "I'm Mae December."

Thank you for joining us, Miss December," the sheriff said dryly. "Listen up people, this is the woman who found Ruby's body. Mae, I'd like to introduce my staff. This big guy to my left is Wayne Nichols, Chief Detective. To his left is Tech Hadley Johns from our lab."

Hadley Johns was tall and gangly looking. His dark hair was military short, Mae noticed. She thought it was probably to protect samples from contamination.

"Next to Hadley is Emma Peters, also from the lab. Going around the table, we have Deputy Robert Fuller in the glasses and George Phelps, who always looks a bit sleepy this early. George, are you with us?" Ben asked and George nodded, looking shamefaced.

Deputy Fuller had given Mae a sharp look when Ben said she was the person who found Ruby's body. It was not the look of a man appreciating a woman.

Deputy Phelps smiled at Mae, seemingly unrepentant at Ben's chastisement.

"It's very nice to meet you all," Mae said, smiling.

"Now, Dory said you have a cellphone for us?"

"Yes, Sheriff."

Ben peered into the envelope. "Damn thing looks more like a computer than a phone. Does anyone here know how to use this thing?"

"I do." Mae smiled. "It's just like mine. I found it yesterday. Don't worry, I used gloves. Her calendar shows that she had an appointment with the road commissioner on March fifteenth at ten a.m. Then she had an appointment with her attorney at one, her doctor at three and a dinner scheduled at the Bistro at six forty-five. I couldn't find a dinner partner's name." Mae smiled.

"Thank you, Miss December. Where did you find this?" asked the sheriff.

"I went to Ruby's before the storm and dialed her cellphone number. When it rang, I followed the sound to the floor of the garage by her car. It was right behind the left front tire."

Ben sighed. "Didn't you see the yellow crime scene tape?"

"Yes, and I know I'm not supposed to enter a crime scene, but the yellow tape was around her house, not around her garage."

"Okay. Our mistake then." He turned to his staff. "Which one of you geniuses put up the crime scene tape and failed to put tape around the victim's garage?" He shook his head when Phelps put up his hand. "Go take care of that right now, George." Phelps left in a hurry with his head down.

"Sheriff, could I stay for the rest of your meeting?" Mae asked.

He shot a glare in her direction. "Absolutely not."

Deputy Fuller gave her a wink. "Oh come on, boss, a pretty lady who brings us coffee, donuts and a Blackberry?"

Ben gave him a stern look. "Fine, but only until we finish discussing what we can learn from this phone, since Miss December seems to be the only one of you smart enough to decode it."

"Thank you," said Mae. "Please help yourselves to the treats. Yesterday I read the names of everyone on her cellphone list, her entire calendar, and her Notes to Self section. I was also able to see all the Internet sites she searched the week before her death. Plus, I figured out how to see her texts. There may be more clues on that phone, and I'll keep looking while I'm here."

"Thank you, but I think my staff is up to it from this point on. Johns, please take the phone and get the fingerprint information. Then I want it returned to Dory so she can make copies of all this information for Chief Nichols. Got it?"

Dory nodded.

"Certainly, Sheriff." Mae smiled. "I have some more information which might help, too. Before she died, Ruby talked to a realtor about selling her property to a big developer. Apparently, she also planned to change her will."

Ben turned to Dory who had entered the room with Mae. "What did you find out about the will?"

The sheriff seemed to be overlooking Mae for the moment. She sat very still, trying not to call attention to herself.

"She planned to leave everything to her brother, Silas, unless she had children. The land and the house came to her in trust from her father. If she died childless, the whole property went to Silas. The only thing she left to her husband was the dog."

This news earned a few laughs, quickly stifled.

Dory went on. "The property was free and clear. No mortgage. I also found out that her doctor is a fertility specialist."

"Lord have mercy," Hadley Johns muttered. "She was trying to get pregnant? How old was the woman anyway?"

"Thirty-seven," Mae said. "She'd never been pregnant. Not for lack of trying." The corners of her mouth raised.

"Thank you again, Miss December," said Ben, firmly. "I need you to leave the meeting now. Dory, can you go with her and track down the other items we talked about?"

They did but Dory left the door slightly ajar, probably by accident. Mae said she needed to go to the ladies' room, but as soon as Dory walked around the corner to follow the sheriff's instructions, Mae slipped back down the hall to the conference room. She stood outside the door and listened.

"All right, everyone," Ben said, "let's get down to business here. The purpose of this morning's meeting is to get everyone's input and settle on a list of tasks. As all of you know, murders are usually solved within the first forty-eight hours, if at all. Since Ruby had been dead for four days when Miss December found her body, we are already starting with a handicap.

"Just as a reminder, everything discussed in this meeting, as well as the detailed reports, are confidential. The press is pushing very hard for answers, but only Detective Nichols and

I will be meeting with them. Nobody else is to say anything. Understood?"

Section by section, Ben received reports. Mae waited fascinated and completely silent. She did feel a little guilty for ignoring the sheriff's directive to leave. She knew whatever she heard by eavesdropping would have to kept completely confidential. She wouldn't even be able to tell Tammy. Listening in on the meeting was rash if not illegal, but the open door proved too much of a temptation to resist. She learned that Ruby had sued Lucy Ingram a few months before her death. Even Mama didn't know that! Ruby apparently died sometime after eight p.m. on the night of March fifteenth. The cord that Mae had seen with her body was a piece of vehicle counting equipment.

"What was the actual cause of death?" Emma Peters asked.

"Ruby died from blunt force trauma caused by a blow to the back of her head. The murder weapon is still missing," Ben said his voice was low and angry.

"Why would the perp leave her body outside in a grove of trees, instead of hiding her more carefully or burying her?" someone asked.

"Good question." The voice sounded like Detective Nichols. "We think the perp chased Ruby and then clubbed her near the grove. He probably left her body in the closest possible place where it wouldn't be spotted immediately. This might indicate a perp who wasn't strong enough to haul the body very far."

"So why would she have the traffic counting cord around her neck?" This sounded like Deputy Fuller.

"We think the perp might have done that to tie Ruby's death to the controversy about widening Little Chapel Road," Ben said. "Johns, did David Allison's shirts show anything suspicious?"

"No, but he might have changed clothes after work. I'm going back today to pick up whatever hasn't been washed."

"Has the car been gone over?" That was Ben's voice again.

"Yes. Nothing but evidence of the vic and her dog."

Mae covered her mouth so they couldn't hear her laugh. Elvis shed up a storm during every car ride. In fact, there was enough red fur left in her tote bag to knit a sweater.

After everybody gave their opinions and ideas, Ben asked Detective Nichols to summarize what the next steps would be.

"Our first step is to meet with all the people Ruby saw on the fifteenth. We've already talked to everyone who lives on Little Chapel Road. So far, we've interviewed Lucy Ingram, the Ryans, David Allison and Beth Jensen. The Connollys are gone for the month. MaryLou Dennis has been in a medical rehab facility for several weeks. Both those houses were supposedly empty at the time of the murder."

Ben said, "Where's that plat map, the one that shows all the lots on Little Chapel Road? Hadley, put that up on the board, will you? Everybody, please note the names of all the homeowners on Little Chapel Road as shown in this diagram."

"I see there's a Connolly. Any relation to James Connolly, Ruby's attorney?" Wayne asked.

"Yes, he's their nephew. Here's the Dennis property. MaryLou is Joe Dennis' mother. All these people have a history—Joe Dennis grew up in this house and he's currently remodeling Mae December's house."

"Joe Dennis and Ruby dated when they were young and may have been sexually intimate at that time." It was the detective's voice. "We can't exclude the possibility that they might have been having an affair currently. This makes him a person of interest."

"Right, I talked to Joe, and he still seemed to have feelings for her," Ben said.

Mae silently disagreed. The only feelings Joe still had for Ruby were those of aggravation and maybe a little protectiveness. If Ben had ever seen Joe and his wife Neesy together he would have known better. The two of them were obviously very much in love.

Detective Nichols went on. "Ruby had some kind of connection with each of her neighbors, except possibly the Van Attas, Anne and Jason. We talked to them yesterday. If they have any ties to our victim, I couldn't find them. There was one interesting thing we got in the interview, though. Do you have your notes, Robert?"

There was a pause. Fuller cleared his throat. "Jason Van Atta reported seeing lights on in MaryLou Dennis' house the night of March fifteenth. He assumed Joe was working late. Mrs. Van Atta told us she saw lights in the Connolly residence that night as well."

Standing out in the hall, Mae was taken aback. She never realized Ruby had been so involved in the lives of all the Little Chapel Road residents. *Of course, she wouldn't talk to me if my hair were on fire, unless she needed somewhere to stash Elvis.*

Detective Nichols spoke up. "We need to find out if the Connollys had a house sitter, or if anyone was supposed to be there that night. We'll also need corroboration that Joe Dennis was working at his mother's house the evening of the fifteenth."

"The most critical detail to get now is the name of the person Ruby dined with the night she died. I would also like to have more information about her appointments with the lawyer and the doctor. Let's get going."

Chairs scraped back from the table and Mae ran down the hall to the ladies' room. When she returned, the conference room was empty. She retrieved her coffee urn and tossed the empty donut container into the trash.

On the way out, she stopped at Dory's desk. "I'd really like to help the sheriff with this investigation. Nobody should die like Ruby did, alone and terrified."

Dory's expression reminded her of Tammy's when she smiled. "Maybe you and the sheriff can help each other out, Honey."

"I thought he and I had a meeting?"

"He's left, Mae. Guess he thinks you've already shared what you know."

MAE LEFT THE station and headed home. For the first time since the murder, her mind wandered to what was happening at her house. She wondered how Tallulah was doing with the newborns. She began to think about some possible names for the new puppies. They were all black with white ruffs except one, who had inherited a red coat from his father. She might call him Eric the Red. People who came to buy the puppies often wanted to hear what she had named them.

Of course, even the thought of puppies, adorable as they were, could only distract her for so long before she again fixed on the subject of Ruby's death. Sheriff Bradley said he needed to know the outcome of Ruby's appointments, so Mae decided to drop by the doctor's office on her way home.

The new fertility clinic in Rosedale was in a large multi-specialty medical complex used by several doctors. The modern facility was decorated beautifully with Asian scrolls on the walls, large plants, and a pond swimming with lovely red and white koi fish. Mae took a deep breath as she walked into the building, enjoying the scent of the fresh green plants. Checking the directory posted on the wall, she found the fertility practice on the third floor. The office décor was über modern with purple leather seating and large abstract paintings. It seemed more like a living room than a doctor's office. Mae had known Sheri, the woman at the front desk, since high school. Her shiny black hair was expertly cut and perfectly framed her small face.

"Hi Sheri."

"Oh, hi Mae, did you have an appointment? You're not trying to get pregnant, are you?"

"Sheri, I'm shocked." She smiled. "You know I'm not even married. I wanted to ask about something. My neighbor Ruby Mead-Allison is a patient here. Did you hear she passed away?"

Sheri sighed. "I know. How awful!"

"I found her body. I was out walking my dogs at the time. It was horrible." Mae felt the heat suffuse her cheeks. The retelling brought back the horror. "I can hardly talk about it. The reason I stopped in is that I wanted to know if Ruby made her last appointment on the fifteenth."

"Mae, I'm sure you know I'm not supposed to give out patient information."

"I know, but the sheriff's people will be here shortly with a subpoena. Could you shake your head or nod in answer to one question?"

"I'm sorry Mae, but I can't help you. I could lose my job."

"Thanks anyway, Sheri. I have to get going. My pug had her babies yesterday. I need to go home and check on them."

As Mae drove the rest of the way home she noticed that everything had turned green after yesterday's rain. Spring was her favorite time of year. She mulled over all the details she had learned at the staff meeting. *Too bad Sheri couldn't tell me anything. However, I can still check into Ruby's other appointments.*

When Mae got home, she called Tammy and asked her to come over. Then she made sure all the dogs went out and that they had full water dishes. Then she sat down and held each of the puppies for a while. Nothing made her happier than holding their warm little bodies. Puppies smelled so wonderful. You could almost sense their personalities even at a few days old.

Chapter Ten

March 21
Mae December

TAMMY BREEZED IN within the hour wearing stiletto heels, gray jeans and a silky blouse. Mae took one look at her and told her to come upstairs while she freshened up. Tammy followed Mae upstairs, sitting on her bed while Mae touched up her lipstick and attempted to smooth her hair. Once she felt a little more presentable, she told Tammy her idea for finding out what happened between Ruby and her attorney the day she got back. Deciding to go out to lunch, they took Tammy's car and ate at Crepes, the new café in Rosedale.

After lunch, they went to James Connolly's office. Mae assumed he would have been the one to handle any property transactions and knew financial matters often figured as a motive for murder. Tammy knew a legal tech there named Mary and she went inside to talk to her. Mae waited in the car until Tammy returned. She wasn't gone very long.

"So, what did you find out?" Mae asked.

"Ruby showed up to meet with her attorney, but she only stayed in his office for a little while. After Ruby left, Connolly came out and showed Mary a gift Ruby had brought him. An expensive cigar, a 'cohiba,' I think she called it. Apparently, they cost about fifty dollars apiece. She said that Connolly seemed preoccupied the whole afternoon after Ruby left."

"That's weird. I wonder if she even made her ten o'clock appointment with the road commissioner. I can probably get Dory to tell me."

The sheriff's office and the road commissioner's office being in the same building, Mae assumed that Dory would know Mr. Stillwell's secretary. She dialed her number.

"Hi, Dory, it's Mae. I've been wondering about something. Ruby had an appointment with Aubrey Stillwell on the morning of the fifteenth. Can you find out if she kept it?"

"I'll go ask his secretary. Give me a minute."

Dory put Mae on hold for about five minutes and then came back on the line.

"She kept it all right. Commissioner Stillwell was real sorry she did."

"I'm sure he was. Mama told me Ruby was a total pain to the Commissioner. Thank you very much for the information. Bye."

Riding along in the warm spring sunshine, the women reviewed what they knew.

Ruby had kept her ten o'clock appointment with the road commissioner and then she had seen her attorney at one, but only briefly.

"I wonder if she kept her dinner reservation at the Bistro?"

"Well, nothing ventured, nothing gained." Tammy smiled and called information for the number. Then she dialed the restaurant. "Hello. Could you look something up in your reservation book for me? Thank you. On March fifteenth, two of my friends were dining at your wonderful restaurant. Their reservation time was six forty-five. I need to know if they kept their reservation. Can you check for the name of Mead-Allison? Sure, I'll wait. Yes, they did? Okay, thanks for telling me." Tammy hung up and turned to Mae. "She kept the dinner reservation."

"Did they know who she had dinner with?"

"No. Maybe we can find out some other way. Can you drive over there?"

"Sure, but they aren't open for lunch, only for dinner. It's two-thirty now. They may not let us in."

They pulled into the mostly vacant parking lot of one of the hottest dining spots around. There were only three cars in the lot. A sign on the door read, "Closed until four." Mae tried the door and, to her surprise, it opened. They went in, flipped through the reservation book, and read the name in the six forty-five time slot on March fifteenth. The entry read, Mead-Allison/Hunter.

"Hunter? Who do we know named Hunter?" Mae asked her friend. They were talking in hushed tones in the darkened entry of the upscale eatery.

"Besides Arlen Hunter?"

"Arlen Hunter." Mae shook her head. He was a big country music star, about thirty-five and unmarried. Known for dating glamorous young women in their early twenties, he was also the singer who had first recorded Noah's music.

At that moment, the Maitre d' approached. Mae blushed but Tammy piped up saying, "Oh hello. We were hoping to find out when you were open and take a look at the menu. Sorry, this isn't the menu, is it? It's the reservation book, my silly mistake."

The Maitre d' looked dubious. "Menus are always posted outside restaurants," he said.

"We'll take a look at it," Mae said, determinedly pulling Tammy along with her.

"We'll come back another time," Tammy called back over her shoulder. Mae shushed her.

"What would Arlen Hunter be doing with Ruby?" Tammy asked when they got to the car.

Mae frowned. "Maybe Ruby wanted to be his manager."

"Well that makes sense. She was way too old for his taste, which I understand runs to barely above jailbait."

Mae dialed the sheriff's office again. "Dory, it's Mae again. Could you give the sheriff a message for me?"

"Go ahead." Mae thought she detected a note of exasperation in Dory's voice.

"Please tell him I found out that Ruby met with the road commissioner—thanks for that information—then she met with her attorney, but I don't know what happened at her doctor's appointment. My friend wouldn't tell me."

"Imagine that," Dory said, her voice heavy with irony.

"I did find out that Hunter was the name that the restaurant had listed as Ruby's dinner partner. I think it was Arlen Hunter."

"Slow down. I'm writing all this down. You mean the singer?"

"Yes, that's right, the singer."

"Hmm, interesting. I'll pass this on to Sheriff Bradley. Bye now."

A few minutes later, Mae's cellphone rang. Recognizing the number of the Rosedale Sheriff's Department, she put the phone on speaker so Tammy could hear the conversation.

"Hello," she said.

"Miss December." The sheriff didn't sound happy.

"Hello, Sheriff."

"What do you think you're doing? You need to stop running all over the county asking questions about this case." His tone was quite unpleasant. Mae glanced at Tammy, who lifted one perfectly arched brow.

"What? You don't want me to help you find Ruby's murderer? I thought you were in favor of community involvement in stopping crime in the county." Mae used her sweetest voice. Tammy rolled her eyes.

"I guess I haven't made myself clear. This could be dangerous and you need to stay out of it."

"I'll stop if you tell me to, of course, Sheriff, but I have an appointment with Arlen Hunter at his office this afternoon." A blatant lie.

"Fine then." The sheriff gave a loud sigh. "Just let me know what he says, but after that meeting, you need to stop."

"Yes, of course. I'll call you afterwards. Or better yet, I'll be home around six tonight if you'd like to stop by for some wine and cheese." Her mother's training was finally paying off.

"You go girl," Tammy whispered.

"Deputy Phelps and I will stop by."

"Fine. If you feel you need to bring a deputy. It's up to you. See you at six."

Mae closed her phone and smiled at Tammy, who grinned back.

"Nicely handled. How are you going to get an appointment?"

"I don't need an appointment. I'll call Rhonda, his assistant. She and Noah were friends. She'll help me out."

"I need to get going," Tammy said.

"Call me later." Mae responded as she hopped out of the car and carefully shut the car door, mindful of Tammy's protective feelings about her prized convertible. She waved at her friend as she barreled down the driveway and went into the house. After checking on the puppies, she decided to call Dory again.

"Hi, Dory. I hope you don't mind me bothering you again." Mae wondered if Dory was getting tired of all the phone calls and hurried on before she could protest. "Is it possible that Ruby was pregnant when she died? It didn't really hit me until just now, but I saw a home pregnancy test box in Ruby's car. Don't tell me if you're not supposed to."

"You're an observant girl, and you're right. The autopsy confirmed that Ruby was pregnant, but keep that to yourself. I probably shouldn't tell you this, but I talked to Nancy in Stillwell's office again, too. She heard Ruby and Stillwell arguing. After Ruby left, Stillwell called Nancy into his office and told her that Ruby was going to be the death of him. Apparently, Ruby had threatened the commissioner with some new trumped-up lawsuit. She'd found another reason to delay the road widening."

"I don't understand why the fight was so important to her."

"I think she was an unhappy woman, honey. Seems like it's always some man—or some money—at the bottom of that kind of a mess."

MAE HUMMED AS she got out of the shower and towel-dried her hair. She laid a black sundress with a red and yellow poppy print on her bed. Then she put on a black bra and panties and slid the silky dress over her head. Glancing into the mirror, she once again felt grateful for the color black. If she could just lose five pounds she could wear those aqua jeans again, she thought.

Putting on her silvery sandals and grabbing a yellow sweater for the cool night, she came downstairs to the kitchen and poured merlot into a decanter. She got out some crackers, red grapes and a round of Brie. Nearly six o'clock and for the first time in more than a year, she was entertaining a man.

At six on the dot, the sheriff's car came up the drive. Ben was alone. Mae smiled, pleased he felt comfortable enough to leave his deputy behind. He came up to the screened porch and knocked.

"Come on in," Mae called. He did, but there was a thundercloud on his face.

"Oh, Ben, what is it?"

"I can't tell you how upset I am. I only came over to tell you in person to stay out of this case."

Mae looked at him, crestfallen.

"You barge into my meeting, make a fool of me in front of my staff, produce a cellphone after having trampled all over the crime scene and then you go to Ruby's doctor's office and the restaurant!"

"Did someone complain from the restaurant?" Mae asked him with a guilty look.

"No, Dory told me. But this has to stop."

Tears started to sting Mae's eyes.

"Miss December, you may mean well, but a murder investigation isn't for amateurs. These are things my staff is supposed to do, not you. I'm going to leave now."

"Sheriff…"

"What?"

"I'm really sorry if I caused you any embarrassment by coming to the office with Ruby's phone. I only wanted to help. I just feel so terrible about what happened to Ruby and to our beautiful little neighborhood. I thought since I know everyone, maybe I could find out a few details that your office couldn't. I'm good at reading people, too. Finding the phone was some help, wasn't it?"

"Yes," he sighed.

"Please stay for a while. I wanted to tell you what I found out about Ruby's dinner partner."

He hesitated. "Miss December," his voice was low, "I need you to promise me you'll stop all this nonsense about trying to solve this crime. You might be putting your life in danger. This isn't a… a hobby. It's a murder."

"I will. I promise. Please sit down and have a drink, won't you? You look like you could use one." He wasn't wearing his uniform, and in street clothes he seemed thinner and less intimidating. He also looked younger and very tired.

They sat in the two wicker chairs on the porch facing Mae's backyard. The tulips were opening, the light shining through their blooms casting colors on the grass.

"What did Arlen Hunter have to say about his dinner with Ruby?"

"Nothing. It turns out Arlen Hunter wasn't her escort. I talked to his assistant and she said he cancelled his appointment with Ruby around four that day. She had dinner with someone, though. She wouldn't waste a reservation at the Bistro. I wonder who it was."

"I'll get my men on it first thing tomorrow."

"You might want to go over there tonight. They're only open for dinner."

"Right. I'll finish up this drink and go over there now."

"With me?" Mae heard the hope in her voice and looked away to disguise the warmth that flooded her face at her forwardness.

"No, by myself." His eyes showed some regret and a bit of amusement. "Before I go, is there anything else you want to tell me?"

"Before I brought the phone to the station, I read some of Ruby's emails to her brother. There were also some to her husband and to another man. At least I assume so. They were pretty spicy. I think Ruby had a new boyfriend."

"Somewhere in all this there's a motive for murder. I'd better get going."

She walked him to his car and touched his shoulder as they said goodbye. He drove away. It was a beautiful evening, and Mae didn't want to be alone. She had given Ben her word, though, so she couldn't follow him to the Bistro. What are friends for? Mae thought and called Tammy.

Tammy called Mae back on her way home. She had arrived at the Bistro before Ben. The hostess and a waiter remembered the reservation because they thought Arlen Hunter would be dining. When Ruby arrived with another man, the staff had been disappointed. Tammy got a description. He was tall, dark haired, and wore glasses. The waiter thought he might be a member of Hunter's band, but the receptionist thought the server was dreaming. She insisted he was a local businessman.

Chapter Eleven

———

March 22
Sheriff Ben Bradley

BEN STARTED HIS staff meeting that morning by asking everyone for their reports. Deputy Fuller informed the group that he located Ruby's purse and had given it to the lab for testing. Although the M.E. informed Ben the previous day about Ruby's pregnancy, he announced the information to the rest of the staff. He also told them that on the night she died, Ruby had dinner at the Bistro with a tall, dark-haired man wearing glasses.

Robert volunteered to take a photo of David Allison to the restaurant to see if the wait staff could identify him as Ruby's dinner partner. Ben asked him to get the receipt for dinner to see who paid for the meal. He had asked for it the night before, but nobody could find it. Perhaps they had paid with cash? The sheriff asked Detective Nichols to summarize their progress to date.

"As I see it, there were plenty of motives for someone to want Ruby dead. Her ex, or soon-to-be-ex, David Allison, told us he dined with people from work that night. We'll be asking for corroboration of his alibi. He may not have wanted Ruby to have a child. If it turns out that David had dinner with Ruby on the fifteenth, he might have been the last person to see her alive. We're going to get a cheek swab and then we'll know if he fathered Ruby's child."

He paused for a moment.

The sheriff nodded. "Go on, Detective."

"In interviews with her neighbors, we learned that Ruby had two visitors the night she died. Lucy Ingram saw a sedan parked in her driveway around eleven and then a pickup truck around one in the morning. Eveline Ryan identified the sedan as David Allison's car."

"We're considering several suspects at present," Ben said. "As Detective Nichols mentioned, the most likely is David Allison. Our second suspect is the road commissioner, Mr. Stillwell. Everyone knows that he was furious with Ruby. There have been articles in the paper detailing their feud. We also plan to investigate the people who stand to inherit money from Ruby's estate. Her attorney might be involved, too. What do we know so far about these primary suspects, Wayne?"

"Most of them have alibis for the fifteenth. Commissioner Stillwell's alibi seems solid. He played contract bridge with eleven other couples over at the Hilton. His wife told us they left the hotel at about ten o'clock and went home. He wasn't feeling well so she took care of him until around one, at which time they both went to bed.

"Ruby's attorney, James Connolly, also seems to have an alibi. He and his wife were at the symphony in Nashville with another couple and, according to them, he never left the group. They all went home after having a few drinks, arriving shortly before midnight. However, the grapevine says Ruby had some sort of hold over Connolly, since he continued as her attorney after the increasingly contentious road decisions. He also owns a pickup truck and two neighbors said there was a pickup in Ruby's driveway that night."

"Ruby's brother, Silas Mead, moved away years ago," Ben said. "However, since he benefits financially from her death, we're trying to get in touch with him.

"We're also keeping an eye on Joe Dennis, the contractor working over at Mae December's house. He and Ruby were high school sweethearts. He's married now and has four kids. So, we know he's capable of being the father of Ruby's unborn child," Wayne said.

Eyebrows went up around the table. "Oh, and according to Joe, he was working at his mother's house the night Ruby died. Nobody was with him, though, so he has no alibi. And Joe drives a pickup," Phelps added.

"Okay, here are the assignments, everyone. George, I want you to go over Ruby's property again with a fine-toothed comb. We need the murder weapon.

"Wayne, I'd like you and Emma Peters to go to the Connollys' and get James' clothes from the night of the murder. I'll talk to Allison and get a cheek swab. We need one from Joe Dennis and James Connolly, too. Johns, you're with me. We're returning to see David Allison."

Detective Nichols cleared his throat and said, "I'll also start checking out those pickups after Emma and I get James Connolly's clothes."

"Good. One last thing. We know Ruby sued Lucy Ingram. The argument was about drainage, but Ruby also wanted to purchase a lot that Lucy owned, which Lucy refused to sell. I'm going to check on whether Ruby was involved in any lawsuits with the other residents on Little Chapel Road. Who knows how many folks she stirred up."

On his way out, Deputy Phelps came over to Ben. "Sheriff, I sure hope you didn't upset the December woman. We loved her coffee. I hope you don't mind my saying this, Boss, but the guys and I were talking and they thought I should remind you that you haven't had a date in months."

"No comment."

Ben felt a bit sheepish. His deputy was right. He hadn't felt much like dating for a long time. Mae was single and hot. Would she go out with him if he asked? Probably not now thanks to his rude behavior, first at the staff meeting and later at her house. He had been angry enough that she had apologized profusely. What happened then? Did you say you weren't mad at her anymore? No, Mr. Sensitive, you drove away, even after she offered to go to the restaurant with you.

Sheriff Bradley and Tech Johns drove to Steven Fanning's residence on Little Chapel Road. They knocked on the door. David Allison answered.

"Good morning, Mr. Allison, you've already met CSI Tech Johns. May we come in?"

"All right," David said reluctantly and backed away from the door. He led the men over to the kitchen table.

"Mr. Allison, were you aware your wife was pregnant?"

David's throat moved as he swallowed. "Yes. Do I need an attorney?"

"That's entirely up to you. At this point, we only need to ask you a few more questions and get a cheek swab."

David's eyes widened. "What for?"

"To determine whether you're the father of Ruby's unborn child through DNA analysis."

David Allison flinched but allowed the technician to take the sample. Tech Johns used a large Q-tip on the inside of Allison's cheek. He put the swab inside a glass tube and capped it competently.

"Are you the father?"

"I… yes, of course." David hesitated. "Well, I guess I'm not sure."

"Was your wife seeing other men? I need to know if you have any information that might clear you of suspicion." The sheriff deliberately softened his voice. "I appreciate how difficult this must be for you."

David was quiet for a moment. "I really don't know. I wanted to reconcile with Ruby. I still hoped we'd have a family. I went over to the house about a month ago to talk to her. There was a car in the driveway I didn't recognize. When she opened the door, I could hear music playing in the background. She didn't invite me in, so I assumed there was a man in the house." David grimaced at the memory. That really made him angry, Ben thought.

"Why do you think Ruby was opposed to the road widening? You were still together when all this started, so you must have some idea."

"Ruby didn't want to lose even a foot of her property. That land was all she had left from her father. She wanted to limit development as much as possible. She is, I mean she was, a real fighter. She saw 'eminent domain' as an injustice and an attack on the residents of the street. I think she probably would have made a fine lawyer." The sheriff noted a faint look of pride on David's face.

After a brief silence he added, "Ruby wasn't as successful financially as she wanted to be. She also thought she might get more money from the county for the easements if she held out longer."

"Were the two of you having financial problems?"

"Not really, but she would have had trouble keeping the place up on her income alone. The house needs a lot of work."

"Why were you divorcing?"

"She was a difficult woman to live with, Sheriff." David sounded resigned. Despite the long silence that followed, he said nothing more.

Johns asked David Allison if he had any other laundry from the evening in question. He followed Allison out of the room and when they returned, Hadley had a pair of sweats, socks and underwear bagged.

"We'll be getting back to you." Sheriff Bradley said.

Chapter Twelve

March 22
Detective Wayne Nichols

After their early morning meeting, Detective Wayne Nichols called James Connolly's home. A woman answered and he asked her if Mr. Connolly was at home. She told him her husband was at his office.

He introduced himself and said, "Actually, I'd like to stop by and ask you some questions, Mrs. Connolly."

"Me? What's this about, Detective?"

"We're investigating Ruby Mead-Allison's murder. I have a few questions for you."

"I don't know that I should answer them."

"This is very informal, Mrs. Connolly." He kept his tone light and reassuring. "Could we stop by in about fifteen minutes? We won't stay long."

"Well, I guess that would be all right."

Detective Nichols and CSI Tech Emma Peters arrived shortly thereafter at the imposing residence. Emma was in her early twenties with dark curly hair. She was skilled at the tedious work of DNA analysis, but always seemed pleased if she was asked to do a site visit. Connolly's housekeeper answered the door and showed them in. At a gesture from Wayne, Emma engaged the woman in conversation and the two of them disappeared down a wide hallway.

At that moment a tall, thin woman, wearing what looked like designer exercise clothes walked into the foyer. She wore her blond hair tightly pulled back from her face.

"What's going on here?" Laura Connolly's voice combined tension and belligerence in equal quantities.

"I want to reassure you, Mrs. Connolly, we're only here to eliminate your husband as a suspect in this investigation."

"My husband?" She seemed surprised but then rapidly changed her attitude. "Oh, fine then."

She closed the door behind them and led Wayne into the living room, where she gestured to the dark leather couch and they both sat down. Laura Connolly sat at the edge of the sofa, her back ramrod straight. Tightly wound, Wayne thought, or she has something to hide.

"Were you with your husband on the night of March fifteenth? We already talked with your husband's secretary. That was the evening you went to the symphony, correct?"

"Oh, yes, you're right."

"Did your husband wear a suit to the symphony?"

"Yes, he did."

"I assumed so, and that's why your cleaning lady and the crime scene tech are talking. We need to get his clothing from that night. Again, this is merely to eliminate him from suspicion."

"She should be able to get his suit and shirt. I haven't taken them to the cleaner's yet."

"Thank you." Wayne heaved an inward sigh of relief.

"Do you and Mr. Connolly have children?"

"Yes. We have two children. Our son Clayton is seven and Marie, our daughter, is three."

"Who took care of your children the night of March fifteenth?"

"Nora Takichi sat for us that night."

"How did she get home?"

There was a brief hesitation. "James drove Nora home. Nora had some trouble getting Marie to sleep so she put her down in our bed. I went in and slept with her. James slept in the guestroom after he got back from taking Nora home."

"Did your husband change his clothes before taking the babysitter home?"

She hesitated again. "No, they left right away."

Emma returned with the clothing. Wayne thanked Laura Connolly and they departed.

"I'm going to drive over to see Joe Dennis," Wayne said. "Are you free to go along? We can get that cheek swab."

"That's fine. I'm pretty much caught up with my lab work at present."

"At present." He grinned at Emma. "But not for long. We'll have plenty for you to analyze soon." Emma was dressed casually, in a lab coat over t-shirts and jeans. Very cute. Way too young for him though.

They drove to the address that Dory had given them for Joe Dennis. Joe's house was on the small side for a family with four kids, Wayne thought. It was a white, ranch-style home with dark red shutters and a three-car garage. Beside the house stood a dog run with a large black lab in it. Nichols rang the doorbell.

A small-boned redhead with a baby in her arms answered the door. "Yes?"

"Mrs. Dennis?"

"That's me." She turned to look at a toddler, who was walking determinedly toward a nail polish bottle sitting on the kitchen counter. "Bobby, stop. Leave that alone."

"I'm Wayne Nichols, Sheriff Bradley's Detective and this is Tech Peters. Is your husband home?"

"Sorry, Detective. He's on a job site." She glanced back into the kitchen, took a step away from the door and scooped up the toddler in her other arm. "It's over on Little Chapel Road, his mother's place. The fourth house on the right from the River Road end."

"Thank you." They went back to the car.

"Busy woman," Wayne said.

"How many kids do they have?" Emma asked.

"Four, all under the age of five, I think."

They drove in companionable silence to Little Chapel Road and found the property easily. Joe had parked his truck on the gravel verge by the driveway. He was unloading four-by-eight sheets of plywood. Was it Joe's truck that Mrs. Ryan and Lucy had seen the night Ruby died? Joe looked up as they drove in.

"Joe Dennis?"

Joe was on the short side, tan with a wiry build. "Yes."

"I'm Wayne Nichols, Sheriff's Detective. This is Emma Peters. She's from the lab. I have some questions for you. Can we go inside?"

Joe nodded and they walked up to the older home. As they passed through the entryway, Wayne noted all of the construction material stacked neatly on the floor in the kitchen. Despite the ongoing remodeling, there wasn't a speck of sawdust in the room.

Joe gestured to the kitchen table and they sat down. "Sorry I can't offer you anything. The water's turned off."

"No problem. We need to get a cheek swab and clarify some information you gave the sheriff. Can we get that now?"

"Sure."

"Open your mouth please, sir," Emma said.

Joe did and she expertly obtained a cheek swab and placed it in a labeled envelope.

"Thank you," Emma said.

"Joe, I know it's been a while, but I need to take you back to your high school days," Wayne said. "You and Ruby Mead-

Allison were high school sweethearts, correct?"

"Yes." Joe looked pensive. Wayne saw both nostalgia and regret in his face. "We were a couple in high school. Ruby was a free spirit, always a lot of fun in those days. Toward the end of our senior year, she got pregnant. A few weeks later, she told me she had lost the baby, but I think she may have had an abortion." Joe looked down, not meeting Wayne's eyes.

"Is that why you two broke up?"

"In a way. She didn't seem the same after that and when she left for college, I started dating another girl, a friend of Ruby's."

"Have you stayed in touch since?"

"On and off. She contacted me when she got engaged to David Allison. She thought I'd be upset about her marriage. Maybe she wanted me to be upset. I don't know. Anyway, I told her I was also getting married. After that, every now and then Ruby would call or send me an email. Sometimes we would have coffee or lunch. My wife … didn't know."

"So I'm thinking you resumed your sexual relationship at some point." Wayne's voice conveyed acceptance and understanding. Joe started to protest, but the detective held up his hand. "I know Ruby and her husband couldn't get pregnant. She had conceived a child once with you. I imagine she thought she could again."

"Yes, that's what she thought, that I could get her pregnant, but I'm married now and I love my wife. I didn't want to jeopardize that." Joe's voice strengthened as he said this.

"I imagine it's pretty hard to turn down such a striking woman who's determined to sleep with you." Wayne raised his eyebrows inquisitively.

"It was. Now she's dead. And I…" His voice faltered. "I'll miss her."

"Well, we'll soon find out if you were the father of her child." Joe looked as if he were about to protest but didn't.

"You knew she was pregnant, I assume."

"She called to give me the news when she got back from

Hawaii." Joe's face was awash with confusion and remorse.

"Ruby was pregnant and in the middle of a divorce. What did you think she really wanted when she called? For you to leave your wife and marry her?"

"She didn't say that outright, but I gathered that was the purpose of telling me."

"I'd like to believe you, Joe, but if Ruby was pregnant with your child, it could have destroyed your marriage, a marriage you obviously value. Did you go over to talk to her that night? Did things get out of hand? Is that what happened? Was it an accident?" He deliberately kept his voice low and supportive.

"I didn't kill Ruby." Joe leaned forward. "It wasn't my child she carried. I could tell she was in over her head, though. She seemed afraid and wanted me to save her."

"You were the white knight. You were supposed to waltz in and rescue her. Maybe there was someone she needed help with? Someone she was afraid of, perhaps? If it wasn't her husband's child, he would have been furious."

"Probably, but I told her I couldn't get involved. Although I considered her a friend, she was a ticking time bomb. I didn't need it. I never could save Ruby from herself."

Again, he saw the unhappiness writ plain on Joe's face.

"Thanks for your cooperation, Mr. Dennis. We'll show ourselves out."

They left him sitting in silence at his mother's table.

"I don't think he did it," Emma said, looking at Wayne over the roof of the car as they opened the doors to get inside.

"We need to find out if Joe was the father of the child, and I also want to ask Mrs. Ryan if it was Joe's pickup she saw the night Ruby died, but, at a gut level, I agree with you. He doesn't look like the killer to me."

Chapter Thirteen

———

March 22
Mae December

MAE RESOLVED TO concentrate on her own life, since Ben clearly didn't want her help with the case. She dialed Joe's cell to check on the remodeling but got no answer, so she called his home number and spoke with his wife. Her name was Denise, but since the full name Denise Dennis was such a mouthful, everyone called her Neesy. She somehow managed to run Joe's contracting business and keep his books, while staying home with four small children. She gave Mae a quick run-down on the next phase of the remodeling. However, Joe was working on his mother's house and wouldn't be back at Mae's for a while, she said. Mae asked Neesy to send her a bill. Their conversation was almost over when Mae asked, "Neesy, has Joe heard from Silas Mead lately?"

"Ruby's brother? Funny you should ask. They hadn't talked in years, ever since Silas moved out west, but he called last week and left Joe a message. I think he may be back in town, because he left a local phone number on our machine."

"Could I have the number? I'd like to ask Silas something."

Neesy gave her the number and they said goodbye. Mae wondered if she should give Ben the number or if she should just try calling Silas herself. Although she was leery of making the sheriff angry again, she decided to call Silas and then tell him if she learned anything useful. Maybe she could get something relevant from Ruby's brother and it would be her chance to get back in Ben's good graces.

Silas answered the phone on the second ring, in a shaky voice. Mae reminded herself to be tactful.

"Hi Silas, it's Mae December calling, Ruby's neighbor. I wanted to tell you how sorry I am about your loss."

"Thanks Mae, I appreciate that. How did you get this number, by the way?"

"From Neesy Dennis. Did you know that I was the one who found Ruby?"

"Her body? Yes, the grapevine's still going strong around here." Silas gave a short bark of a laugh. It was devoid of humor.

"Anyway, when did you get back into town, Si? Did you get to see Ruby? Where are you staying?"

"Well, aren't you the inquisitive one?" Silas always had a sharp tongue. "I've only been here a few days. I came back at Ruby's request. She said I could crash with her, but I preferred to stay at my friend Jon's instead. My partner, Terry, is with me. Ruby said she needed to discuss something important, but I never got a chance to find out what." He sounded close to tears. "We planned to meet the other day, but she never showed—I guess she couldn't."

"Well, you take care, Silas. I am truly sorry for your loss. I'll let you go."

"Goodbye, then."

Mae put the phone down and stood in her kitchen, deep in thought. Her reverie was interrupted by slamming car doors and scraping metallic sounds. She looked out the window to see the painters unloading their ladders. She let them in and double-checked the color of the paint. The soft gold should look beautiful in the dining room, particularly in the evening. After making sure they had everything they needed, she opened some windows and placed a fan in the laundry room doorway to blow any fumes away from Tallulah and her babies. Mae preferred to be out of the house when workers painted or stained so she decided to take her mother's dogs with her and go to her parents' house. Kudzu and Lil'bit, Suzanne's Jack Russell terriers, were always happy to go for a ride. They jumped into the backseat of her Explorer when Mae opened the door, but as soon as they were inside, they leaped up into the driver's seat.

"You ride in the back, or you don't ride at all," Mae tried to convey this as sternly as she could. Kudzu obediently hopped in back, but his sister, Lil'bit, continued to sit in the driver's seat, wearing her cutest expression.

"Don't give me that look." Mae couldn't help softening when she noticed the dog's stumpy little tail wagging away. "Fine. You can ride shotgun. It's the best I can do."

Lil'bit reluctantly moved to the passenger seat, where she assumed a hunched and dejected pose.

"I think you were robbed of the Oscar for best actress, Lil'bit. Let's go see Mama."

Her mother's car wasn't in the driveway so she walked back to the studio, a separate building at the back of the property, to see if Daddy was working at home. He was at his desk, reviewing the proofs for his new book, a retrospective of his photos of Country Music legends. He met Mae's eyes with a smile. Mae's breath caught for a minute. The lines on his face were highlighted by the sun. Her tall, handsome father was getting old. She had inherited his thick, wavy blond hair, but his now had a lot of silver mixed in with the gold.

"Can we come in?" Mae tried to hold the dogs back with one foot. Lil'bit squeezed past her, followed by her brother.

"Please do, sweetie. I'm sick of looking at this. I'd much rather see your pretty face. Let the dogs run out in the yard."

"Daddy, you know how Jack Russells are. They'll smell the fresh dirt around the new fountain and start digging everything up."

"We may as well get it over with then. Sit down and tell me what's new."

Mae shooed the dogs out and closed the door behind them. She sat down in one of his comfy old chairs and filled him in on the case, reminding him again of the confidentiality of the information.

"Do you think it sounds suspicious that Ruby asked her brother to come home?"

Her father sat back in his chair and swiveled back and forth a few times. "I don't think Silas would get involved in anything shady. That man has always been honest to a fault. He fought with his father about being gay, but he didn't lie, even though coming out cost him the property. Their dad left everything to Ruby, because of his contempt for homosexuals. After that, Silas moved away. If he says he came home at Ruby's request, I'm sure it's true."

Mae leaned forward in her chair. "Do you think you or Mama could pass all this along to the sheriff for me? He's very upset with me for getting involved in this case."

"I think your mother is perfect for the job, sweetie. I'll ask her as soon as she gets back. I'm glad you came by, though. I'm almost done with this book and I wanted to talk to you about my next project." He stopped and looked at her.

"What is it? Do you need my help with something?"

He shook his head. "More like your permission, actually. I've been thinking about putting together some behind-the-scenes shots from the Opry and the Bluebird. You know, images of the songwriters and session musicians. Would you be all right with me including Noah in the book?"

"Of course I would. Actually, I'd be pleased for him. Do you have any pictures of him working?"

"Yes, I took several. Do you remember Uncle Phil's friend

with the recording studio in Rosedale, John Ayers?"

Mae nodded. "Noah took me there a few times when he and Uncle Phil were co-writing. Mr. Ayers introduced Noah to a lot of industry people. He's a nice man."

Her father tapped the photo. "Sure is. I was out at his place on a shoot for Artesian Records a while back, and Uncle Phil and Noah were in the barn. I could hear them laughing and I got curious so I went out there and they were goofing around, coming up with the worst lyrics you've ever heard. They were a little slaphappy and I started taking pictures." He smiled at her. "Just looking at all the photos made me realize that the songwriters and musicians don't get much of the glory in the end. It all seems to go to the singers. I'd like to pay them a tribute, but I don't want this to be painful for you."

"It's certainly bittersweet, but I'm happy Noah will be part of the project. You don't really need my permission, but I'll be fine."

"Good to hear." He rose to his feet, patted her knee, and started to leaf through the stack of photos again. "I came across some pictures of you and Noah, but there was one person I don't know." He held the picture out to Mae. She took the photo from his hand and studied it.

"Do you recognize this man?" he asked.

The man in the photo was blond and heavyset, not fat but muscular, with a thick neck. He was standing beside the barn, looking out toward the open door.

"No, I don't think so."

Dad handed her three more pictures. "Are you sure?" He tapped the top of the stack. "In this one he's looking right at you."

Mae took a second look, but the man was a stranger. The picture had been taken almost three years earlier. She was younger in the photos and quite obviously in love.

"Sorry, Daddy. I have no idea who he is. I only had eyes for Noah back then."

He smiled and nodded. "It sounds like you might be moving on a little bit. This sheriff character could be interesting." He tilted his head inquiringly.

"I guess so. He read me the riot act last night, though." Mae stood up. "I need to get going."

"Thanks for coming by, hon. Remember, sometimes a bad reaction from a man is better than no reaction at all."

They hugged and said goodbye. As she was backing out of the driveway, Mae saw dirt flung high in the air from two different areas around the new fountain. Mama would be peeved at Kudzu and Lil'bit's antics, but given all the construction going on at Mae's place and a crime scene down the road, Mama's dogs needed to stay at home.

Chapter Fourteen

———

March 22
Mae December

O N HER RETURN from her parent's house, Mae picked up a turkey and cheese Panini from her favorite deli to take home for lunch. She sat down on the laundry room floor with Tallulah and her babies and ate the sandwich. Holding first one puppy and then another, Mae thought again about how much the dogs had helped her recover from Noah's death. They were still a joy whenever she came home.

But even the puppies couldn't fully distract her from the thought that nagged at the edge of her mind. She called her father.

"Hi, Daddy. I've been thinking about that guy from the photographs some more."

"Did you remember something?"

"Not really, but maybe you should ask around. Mama might have seen him before, or Mr. Ayers may know him."

"Good idea, hon. I already asked your mother, but I'll call John Ayers and Sheriff Bradley. Something about the guy reminds me of a case I did some police photos for."

"Let me know what you find out, will you?"

"Will do, Mae. Bye."

After the call, she decided to take a run down the street and up the big hill behind her house to give Rusty some exercise. He was a big dog with high demands for activity and Mae wondered, not for the first time, why busy people who lived on small lots got such large dogs. She changed into sweats and an old t-shirt and got the Rhodesian Ridgeback out of his kennel.

Rusty seemed to thoroughly enjoy running on Little Chapel Road. They went down to the river and then cut back up the hill along the ridge, arriving at the small stream that ran down from the hill above her house. After a short rest and a drink in the stream, Rusty seemed calmer. But on the way down the hill he abruptly stiffened and growled low. What a frightening specimen. No wonder these dogs could hunt lions on the Serengeti.

The big dog began to run down toward the house, pulling her at a terrible clip. By the time they reached her backyard, she was out of breath. "Rusty, what was that about?"

Remembering Elvis' disappearing act, Mae turned to count the four heads in the kennels: Toulouse, a black French bulldog; Clementine, a mix; Baxter, a golden retriever; and Christensen, the Great Dane. They were all there and seemed fine. Then she caught sight of a small red ribbon on Toulouse's kennel door. Her breath caught in her throat. Someone had tied red ribbons on each of the kennels.

She untied and removed them. She checked the dogs over carefully. They were unhurt but seemed a little agitated. Could it be some sort of practical joke? She put Rusty into his kennel and headed into the house. There was another red ribbon pinned to a note on the back door.

"MYOB or ..." At the bottom of the note, there was a drawing of a dog lying on its side in a pool of red. Someone had left a death threat for her dogs. Feeling lightheaded, she sat down on the back steps and held on to the porch railing. She had to check on Tallulah, Titan and Thoreau. They were all inside. Did I leave the house open? She tried to turn the handle. The back door was locked. She dashed around to the front door. Also locked. Using her key, she went inside and called her dogs. Mae drew a deep breath of relief. Titan and Thoreau were unmarked by red ribbons.

What about Tallulah and her puppies? She ran to the laundry room. The pups were all nursing quietly. She picked them up, one by one. There were no ribbons inside the house. Carrying Little Red into the kitchen, she picked up the phone and called Mama.

"Mama, I'm sorry, I can hardly talk. I'm so upset. Can you or Daddy come over right away, please?"

"Mae, what is it? What's wrong?"

"I've been threatened and the person is targeting my dogs. It's terrible, Mama. Whoever did this awful thing left a drawing of a dog in a pool of blood."

"Oh sweetheart, I'm so sorry. I'm not home. I'm in Belle Meade conducting an interview. I'll send your father right away and I'll get there as soon as I can."

Mae was in a panic. She called Tammy at work, asking her to come over as soon as she could.

"I'll take a break now. I'm on my way."

Mae paced the kitchen and then the driveway until her father and Tammy arrived. The three of them sat at the kitchen table, now clear of paint and tarps, and appraised the note.

"Do you think we need to call the sheriff's office?" Mae asked.

"I do. Perhaps there's a link here to Ruby's death." Tammy tapped the table beside the note with her shiny silver fingernails.

"I'm scared. Whoever did this is really angry," said Mae.

"I must be getting senile," Daddy said. "I've forgotten what MYOB means."

"Mind your own business," Tammy said. "It seems like something a woman would do. All those little red ribbons don't seem like a man's kind of threat."

Mae's father nodded in agreement. "You could be right. I also wonder if the intent is to damage Mae's reputation."

"Yes, I thought of that, too. If a dog was injured while in Mae's care, her business would be destroyed."

"Maybe someone who felt threatened by me looking into Ruby's death left the wretched thing."

"I agree." Tammy's breathy little voice sounded stronger than usual. "Who has the most to lose by being investigated?"

Daddy wrinkled his forehead. "What about Silas? Because he was gay, he didn't inherit the property. His father thought having a homosexual son made him look bad. Silas' partner is also in town. I don't think we can rule either of them out because of their interest in the Mead property."

"What about Joe?" Tammy asked. "If he killed Ruby and thought you might find out, he might have left the note to warn you off. Or maybe Neesy left it, trying to protect her husband. Joe does have a key to your house."

"Tammy, that's horrible. How could you say such a thing? I don't believe either Joe or Neesy would do this. They're my friends. There must be some other explanation. Besides, there were no ribbons inside the house, so having a key doesn't put Joe under suspicion."

Tammy continued, despite Mae's plea. "Do you think Joe might have been having an affair with Ruby? You told me she was pregnant when she was killed, and Joe and Neesy have four kids—"

"Stop it. Joe is my good friend. He wouldn't do this to me."

"Ladies, I'm going to go out and look at the security of the outdoor kennels."

"I'll go with you." Mae and her dad walked to the barn, while Tammy continued to study the note and the ribbons.

WHEN MAE SET up her boarding business, she had a small barn built behind her house, fitted out with dog runs. There were four runs on each side. Each run had an area inside the barn and a small door at the back with a leather flap on it, leading to an outside run. This allowed the dogs to go out and do their business. The leather flaps kept the runs cool in the summer and warm in the winter. A wide cement pad ran down the middle of the barn. Each dog run was good-sized, with a top and a door. A fence beyond the barn enclosed the outdoor dog runs and a large grassy area. Two big wooden stable doors, which opened wide enough to get a tractor into the building, served as the barn's entrance.

"Mae, can you lock the barn?" Mae's father asked as they approached the doors.

"Yes, I can lock it, but I don't very often. I guess I will now."

"You absolutely need to lock the barn, and I'll get a lock for the outside gate. I'm also going to get some motion lights to put up on all four corners of the barn. I'm thinking of installing an electric wire on top of the fencing, too."

"You really are taking this seriously then?"

"Yes, baby, I am."

When Mae came back into the kitchen, Tammy said she was going over to talk to Neesy.

"Tammy, no."

"I'm just going over to their house. I'll tell her what happened and then watch her face. She may know something."

Daddy came back into the kitchen. When he spoke, his voice was solemn. "I found a man's footprints in the mud by the back door of the barn. I'm going to the hardware store to buy security equipment."

"I guess I should call Ben." Mae tried to keep her voice steady.

Tammy gave the note back to Mae and grabbed her things. Mae was exasperated at Tammy's insistence on talking to Neesy, but still they hugged each other before Tammy left. Sitting alone in the kitchen, Mae dialed the sheriff's office. Her hands were shaking from all the adrenaline in her system. The sheriff wasn't available when she called so she left a message with Dory.

Mae rubbed the back of her neck for a minute. Then she started to cry. If Noah had survived the car crash, he'd be rubbing her neck and she wouldn't be here alone. She closed her eyes, trying to remember what his hands felt like, when the phone rang. She jumped up, thinking it would be her mother.

Ben's voice came forcefully over the phone. "Mae, do I need to send someone from the department over? Dory called. She said you sounded terrified."

"Oh, Ben, I guess I am. Somebody came here while I was gone and left a threatening note. It has a horrible drawing of a dog in a pool of blood."

"Was the note inside the house?"

"No. On the back door."

"Have you checked the rest of the house? Are you alone? Have you told anyone else about this?" The volume of Ben's voice rose with each question.

"I checked on the dogs, not the house. My mother's arriving now."

Suzanne came charging in. "Mae, are you all right? Who are you talking to?"

"It's Ben, Mama. I'm okay." Her mother reached for Mae and hugged her fiercely.

Pulling the phone from her hand, she said in a strained voice, "Sheriff, could you come out here? This child is white as a sheet." She listened for a minute. "That's fine. We'll stay in the kitchen until you get here. Thank you."

"Mama, you can let go of me now. Let's sit down and wait for the sheriff."

They sat across from each other at the kitchen table. Strange thoughts floated through Mae's mind. Her mother was a petite woman, pretty in a delicate way. July looked much like her, with her smooth, dark hair and brown eyes. Mae had always felt like she didn't fit in with them, even though her eyes were also brown. She always forgot how strong her mother was. She seemed to take most things so lightly that Mae was surprised when she got serious.

"Can I see the note?"

Mae laid the note on the table and they studied it in silence.

Mama's eyes glistened with tears. "Honey, do you want to come and stay at our house until Ben gets this thing figured out?"

"I can't. Tallulah and the puppies can't be moved yet and I have four boarders right now, plus Titan and Thoreau. I refuse to allow this horrible person to drive me out of my home. Maybe I should change the locks. Daddy left for the hardware store to get some security equipment for the kennels. I could call and ask him to pick up new locks for the house, too."

Just as Mae had finished speaking, Ben rapped on the door and walked into the kitchen.

Mama pinned him with a look. "Don't you think Mae needs to get out of here? Could you please convince her to come and stay with me?"

"Let me look around first, ma'am." Ben walked over to stand behind Mae. He touched her shoulder lightly. "Do you feel up to coming with me while I go through the house?"

Mae nodded and stood up. Titan walked right beside her and, as they walked past Thoreau's bed, the old Rottweiler hauled himself to his feet and joined them. They opened the door to the laundry room to check on Tallulah and her puppies. Ben stroked Thoreau on the top of his head.

"Do you feel a draft coming down the hall?" he asked.

Mae looked down the hall and remembered opening the window for the painters. The hall window still stood open.

"Well, clearly they could have gotten into the house, but you didn't see any ribbons inside, did you?"

She shook her head. Ben walked down the hall to examine the windowsill.

"Nothing leads me to believe that anyone got inside. I'm

going to look outside for footprints. While I'm doing that, would you get the ribbons and the note for me? Make sure all the other windows are latched, too, okay?"

Mae nodded as Ben walked away. Titan stayed with her, but Thoreau followed Ben and they went out the door together.

Now that she knew the trespasser hadn't been inside the house, Mae called Tammy and told her about the open window.

"They wouldn't have needed a key and Ben doesn't think anyone was inside. If you combine that with the man's footprint Daddy found, Neesy doesn't make any sense as a suspect. I insist that you leave her out of this."

"Fine. Are you planning on staying there tonight?"

"Yes. Mama asked me to stay with her, but I have to stay here. The puppies, you know."

"Okay. I have to check on some things at my office, reschedule two appointments and pack a suitcase. I'm inviting myself to sleep over tonight. I won't take no for an answer."

"I'm glad you're coming. I've been alone enough."

When Mae got off the phone, Mama said, "It's good she's coming to stay, Honey. You've been dealing with a lot by yourself lately."

"I know. Tammy will distract me from feeling sorry for myself. I'm afraid I blew it with Ben. All I wanted to do was help. He said I made him look like an idiot in front of his staff."

"You like him, don't you?" Mama took Mae's hand and began rubbing her thumb gently across it. Mae's breathing started to slow, along with her heartbeat.

"Yes, I do. The day I went to his office and we saw each other for the first time, I noticed a definite spark. I'm sure you get what I mean. It's only happened once before. You know, the feeling when both people are instantly attracted? I felt that connection with Noah. Despite the spark, I don't know if I'm ready for another relationship. I still miss Noah so much. Sometimes I wonder if I'll ever bond with anyone else."

"Mae, can you bond with the new puppies?"

"Sure, every time. Why?"

"Then you can bond to another man. Seriously, Mae, if something happened to your father, I'd be on the next plane to a singles resort in the Caribbean."

"Mother! I'm shocked. What about grieving and saying goodbye?"

"I'm exaggerating. Of course, I'd miss your father very much, but I can see your attraction to the sheriff. I want you to know I hope you'll pursue this."

"Do you really think chemistry is enough?"

She smiled. "I think it's an essential beginning. Even when I'm really irritated with your father, I'm still drawn to him, you know… physically."

"I wish that was news to me. You and Daddy obviously have chemistry. July and I've been mortified by the pair of you for years."

"Well, there's nothing wrong with having a strong physical bond in a marriage. For one thing, it's very good for your complexion. I'm the only one of my friends who doesn't get Botox injections. I think you should let Ben know."

"Let me know what?" Ben walked back into the kitchen.

"Nothing." Mae shot her mother a horrified glance. "I know you have to get going now, Mama. I'll call you tomorrow." Mae ushered her mother out the door.

"Goodbye, Ben." With a little smile at Mae and a wave for Ben, Mama departed.

Ben grinned like a mule.

"Did you find anything outside?" Mae hoped to distract him from whatever he might have overheard.

"I found some footprints in the flowerbed under the open window. They look like a match for the ones by the barn. Your dad came back and showed me those. Maybe the person who did this saw the open window but decided not to come into the house for one reason or another. By the way, I like your dad. He's out there turning your barn into a fortress."

"That's good, I guess. Thoreau seems to like you." She glanced down at the big brown and black dog sitting on Ben's foot.

"Yeah, he's a good old dog, isn't he?" Ben reached down and fondled Thoreau's ears. "Could I have the note and the ribbons? I need to get going."

"Here they are. I'm sorry, but both Tammy and I handled them. Tammy's going to stay here with me tonight. I'm sure with all of Daddy's security measures, we'll be fine. Would you let me know if you find out who did this?"

"Of course I will." He turned to go. "Goodbye, Miss December."

"Stop calling me that!"

Ben stopped and turned back toward her. He wasn't smiling. "You've got to be the most irritating woman I've ever known. I've been trying to maintain a professional detachment toward you since we met." He stepped closer. His belt buckle squeaked and a beam of light reflected off his badge. "It hasn't been easy, but I have tried. Is there some reason I can't call you by your name?"

"It's that stupid song," Mae blurted out. "You know, the one about the guy who dates eleven centerfolds."

"…and I saved the best for last, Miss December." He sang the end of the line. "So that Arlen Hunter song is about you?"

"It's not about me. I'm not a centerfold." Her tone was frosty. "It's about my name. I never liked the song. It's bad enough to grow up with a name like Mae December, without your boyfriend putting your name in a country song. Then to have Arlen Hunter turn it into a hit; well, don't get me started on that dirt bag."

"Okay, okay. I'm sorry. I didn't know." Ben bit his lip.

"No one really knows how I feel about the song. I never even told Noah. 'Miss December' was his big break as a songwriter, and I didn't want to hurt his feelings. I thought I'd take Noah's name after we got married and people would forget about those dumb lyrics. I feel guilty even telling you this. When

Noah died, I inherited the rights and royalties to all his music, so even the house I live in was paid for by that damn song."

"You poor thing." Ben stepped even closer and put a hand on her shoulder. "I promise, I'll never call you Miss December again."

"Have you forgiven me for crashing your staff meeting? I really am sorry."

He put his hand under her chin and tilted her face up. For a second, she thought he'd kiss her. The bright blue in his eyes darkened to navy.

"Hey, y'all, should I knock next time?" Tammy was back and using her whispery little voice, which annoyed Mae to no end. When they were in high school, one of the boys told Tammy she sounded like Marilyn Monroe, only cuter. Mae wished he'd kept his big mouth shut.

Ben mumbled something under his breath and fled from the house. Mae and Tammy looked at each other and started to laugh. By the time Daddy stuck his head in to say goodbye, the two friends were in a heap on the kitchen floor with tears rolling down their cheeks from laughing so hard.

"Goodbye, you two. Maybe you should try to relax and have some fun." Daddy shook his head and left.

Chapter Fifteen

———

March 23
Sheriff Ben Bradley

WHEN BEN ARRIVED at the office that morning, he tracked Dory down in the break room. "Can you find out where Silas Mead is staying?"

"I already have the phone number and address on my desk. Follow me."

She turned and walked down the hall. Seating herself at her desk, she reviewed a legal pad filled with her elegant cursive.

"Here it is."

"Thank you, Goddess of Information."

"Actually," Dory sounded a little sheepish, "Mae's mother gave me the number yesterday. She got it from Mae."

"Did Mae talk to Silas?" *What do I have to do to keep that woman out of this investigation?* Ben wondered.

"She only spoke to him real briefly, to give her condolences."

"That better be all she did. What's the address?"

"Here you go." Dory read off the numbers.

Ben got Deputy Fuller and they drove to the address

Dory provided. On the way over, Ben told Robert about the trespassing at Mae's house.

SILAS MEAD WAS staying at a fine old antebellum home with a long circular drive. Ben and Deputy Fuller spoke with the housekeeper at the front door who directed them back to the carriage house. They walked through the garage toward a staircase leading to the upper floor. The light coming through the dusty windows seemed to turn everything green, reflecting the color of the grass and trees outside. They walked up the staircase at the back of the garage and knocked.

A tall, thin man with a receding hairline answered the door. "Are you Silas Mead?" the sheriff asked.

"I am."

As far as Ben could see, Silas bore no resemblance to his sister. Besides having seen her body in the grove of trees and at the morgue, Dory had gotten pictures of Ruby from her grandmother and put them up on the conference room bulletin board. Even in the photos, Ruby possessed more vitality in her little finger than her brother seemed to have in his entire body.

"I'm Sheriff Ben Bradley and this is my deputy, Robert Fuller. We'd like to talk with you about the death of your sister, Ruby."

Without a word, Silas opened the door wider, gesturing for them to come in.

They sat at a small round table by an open window that overlooked the large backyard. In the quiet, the bubbling of a fountain could be heard.

"I'm very sorry about your sister, Mr. Mead."

Silas nodded, looking fatigued. His skin was almost gray. He offered them water or lemonade but didn't say anything about Ruby.

"I understand that you will now inherit her property, as long as you're not implicated in her murder." There was a pause, and Ben fixed his eyes on Silas. "I'm sure you're aware that you cannot see or even walk the property until her murder is solved. At present, the entire site is a crime scene. May I ask when you returned to town? ”

"Ruby called and asked me to come home. I hardly need to see the property, Sheriff; I grew up in that house."

"When did you get back?"

"I got here on March thirteenth after checking with my friend to see if Terry and I could stay for a while."

"Terry is?"

"He's my partner."

"Did you take vacation time to come back to Tennessee?"

Silas shook his head. "I'm a Web designer. As long as I have Internet access, I can work anywhere."

"What does Terry do?"

"He's a graphic designer. He freelances."

"So he can draw, then?"

"Yes, he does beautiful sketches." Like the beautiful drawing of a dog lying in a pool of blood?

Ben kept his focus on Silas and watched as he folded his arms on the table and rested his head on his arms. It was the defeated posture of a depressed man.

"Where is Terry right now?"

At Ben's question, Silas picked up his head. "He went out to do some errands. He should be back in an hour or so."

"What time did he leave?"

"Before nine this morning."

"Were both of you here yesterday afternoon?"

"What's this about, Sheriff? Ruby died over a week ago. I don't think we need to account for our whereabouts at this point."

"Yesterday afternoon someone trespassed on Mae December's property and left a threatening note on her back door."

His eyes grew wide. "What?"

Ben felt Silas' surprise was authentic. His body posture conveyed astonishment. "The person drew a picture of a dog in a pool of blood. Would you know anything about that?"

"No, I've been here the whole time. I wasn't feeling well and was asleep until you knocked." His face did look drawn; maybe the man didn't normally look this listless, Ben thought.

"Was Terry here all yesterday afternoon?"

He sighed. "I think so, but I've been pretty much out of it."

"Does he know this area? Would he know Miss December, for instance?"

"After Mae called yesterday, I told Terry she seemed awfully nosy."

Certainly couldn't argue with him there. "Do you think Terry might have been angered by her asking questions, enough to want to threaten her?"

"Of course not." Silas shook his head.

"Somebody did. There were footprints by her barn. I need to know your shoe size and Terry's, too."

"I wear a ten and a half and Terry wears a nine."

"I'd like to borrow one of his shoes and one of yours."

"I don't think so. I don't think I should give you anything without a warrant."

"I would prefer it if you would simply cooperate with us and give us the shoes. We'll be able to return them within a day or two, unless one of you is the guilty party in the trespassing incident."

"Fine." Silas stood up and went back to the bedroom. Robert and the sheriff exchanged glances. Silas returned carrying a sneaker and a loafer.

"Which one belongs to Terry? What's his last name by the way?"

"It's Lerner. That's his shoe." Silas indicated the sneaker.

"That will be all for the moment, Mr. Mead, but I want you to remain in town until this matter, and the investigation into the death of your sister, is resolved."

"When will her body be released? My grandmother would

like to schedule the funeral. She has everything planned and her minister is standing by."

Ben gave him a long, hard look. "The funeral home released the body yesterday. I'm surprised you didn't know. Please notify my office about the time and date of the funeral. I plan to attend." He glared as he handed Silas his card. He wanted to fluster this man about his sister's death and the trespassing incident.

Ben and Robert started driving back down the long driveway, talking about the encounter. When they reached the road, Robert said, "I'm glad he gave us the shoes."

"Yes, me too. You know, I think we should park over by the main house where we can see the driveway to the carriage house and wait just a bit for our Mr. Lerner."

They waited for twenty minutes without seeing any signs of Silas' partner. Impatient and not wanting to waste any more time, the sheriff called Dory and asked her to send a deputy with a car to pick him up. He told Robert to stay there. Ben wanted him to find out Terry's whereabouts the previous afternoon and to take a scraping from the shoes he was wearing. Even if Terry had been the one to leave that note at Mae's, he might not be wearing the same shoes, but it was worth a try. The sheriff got into the other patrol car and drove off for the station.

The sheriff's cell rang shortly thereafter. Deputy Fuller gave him an update. He had talked with Terry Lerner and had taken a scraping from his shoe. He described him as very nervous and almost combative. He had insisted on knowing the reason for the sole scraping so the deputy told him. According to Robert, the man literally backed away when Fuller told him why he needed the debris from the bottom of his shoe.

"Is he still there?"

"Yes. He's sitting in his car, waiting while I called you. He's on his cellphone."

"Please bring Mr. Lerner into the office. I'd like to talk with him. I'll meet you here."

Robert met Ben at the door to the sheriff's office building twenty minutes later. Standing next to him was a thin man with straight brown hair.

"Mr. Terry Lerner? I'm Sheriff Ben Bradley."

"Yes, I'm Terry Lerner. Why did you have me dragged in here?"

"Please come back into our conference room. We need to talk." The sheriff spoke softly, hoping to calm the man down a bit. They went into the conference room.

After getting Terry some coffee, Ben asked him what he had been doing earlier.

"I went shopping. It's a good thing your deputy let me call Silas. He came right away; otherwise those groceries would have spoiled."

"What about yesterday afternoon? What were you doing then?"

"I was running some other errands."

As the questioning continued, Terry's face reddened. He began to sweat. For the next twenty minutes, the sheriff asked questions, listening carefully to the answers and watching Terry's nonverbal behavior.

At one point, Robert knocked on the door and handed Ben a slip of paper. It was the analysis request for the sample taken below the window at the December place. He'd scribbled a note at the bottom of the page. The size of the footprint they found was a nine and Lerner's sneaker was a match in size and tread.

Ben looked at the sheet of paper. There had been no time for an actual lab comparison between the scraping from Terry's shoe and the soil sample from the December house, but this would be enough to intimidate him.

"Mr. Lerner, it's time you stopped lying to me. I know you were at the December house yesterday. You left the threatening note for Miss December and the drawing of the dog in a pool of blood. The footprints behind the barn were your size. The dirt on your shoe is identical to the soil near the window of her house."

Terry's eyes flicked from side to side.

"I could arrest you for Criminal Trespassing and keep you here in the county jail until such a time as you could come before the judge. However, I doubt you want jail time. Since this relates to a murder investigation, you're now at the top of my list of suspects." Terry's eyes opened wide.

"I just wanted her to leave Silas alone," Terry burst out. "I had nothing to do with Ruby's death." He paused. "Do I need a lawyer, Sheriff?"

"It's up to you, Mr. Lerner. I'm going to call Miss December to see if she wants to press charges. You can go for now. I'll let you know what she says. Don't leave town."

Chapter Sixteen

———

March 22
Mae December

M AE HAD ENJOYED her night with Tammy enormously. It was like the sleepovers they used to have in middle and high school when they talked about boys for hours, a scene often repeated over their seventeen-year friendship. This time, though, they had something more than gossip and rumors to discuss. Tammy's database from Local Love really came in handy.

Five minutes after Tammy arrived, Mae asked to see Ben's profile.

"What makes you think I have it?"

"C'mon, you have it. I know you do. He got to see mine."

"Already? You work fast," her alleged best friend said.

"No, my profile, remember? You gave Ben a copy. If you have a profile for him, I think it's only fair to let me see it."

"Well, I did bring some files with me from the office," Tammy said in her faux reluctant voice. She reached for her bag but Mae got there first.

"Some files? Looks like there's only one."

"I know." Tammy dropped all her pretenses. "I knew you'd want to see Ben's profile, so I brought the file with me. Real professional, right?"

"Don't worry." Discretion was a major issue in her line of work. "I won't tell anyone I saw it. I promise."

Mae read Ben's information, wondering why Tammy hadn't kept him for herself and why he was still single. He grew up in Rosedale but attended Green Road Academy instead of public school. He went to Texas for college, then started law school but had obviously changed his mind partway through. He then entered the police academy and returned home to work in the sheriff's department. When criminal allegations drove the former sheriff from the job, Ben stepped in as interim sheriff. He won the office in the next election. At thirty-two, he was the youngest sheriff in the history of Rose County. His profile said nothing about his romantic history.

Tammy flipped the page over. On the other side, in the optional section, were fill-in-the-blank statements. One caught Mae's eye. The item read, "I think long engagements are ..." Ben had written "stupid."

"How funny." Mae pointed out the engagement comment to Tammy. "He seems like such a cautious type. I would have guessed he'd be all about long engagements."

"He was engaged to his college girlfriend, Katie Hudson, for years. She was involved in youth ministry, always going on mission trips. On one of the trips, she met a handsome young doctor. They flew from Guatemala to Vegas to be married. She called Ben to tell him right after the honeymoon."

"Wow. That sounds like a country song; a bad one. How do you know all this anyway, Tammy?"

"I have my sources," Tammy said looking at Mae out of the corners of her eyes. Mae laughed.

"Why didn't you go out with Ben after he applied to your service?"

"He really is cute, isn't he? I suppose I do date quite a few of the men in my database." Tammy grinned.

Mae rolled her eyes.

"Ben is really a great guy. There's nothing wrong with him at all, except this." Tammy pointed to a line near the bottom of the page.

"Oh, I get it." Ben had checked "allergic to cats" and noted that he disliked them. "It's because of Gladys, Knight, and Pips." These were Tammy's three Siamese cats. She preferred to think of their constant yowling as singing and had named them after Gladys and her backup singers.

"Yes, he's not a cat person. We wouldn't be pet compatible. He's yours if you want him. I was trying to save him for you anyway."

"Does he have a dog?"

"He had an old basset hound that died a week after his fiancée dumped him."

"Good Lord. Poor guy."

"All that happened about four years ago. He got heavily involved in his work after that. He's dated a little bit since, but isn't serious about anyone."

Mae remembered the previous day and her face started to heat up. "So, who are you dating these days, Tammy?"

"Jim Goddard. You know, the head of that big construction company that's doing those historical renovations in Nashville."

"And?" Mae knew that Tammy firmly believed in dating more than one man at a time.

"Once in a while I go out with Carter Drake. He's one of those guys who swoops in when he's in town, takes me out to fabulous restaurants and then disappears for weeks. Then sometimes I go out with Johnny Temple. He's real cute. We have a lot of fun together, but Mom doesn't like him much. I like him, though. He's great in bed."

"Tammy, you aren't sleeping with all of them, are you?"

"Not quite." A demure look crossed her face.

Mae chuckled.

When they stopped laughing, Mae said, "I think it's time you picked one of your beaux and had an actual relationship, one lasting more than a few weeks. You're almost thirty, my friend. There's no time like the present."

"You're a fine one to talk, aren't you?"

"Well, it's not like I've never had a long-term relationship. Noah and I were engaged. We bought this house; we even moved in together. He gave me a ring. Seriously, you do know why you aren't bonding to any of these guys, don't you?"

"Why?"

"I think it's because of your dad."

Tammy sat very still, hardly breathing. She never talked about the fact that she had lost her father to a heart attack when she was in elementary school. Tammy's mother had told Mae about it years ago.

"I think you're afraid to get too close to one of these guys, in case you might lose him."

"Oh, Mae," Tammy's husky voice broke. "I still miss him."

"I know, honey. It's been a long time, though. Isn't it time to choose someone to be serious about? Your dad would want you to have someone who loved you."

"Maybe." She tilted her head. "Isn't it about time for you, too?"

"I don't know. I still miss Noah. We were true soul mates. I don't know if I can get that close to anyone else. I sure haven't so far."

"I think you should give Ben a chance. I know Ben's brother and sister-in-law quite well. They really love Ben. He's excellent with their boys and because of them, he's started coaching baseball. Ben really suffered after Katie ditched him, but he grew up a lot. Mae, he even loves dogs! Plus, he's cute and not a skirt chaser. At least he hasn't chased my skirt." Tammy smiled.

"Okay. I'll think about it. But he'd have to ask me out and that's not going to happen, at least not now."

"Maybe you need to let things happen instead of deciding

ahead of time how they're going to play out." Tammy's eyes twinkled.

They ordered and ate a huge pizza and shared a bottle of Chianti while they talked about other things, finally getting to bed around one in the morning. Mae slept like a baby.

IN THE MORNING, after Mae did her kennel chores, Tammy told her she had to get to work. She said she'd come back for another night if Mae needed her.

Mae put all the big dogs out in the front pasture for some playtime. Titan and Toulouse, the French bulldog, played in the fenced barnyard together. Tallulah cavorted with them for a short while and then went back to her puppies. Mae was updating her kennel website when Ben called.

"Hello, Mae. This is Sheriff, er ... Ben Bradley calling. I talked with Terry Lerner, Silas' partner, yesterday. He's admitted to trespassing on your property and leaving the threatening note. I need to know if you want to press charges."

Mae hesitated. "I'm not sure. Tell him I'm going to think about it and would like him to call me tomorrow. If it's okay with you, I'd like to let him worry for a while."

"Not a bad idea. I'm going to have him followed to see what he does. I'll have Deputy Phelps posted at your house, too, in case he tries anything else."

"I'll be here for the rest of the day. I have a lot of work to do. Don't worry. I'm not working on the case. I'm trying to stay out of it."

"I appreciate that, Mae. Did you know Ruby's funeral is tomorrow? Dory put it on my calendar."

Mae said she planned to attend and asked him to have Terry call her after the service.

"Goodbye, Ben Bradley." Mae hung up the phone. She sat thinking for a long time about what she should do about Terry Lerner.

Chapter Seventeen

March 24
Mae December

THE MORNING OF Ruby's funeral a gray mist lay on the grass in shredded veils. Mae hadn't slept well, despite the officer watching her house. An idea about the case was hovering just out of reach, but she didn't have time to lie in bed and think. She put on some sweats and went downstairs to take care of the dogs.

As Mae went from one dog run to another, she thought of the dogs in her care that would be leaving soon. Two of them were going home tomorrow, which would mean less work. Still, Mae knew she'd miss her boarders. There were many wonderful breeds of dogs and caring for them gave her the chance to observe all their characteristics.

She was having a problem with Tallulah, who seemed to be losing interest in nursing her puppies. This was a perfectly normal reaction once the babies started to get their needle sharp teeth, but it was happening way too soon. Tallulah needed to hang in there for at least another two weeks. Puppies did best if their mothers nursed them for four to five weeks, but they could survive and thrive on only three weeks of nursing, as long as they were fed carefully from then on.

Mae cleaned the dog runs and fed her dogs, all the while thinking about the funeral. Silas would be there. She dreaded seeing Silas' partner, Terry, and hoped Silas would have the sense not to bring him. David Allison, Steven Fanning, and Steven's wife, Robin, would all attend. Joe and Neesy Dennis would also be there. James Connolly would probably attend, as his duties involved the handling of the will. Ben was going, too. Mae envisioned him taking a very low profile. He'd most likely stand at the back of the church and not even come to the cemetery.

The service was scheduled for eleven a.m. Mae dressed with care in a slightly longer than usual black dress, black heels and an off-white A-line coat. After twisting her dark blonde hair up, she put on a pair of pearl earrings. Finally she grabbed her favorite umbrella, black on the outside and blue with white clouds on the inside. The rain came down in sheets of solid gray as she drove to Rosedale.

Rolling into the parking lot of First Presbyterian, she saw her parents, her sister with her husband and several neighbors standing nearby. They all greeted one another pleasantly, though the mood was somber.

Silas and his grandmother, Henriette, were in the vestibule of the church welcoming everyone. They were the only people left from the great Mead family. Ruby and Silas' parents had both died in their early fifties. Their mother had succumbed to breast cancer after a long battle. Three months later, a heart attack took their father.

Mae waited in line to say hello to Henriette, whose husband raised racehorses and farmed tobacco. People said the family fortune originated from moonshine, back in the twenties and thirties.

Mae had known Ruby's grandmother since the sixth grade, when Henriette was her Junior Cotillion instructor. Although she hadn't liked the class, especially the ballroom dancing, she had always loved Miss Hen.

"I'm terribly sorry for your loss." Mae clasped her small hand.

"Thank you, Mae, and thank you for coming." Henriette Mead had a warm resonant voice. Everyone knew that she had opposed her son's decision to give the Little Chapel Road property to Ruby. She loved both her grandchildren and wanted the property split between them. Today she appeared so small in her dark gray dress with white gloves. After all the losses Henriette had already endured, Ruby's funeral was going to be an awful ordeal for her.

The service was simple and quiet. After the conventional remarks, the minister asked if anyone would like to talk about Ruby. Her brother rose and went to the front of the sanctuary.

"Ruby was my sister." Silas gazed out at the congregation with a half-smile. "My big sister. I looked up to her and followed her around like a puppy. I adored her. I remember her well as a kid. She was always getting into trouble. Once, when she was only fourteen, she took Dad's car out for a drive. She got into a fender bender with his new Caddie and Dad was so mad I thought he'd kill her. She always got the beer for the high school parties, often from Dad's private stash. My sister had a vibrant and fierce personality. I will always miss her. My family is much diminished without her spirit." His voice broke; he appeared close to tears.

After he stepped down, two others spoke about Ruby. One was a teacher who remembered her skipping school but always getting decent grades. Joe Dennis talked about what fun he and Ruby had as teenagers. He spoke quietly and was obviously struggling with his grief. David Allison didn't speak, which was a little surprising.

After the closing prayer, the organist played a familiar tune. As the mourners passed down the receiving line, Mae tried not to look at the man who stood next to Silas. She assumed it was

Terry Lerner. She was still furious with him, but this wasn't the time or place for a confrontation.

When Mae got to Henriette Mead, Ruby's grandmother thanked her again. "I know you found Ruby. I'm glad she'll be laid to rest now." She then turned to Annie and Jason Van Atta, who were behind Mae in line, to thank them for coming.

ALMOST EVERYONE AT the church service followed the hearse out to the cemetery. The wind rose and Mae's hair curled into tendrils around her face. They stood by the open grave as the funeral attendants lowered Ruby's coffin into the dark red earth. David Allison walked slowly up to the grave, picked up a spade and threw a handful of dirt on Ruby's coffin. Others came and dropped single flowers. Then Ruby's grandmother, with the help of Silas, lowered a large bouquet of red roses on top of Ruby's coffin. Tears poured down Henriette's face. "May you find peace at last, Ruby girl."

To Mae's immense surprise, Ben stepped up to the graveside. He wore a charcoal gray suit and a white shirt with a gray and black striped tie. His hair was combed back from his forehead, and his expression was serious.

"Hello. For those of you who don't know me, I'm Ben Bradley, Sheriff of Rose County. I don't suppose many of you thought I'd speak at this event, or even attend. I wanted each and every one of you to know that my whole staff is working very hard to find the person who did this to Ruby. We're getting closer to making an arrest every day. This will not be an unsolved case." Ben's voice resonated with quiet passion.

People whispered in shocked tones. Everyone was surprised to see the sheriff speaking out at her funeral. It was a controversial act, probably intentionally so. If the perpetrator was nearby, the sheriff clearly wanted him, or her, to be worried.

Mae's neighbor, Robin Fanning, stood next to James Connolly and whispered in her brother-in-law's ear. He looked down and shook his head. As people began leaving, Mae moved closer to them and heard him say, "Of course I know it was wrong, Robin. I regret the whole thing."

As Mae turned to leave, Henriette touched her sleeve. "I'm glad our young sheriff spoke out. Many people think no progress is being made. I'm not of that opinion. Ruby was my granddaughter and I loved her dearly. I'm glad to hear Sheriff Bradley isn't giving up." She gave a little grin. "He reminds me of an old hunting dog we had many years ago. That dog would track a fox or coon for ten, twelve hours. He always got the game in the end."

Mae gave her a hug. She had little bones, like those of a sparrow. Tears welled up in Mae's eyes, more for Henriette than for Ruby.

THE RAIN HAD increased in intensity during the service and Mae was forced to pull over several times on her way home. The trees along the road whipped back and forth in the wind. Once home, Mae changed into jeans and a sweatshirt and fixed herself a sandwich. Standing at the counter, she ate quickly, without really tasting the food. Putting on boots and a barn jacket, she took her three dogs outside. She had them trained to go to the bathroom on command. The magic words "hurry up" always did the trick. As soon as they were finished, she took them back inside and toweled them off. Titan and Thoreau went back to their beds and Tallulah went back to her puppies. Mae walked out to the barn to check on her boarders.

Mae made sure that all the dogs took a potty break, since some of them would go inside their runs when it rained. Then she checked their water dishes. After settling them back in their runs, she was about to lock the barn door when a thought struck her. Something she'd been trying to remember all morning had finally come to light. There was a shovel hanging on a hook to the left of the door. Mae turned on the overhead light to take a closer look. It was definitely not her old shovel. This one appeared to be new. The handle was shiny and reflected the light from the ceiling.

Why would a new shovel already have rust stains on it? She bent down to take a closer look. The stain was gel-like. She reached out and then froze when she saw a tiny piece of hair embedded in the stain. Ben's angry voice the day of the staff meeting echoed in her mind when he said Ruby had died of blunt force trauma. She was certain she had found the missing murder weapon. She turned off the light, walked out and locked the door. What on earth was that shovel doing in her barn?

Remembering that Deputy Phelps was watching the house, she ran down to the car parked in her driveway and banged on the window. The rain was still pouring down.

"I need you to call the sheriff. I think I just found the murder weapon."

While Mae waited for Ben to call, Beth Jensen rang to let Mae know about the neighborhood meeting, which would be held the next night at her house.

"Do you need me to bring anything?"

"No thanks. Glad you're coming. See you tomorrow."

As soon as she hung up the phone, it rang again.

"Hello, is this Miss December?" She didn't recognize the man's voice.

"This is she. Who's calling please?"

"This is Terry Lerner, Miss December. The sheriff told me to call you this afternoon."

Standing there, wet and cold, a wave of heat flew through her. She was furious. "Mr. Lerner, what do you have to say for yourself? What kind of person threatens innocent animals and a woman who lives alone?"

He was quiet for a minute and then he heaved a deep sigh. "The kind of person who thinks they're protecting someone they love, I guess. I'm very sorry about what I did. I was afraid you'd draw attention to Silas with your investigation."

"I know all about feeling protective," her words spilled

out. "When you threaten my dogs, you're threatening my livelihood, as well as the pets I love. I can't make money in this business if people think their dogs aren't safe here."

"Are you going to press charges? I really am sorry."

"I'm not sure yet." The doorbell rang and the dogs started barking. "Look, I need to go. I'll let the sheriff know my decision." She hung up and went to answer the door.

It was CSI Tech Johns. He asked Mae to show him the shovel. She led him to the barn and unlocked it. The rain came down with such intensity that every step she took made water splash up past her ankles. They stepped inside, and she flicked on the light.

"It's right here. Don't worry, I didn't touch it."

"Good," He pulled a camera out of his pocket. He left the shovel hanging there, took several pictures and then pulled on his latex gloves. "Sheriff Bradley will be here soon. You can go wait in the house if you want."

"Is it the murder weapon?"

"We won't know for a while. We'll need to analyze the blood at the lab. Why don't you go dry off and change clothes? You look really cold."

Mae nodded and went back to the house. Her teeth were chattering. Leaving her wet clothes on the bathroom floor, she put on a robe and dried her hair. She was carrying her wet things down to the laundry room when Ben walked in through the front door. Seeing him there just did her in. Mae dropped the bundle of laundry and threw herself at his chest. He bent down and wrapped his arms around her. They stood there for a minute without saying a word.

"You're shaking," Ben finally murmured. "Are you that cold?"

"No. Freaked out. I saw that shovel in Ruby's garage the day I was over there looking for her cellphone. I think that's what bothered me when I first woke up. I guess I noticed the shovel subconsciously but didn't make the connection until today."

"You look like you might be in shock." Ben pulled back and

observed her carefully. "Do you have any liquor in the house?"

"There's some Jack Daniels in the liquor cabinet. In the living room."

Ben pulled her into the living room and sat her down on the couch. He took the blanket off the arm of the couch and wrapped it around her.

"Stay here. I'm going to fix you a hot toddy."

He went to the liquor cabinet and took the bottle of bourbon into the kitchen. She heard cabinets opening and closing and Ben talking to the dogs. He hummed the tune the organist had played at Ruby's service. After a few minutes, the teapot started its shrill whistle. Ben walked back into the living room and handed her a steaming mug.

"Drink it. It'll make you feel better."

"What song were you humming?"

"'Goodbye, Ruby Tuesday.'"

"That was a good choice."

She leaned her head back on the couch for a second and then sat up with a jerk. "Do you think someone is trying to frame me?"

"I'm sure someone is trying to frame you, but it's a pretty transparent attempt. Try not to worry."

"This is really good." Mae sipped some of the hot liquid. "What's in here?"

"Hot tea, bourbon and sugar. My grandpa used to make these for me when I got sick. Is it helping?"

She drank more deeply and her body started to relax into the couch. Heavy fatigue washed over her.

"Do you want me to build a fire? You're still shivering."

"I had gas logs put in. Could you flip the switch?"

He went over to the fireplace and turned on the fire. Coming came back toward her, he took the mug from her hand.

"Why don't you rest for a while? I need to go to the lab and follow up on the weapon. Someone will be watching your house around the clock. You'll be safe, Mae. I promise."

Mae stretched out on the couch and closed her eyes. Ben's hand lightly touched her cheek and then she sank into sleep.

WHEN MAE OPENED her eyes, the sky was dark. Ben was gone and the rain had stopped. Tammy and Patrick were talking in the next room. Mae walked into the kitchen, still wrapped in the blanket. They stood close together, but stepped apart when they saw Mae.

"You two look like a couple of biddy hens, clucking over me. What are you doing here?"

"Ben called before he left and asked me to come over tonight. I decided to call Patrick. Ben said somebody was trying to frame you. He told me there would be an officer in the driveway, but he thought you'd feel safer with me in the house. I decided we'd both feel safer with Patrick here."

Patrick came over and gave Mae a hug. "We're here for the duration. You still look wiped out. Tammy and I are going to make some dinner."

"Yes, why don't you go take a long, hot bath? We'll call you when dinner's ready and Patrick will tell you all about his tournament. He's dying to tell someone besides me."

"You go relax for a while," Patrick said. "The epic story of my triumph can wait."

Tammy winked at her. "He's right, Mae-Mae. Go take a long relaxing soak in the tub. We know where everything is. We'll get some food going."

Her wet clothes were still on the floor at the bottom of the stairs. She took them into the laundry room and put them in the washer. Tallulah looked up from her babies, her face more scrunched than usual. Mae rubbed the wrinkly spot in the middle of her forehead while the little pug gazed up at her unblinkingly.

"Don't worry, little mama. We're all going to be just fine."

Chapter Eighteen

—

March 24
Detective Wayne Nichols

DETECTIVE WAYNE NICHOLS felt every minute of his fifty-eight years. On this particular morning, his alarm sounded at five a.m. He rolled out of bed and into the shower, where he did most of his best thinking. He hadn't gone to bed until around two and he knew there were many more long days ahead. When he wasn't working a case, Nichols would get to the office later in the day, but he pulled out all the stops when working a murder.

As the warm water spilled over his scar-riddled body—from bullets, knives, and dog bites—he mulled over what they knew about the Ruby Mead-Allison case. She was killed late on March fifteenth. Earlier that day, she met with Commissioner Stillwell. According to Dory, she emerged from the meeting with a triumphant smile on her face. Stillwell was heard talking on the phone to his secretary, saying Ruby was going to be the death of him.

Ruby had arrived at the Bistro at six forty-five in the evening, having missed an appointment with her doctor. She stopped in to see her attorney and presented him with an expensive cigar. They now knew that David Allison had lied to them about being at a dinner meeting. His credit card purchased the meal at the Bistro. The host at the Bistro identified Allison from a photograph. Ruby was killed approximately five hours later. Did Allison kill her? Did someone else come to her house later on in the evening? Mrs. Ryan thought so; she reported seeing a pick-up truck there at around one in the morning. Lucy Ingram had also mentioned seeing a pickup truck parked in Ruby's driveway after Allison left.

Apparently, the murder weapon had turned up in Mae December's barn. Ben's blind spot about her could be a problem for the investigation. Funny what a murder case brought out in everyone involved. His thoughts bounced back and forth between the past and present as they always did when working murder investigations. He knew all too well how easily he himself could have become a killer, one of the hunted instead of the hunter.

The memory never really left him; he still heard the muffled sobs and angry voices of his foster parents.

"I see the way you look at that goddamn half-breed, you slut!"

A scream and heavy steps from the bedroom to the living room. Then the front door was thrown open, slammed, and the truck door was opened and closed. Pressure built behind his eyes. Was he the half-breed? Some of the kids at school called him "Injun" or "chief." He never paid much attention to them, but "half-breed" sounded very ugly coming from his foster father's mouth, almost as ugly as "slut."

If that man hits her again, I'll … the thought ended there, like always. He wanted so badly to save her but was afraid. Was he big enough, strong enough to fight the drunken man? If only I had a gun, he thought. But if he did, he knew he'd use it. He needed to get out of there soon, or he'd find a way to stop the man for good.

"Wayne, come here." Her voice was usually soft and easy to listen to, but at that moment it was high pitched and loaded with pain and fear. He got up and left the bedroom where his little brother lay sleeping. She sat on the edge of her bed with her head in her hands.

He sat down next to her and put his arms around her. She flinched. "Did he hurt you?"

Wordlessly, she pulled down the strap of her nightgown to show the purpling bruises that darkened her white skin. He tore his eyes away from the tops of her breasts. His anger and disgust with his foster father joined with feelings even more disturbing.

"And this, too." She pulled up her nightgown to show more bruises on her thin, pale legs. A dark triangle of hair showed through the thin fabric of her panties. His mouth felt dry.

"Don't …" His voice was low and rough as he pulled her nightgown down. Didn't she know he was almost a man? She looked into his eyes, pulled him close suddenly and kissed him hard, on the mouth. He felt her strong tongue push past his lips. Gasping, he ran away from the room, slamming the bedroom door behind him.

Walking back down the hall, he opened the door to his bedroom, taking care not to make any noise. He knelt beside his brother's bed and shook him by the shoulder.

"Kurt, get up." Kurt was ten, tall for his age and slender with dark hair and eyes. They had come to this house together from another foster family when Kurt was only three. Neither boy belonged to the foster couple. Kurt wasn't Wayne's real brother, but they were as close as two halves of an orange.

"I need you. Come out to the kitchen."

Kurt sat up and swung his legs over the small bed, placing his toes on the cold floor. He followed his brother down the hallway, a sleepy little boy whose world was about to be ruptured.

"This is important. Don't make a sound. He's not in the

house, but he'll be back soon. He's only sleeping it off out in the truck. I have to go. I have to leave the house."

Kurt looked up at him and said a small, fierce, "No."

Wayne hugged the little boy. "When Mom wakes up, give her this." He handed him a note. "I don't want to leave you, but something bad is going to happen if I stay here, something even worse than this." He gestured out at the truck. "Mom knows I have to leave. She knows why. Don't go to school today. Don't get on the bus. Hide in the ditch beside the road. Don't let the bus driver see you. Go to the Wilshire's house. Tell them Dad hit Mom again. Ask Mr. Wilshire if he'll come over. He's a deputy. He can stop him."

"Don't go." Kurt's little voice rasped out, then it changed, became hard. "Please."

Wayne placed his backpack on the table and finished putting some food in it—peanut butter, crackers, apples, a can of tuna fish and a small can opener, along with a thin white blanket. He reached up and lifted a stack of plates, taking down the money hidden under it.

Kurt's eyes widened. "You can't take that. That's Mom's money."

"I have to. I'm going to be gone a long time. I'm only taking a little of the money. Don't wake Mom. Wait until she gets up before you give her the note. Let her sleep as long as she can. If you give her the note too soon, someone might come after me." He ruffled Kurt's hair. "Don't worry, they probably won't. They'll be glad to get rid of me." He hugged the small boy again. "I'm sorry. Someday I'll come back for you. When you're older, you can live with me."

He zipped the backpack shut, put on his jacket and stepped outside into the early summer morning. It was foggy, the kind of mist that lay on the ground in white puddles. He hesitated, looking back through the kitchen window. Kurt peered out at him. His heart clenched. The little boy raised his eyes to his brother and then turned away. Even from beyond the house,

Wayne could sense Kurt's despair. For a moment, he wanted to go back, but he couldn't. He raised an arm in farewell and let the mist take him.

Chapter Nineteen

———

March 25
Tammy Rogers

IT WAS A beautiful morning, sunny and cool. Tammy Rogers drove her two-seater convertible into Rosedale and parked behind Birdy's Salon. Her mother, Grace, owned the historic brick building that housed the salon. Tammy rented one of the storefronts for Local Love and an apartment on the second floor, where she lived with her three cats and countless plants. Other than her cozy apartment, complete with a raised deck overlooking a small courtyard, Grace used the rest of the second story for storage. The other storefronts on the street level housed a coffee shop, a jewelry store and an antique store. Tammy used her building key to let herself in the back door and went up the rickety stairs to her apartment, picking up a bundle of mail on her way.

She unlocked the ornate iron door that the antique dealer downstairs insisted he'd purchased in New Orleans. Though he said he was practically giving the door away at the price she negotiated, he wanted her to have it "for safety's sake." Until Ruby's murder, Tammy had always felt safe in the building where she'd practically grown up, spending time in the salon with her mother and grandmother. Her innate sense of style was strengthened there, and although her mother was skeptical about her living in what she described as "that ratty old attic," Tammy created a sumptuous nest for herself.

Tammy had painted the door a deep blue and distressed it to look old. She pulled the iron filigree outer door shut and locked it behind her. She dumped her mail and pocketbook onto her tiny kitchen table and fussed over her cats, apologizing for her absence. She filled their large crystal water bowl with fresh water and put dry food into three silver bowls. After filling a Mexican pottery pitcher with water, she stepped out onto her verandah to water her outdoor plants. The sun was warm on the sheltered eastern side of the building and she lingered over the pots, pinching off violets and snapdragons that were now past their prime.

"Tammy," a deep voice called from down below. She looked over the railing. Ben stood by the gate of the small courtyard. "Is Local Love closed today?"

Tammy shaded her eyes. "Not for you, handsome. I'll be right down. The gate is always locked. No one seems to know where the key is. I'll meet you at the front door."

Tammy ran down the stairs, after grabbing her keys and cellphone and locking the door behind her. She entered the office of Local Love through the service door and turned the bolt to admit Ben. Standing there in his uniform, he looked very official.

"Is everything all right?" Tammy asked, breathless. "Mae?"

"Everything's fine. Don't worry. I wanted to thank you for staying there last night, and I have a favor to ask." He stopped, looking at her a little self-consciously.

"Don't be shy, honey. You know I'll help if I can." Tammy tilted her head and gazed up at him in amusement.

"I can't believe I'm doing this in the middle of a murder investigation. I wanted to ask you to take me out of your listing for the dating service. I know I paid for another six months, but I don't think I'm going to need them."

He looked straight down at his shoes. Tammy didn't even need to hide her triumphant smile. She couldn't resist toying with him a little bit.

"Have you been unhappy with my services?" She unsuccessfully suppressed a giggle.

"No, not at all. Don't tease me. You know it's because of Mae."

Tammy reached out her hand and gave him a playful tap on his cheek. "I tease everybody I like, you know. Of course I'll take you off the list, but you better be good to my friend, or you'll be on my bad list, Sheriff."

"Of course. Thanks. I better get back to work."

They smiled at each other in perfect understanding. He walked away. Mae's right, thought Tammy. He does have a cute butt.

She locked the door behind him and went back upstairs to curl up on her dark orange velvet couch with her phone. She checked the battery status. It had a full charge. She had already left him multiple messages, if he didn't call back soon, she'd turn it off.

THE CUSHION UNDER Tammy's cheek vibrated. She opened her eyes and looked at her phone. There was a notice on the screen indicating that she had three missed calls. Refreshed from her catnap, she smiled. Two of the calls were from Patrick. Tammy broke her own rule and called him back immediately.

"Hello."

"Hi, Patrick. It's me."

"Hi, yourself. How are you this morning?" He sounded normal; breezy and friendly as usual.

Crap. Maybe she had been imagining things last night. The last few times she had seen him he had seemed to be interested in her as more than a friend, but maybe not.

"I missed three calls from you. Did you need something?"

"I did, yeah. Do you think Mae's all right? She was really quiet last night."

Tammy suppressed a sigh. Both Noah and Patrick were apparently reserved for Mae. "I think she's doing fine. She's finally getting over losing Noah."

"Is she interested in that Ben guy?"

Was he jealous? "She is. I hope you're … all right with that."

She waited for him to say something. "Patrick, are you still there?"

"Yeah. Listen, I need to get going. Stuff to do, you know."

"Wait. I didn't mean anything by that. I know you miss Noah."

"I do. I want Mae to be happy; it's just hard for me to see her with anyone besides my big brother."

This conversation wasn't going at all as she'd hoped. "It's hard to picture for her too, but it's been a long time. I'll let you go. Bye."

"Bye, Tammy."

Someday Patrick would quit worrying about Mae and see what was right in front of him. Maybe.

Chapter Twenty

—

March 25
Mae December

Mae hurried out to the barn. It was a cool, pretty morning. The kitchen was a mess after her dinner with Tammy and Patrick and she was in a rush to get to her chores. Two of her boarders were going home, and a new dog would be arriving. Refreshed by the cool morning air, Mae resolved once again not to dwell on the investigation into Ruby's murder.

Rusty was going home. His owner, Mrs. Blackwell, was coming by at around eleven. She had brought the dog to Mae, saying that he was difficult ("impossible" was her word) to handle and asked for some help in training him to walk more calmly on a leash.

Mae always washed the dogs before they went home. She didn't do a full grooming, since she lacked the equipment and the inclination to do trimming, but she gave them a bath, dried them, brushed them and put a bandana around their neck. When she started her business, she had neck bandanas made that read, "I was a good boy (or girl) at Mae's Place."

All the Rhodesian Ridgeback needed was exercise and he

calmed right down. Since both of the Blackwells worked full-time, Mae started getting the big dog used to standing and walking at very slow speeds on the treadmill she set up in the barn. If they stayed with the program, they'd find him a much easier dog to live with.

Mae finished drying and brushing Rusty. Mrs. Blackwell talked on her cellphone as she walked toward the barn. Mae grabbed a "good boy" bandana and tied it quickly around his neck.

"Hi, Mrs. Blackwell. We're in here."

Mrs. Irene Blackwell walked in through the double doors, dropping her phone into her purse. Her pointy high heels were caked in mud.

Rusty barked a loud greeting.

"Good morning, Rusty." She gave him a timid pat on the head. "Well, how was my boy?"

"Great! He needs a lot of exercise, though. I've been walking him a mile every day, outside when the weather was decent, or inside on the treadmill when it wasn't. Do you have a treadmill?"

"Yes, we do. We never use it. Wait a minute, are you telling me my dog actually walks on the treadmill?"

"Yes, I've only just started him on it. Exercise is definitely the key with him. He's a sweet teddy bear when he gets enough exercise."

Irene put her hands on her hips and stared accusingly at the dog. "Well, he's not very sweet at home. He's actually been eating furniture. I'm about at my wit's end. He even chewed up one of our kitchen cupboards last week. I work full-time and so does Ron, and we can't give him the exercise he needs. I still have bandages on my elbows where I hit the concrete last time I tried to walk him." Desperation was all over her face.

"Irene, do you think you could hire a dog walker? These big guys have to be walked at least once a day. Twice is better."

"Good idea. I'll look into it. I'd like to walk him sometimes, too. He pulls me all over the place, though, so I'm not sure that I can."

"I was going to offer to come to your house one day and show you how to walk him and how to put him on your treadmill."

"Oh, would you? That would be great. I don't know why he's this hard for me to control."

Mae hesitated. How could she be diplomatic about this? "It's possible that he doesn't see you as his leader."

The woman blinked a few times. She looked taken aback. "Am I supposed to be his leader?"

"Definitely. In Africa, Rhodesian Ridgebacks form large packs with distinct leaders. I'm afraid that Rusty sees you and your husband as siblings or littermates, rather than leaders. Let me show you how he walks for me."

Mae snapped the leash to the big dog's collar. "Come on, Rusty, let's walk." She took a step forward with Rusty beside her on her left. He walked with her all the way to the Blackwell's car. There was no pulling or stopping to sniff things. He heeled perfectly.

Mrs. Blackwell's jaw dropped open. "Amazing. How much would you charge for a home visit?"

"I'm not certified as a professional dog trainer, you know. I just haven't had time to take the certification course yet, but I do some consulting about obedience. To be an expert trainer, you have to have the reflexes of a mink, the temperament of the Dalai Lama, and the charisma of a movie star. But I'd be happy to come over for a consultation with the two of you, or the three of you. I charge forty dollars an hour."

Mrs. Blackwell took a check out of her large black purse. "I'll call you for an appointment and here's your check for the week. Thank you. He always seems happy at your place."

No surprise there, Mae thought. She didn't treat him like a houseplant. "No problem, he's a wonderful dog."

Mrs. Blackwell got Rusty into her car as Mae's next client

pulled up. Her business was always like this, with everything happening at once.

It was the Great Dane's owner. Christiansen was ready to go.

"Hi, John."

"Hi, Mae. How was he?"

"Perfect, as always."

Christiansen was a lovely black and white spotted Dane. When Mae first met him, she was glad to see that his owners had chosen not to alter his ears surgically. Cropping was cruel and unnecessary, unless a dog was going to compete in shows. To Mae it was a much more natural look to have his ears hanging down rather than standing up in points. The dog had only one unfortunate habit. When he saw John, he ran at him, jumped up and rested his front feet on John's shoulders. Both John and Christiansen were over six feet tall. They made a startling sight.

John laughed heartily, standing chest to chest with the dog.

Mae looked at them in exasperation. What a moron. Meaning John, of course, not the dog.

"You know, John," Mae's voice was firm. "You need to start curing him of that habit."

"Why? I like it. He's always so happy to see me when I get home."

"I'm sure you like it, but what about Lila? Does she like it?"

"Oh, sure she does."

Was the man demented? She probably liked it about as much as being flattened by a freight train. Mae sighed. John's beautiful wife was petite and Christiansen was a huge silly Marmaduke.

"John, you're asking for trouble by laughing at him and letting him think this is okay. If he jumped on a child, you could really have a problem on your hands. I think we should work on it. I did a little training while you were away."

"Christiansen," Mae called. When he came over, she held

him by the collar. "Okay, now you call him." She released the dog.

As the huge animal dashed toward John, she yelled, "Christiansen, stop!"

He stopped. "Sit." He sat.

"Wow. That's great. How do you do that?"

"No big deal. You say your commands only once and in a stern voice. I'm sure he'll respond."

Was John up to the job? He seemed clueless about how to become the boss in the relationship with his dog.

"Dogs need rules that don't change, John. If he isn't supposed to jump on people, you can't let him jump on anyone, even you."

John left looking humbled. She knew she sounded like a scolding schoolteacher, but better for him to hear this from her than from an angry judge during a lawsuit.

Half an hour later, a small white SUV drove up the driveway. The car belonged to Jerry Freeman, a big man who was crazy about his little dog, a West Highland white terrier named Monica. He gave Mae extremely thorough instructions about his dog's care and left a typed contact sheet. In the event of any emergency, Mae would know exactly what to do.

Monica was only six months old, a soft coated white terrier with black eyes. The pup had diva written all over her. Looking at Jerry, Mae saw all the signs of a man already enslaved by a four-pound puppy.

He kept talking about the instructions until Mae finally interrupted him, taking little Monica firmly in her hands. "I've got it, Jerry."

"It's the very first time I've ever left her anywhere."

"It's kind of like leaving your child at preschool. Once you're gone, she'll be fine."

"You'll call me if there are any problems?"

"I will." She mentally rolled her eyes. Jerry got himself together and walked toward his car.

Mae carried Monica back to her dog run. She held her against her chest to give her a sense of security. When she looked down at the puppy, she could see that Monica's eyes were fixed on Jerry as he walked away. She was clearly planning a takeover. Jerry didn't stand a chance. The miniature despot looked up at her speculatively.

"Oh no you don't, drama queen. Your little act doesn't work on me." She put a toy down in the straw but the puppy regarded it disdainfully and retreated into the corner.

The phone rang and Mae dashed into the house to get it.

"I understand there's a Little Chapel Road neighborhood meeting tonight. Are you going?" Ben asked.

"Yes, do you want to go with me? Would it be helpful for the investigation?"

"I could go as your bodyguard, I suppose. Or undercover as your date …" He chuckled.

Mae was happier than she'd been in a long time. "Call yourself anything you want, Ben Bradley. Pick me up before seven. Bye."

"Bye, bossy, I'll see you later."

Chapter Twenty-One

———

March 25
Sheriff Ben Bradley

Ben got to the office and immediately called Hadley Johns in the lab. "What did you find out about the shovel?"

"We got a hit. I'll read you my report. 'Ms. December noticed a substance she believed to be blood on the blade of the shovel. She did not touch it. She notified the deputy on patrol at her house and he contacted us. I photographed the shovel in place and brought it back to the lab. There were no fingerprints on the handle, suggesting someone wiped it down. Here's the best news, Sheriff. The blood from the head of the shovel matches our victim. We got lucky. Ruby had AB negative blood. It's only in one percent of the population. I'm confident it's the murder weapon."

"Good work. Thanks for sending those images right away. Clearly, the shovel is our murder weapon. A shame someone wiped down the handle. How is it coming with the cheek swabs?"

"We've checked Mr. Allison and Mr. Dennis. David Allison is not the father and neither is Joe Dennis. Chief Nichols and

I went to Mr. Connolly's office to obtain a cheek swab but he refused to let us take one."

"What did he give as a reason?"

"He said we'd have to have a court order before he gave a sample. He was furious that Detective Nichols and I came to his place of business dressed in our uniforms. He said his clients would be aware of our visit and that we could cost him business."

"Were any clients waiting to see him?"

"No, sir. Not a one."

"What about the materials from Ruby's house you were working on. Are they ready yet?

"We found a discarded pill bottle in the wastebasket. The name of the drug was Cialis; that's a drug for treating, you know, what they call erectile dysfunction." He started to laugh. "Hey, I think I'd need something to get it up for Ruby too."

"That's enough, Hadley. She's a murder victim, not a joke."

DORY WALKED INTO Ben's office immediately after he hung up with Hadley.

"Boy, that Nichols is hot." She grinned and fanned herself with her hand.

"Dory!"

"Well, he is. I bet he gets lots of action."

As usual, Dory didn't seem too concerned about his opinion, or observing proprieties.

"What has Nichols done to deserve this conclusion? Is that how ladies talk these days?"

"At least ladies who still like gentlemen talk about who's hot and who's not. He's been slightly more mysterious than usual lately. It drives me crazy that I can't get anything out of the man. We ladies like a challenge and Wayne is definitely a challenge. Plus having a nice ass for a white boy."

"Is Wayne really that attractive to women?" Ben tapped his cheek with his finger, feeling baffled.

"Are you kidding me? He's got to have every woman he questions trying to get him into bed."

She turned his world upside down with this. "Into bed with Wayne? The one who's pushing sixty, losing his hair and has a beer gut?"

"I bet you wish you were getting all the action he gets."

This was just too much.

"Dory, for heaven's sake! You must be ten years older than he is."

She looked at him with a grin and shook her head. "You think the urge to merge dies out? Never does."

"I really don't want to know this."

"You know, Sheriff," Dory gave him the onceover, "we need to work on your attractiveness to the opposite sex."

"So I'm not as sexy as Wayne?"

She appraised him with care. "He's not a pretty boy like you. That man sure enough melts my butter, though."

He had to get some control here. He stood up, motioning her toward the door.

"I'm going, I'm going," she said. "Tomorrow, I'm going to start working on your style, Sheriff. You need my able assistance."

He closed the door behind her. He needed someone's help—that was for sure.

Ben could no longer avoid his overflowing Inbox and decided to spend a couple of hours reducing its height. There were a number of reports submitted by Wayne Nichols. Ben read three of them, struck as always by his Chief Detective's keen insights into human behavior.

Reaching for correspondence from the pile, he paused. The first letter was from an old classmate from his brief stint in law school. Kevin Sabin was now an attorney in criminal practice. He'd started a firm in Nashville and wanted Ben to have his contact information. Ben glanced at his computer screen, noted the one hundred fifty-seven emails and clicked on his "Favorites." The top one was the site of a law school in Texas. There were several other law schools listed as well, one in Michigan and two in Ohio. He clicked idly through the admission requirements pages, noting that his old LSAT scores were still competitive. He printed off several pages.

Another look at the pile of papers on his desk said he needed to get back to work. Maybe he could go to law school at night. He knew that wasn't realistic. Most crimes occurred at night. He crumpled the pages, tossing them into his wastebasket. Maybe his dad would have a suggestion.

Chapter Twenty-Two

March 25
Detective Wayne Nichols

A T TEN IN the morning Detective Nichols and Deputy Robert Fuller arrived at the architectural firm of David Allison and Steven Fanning and asked the receptionist if either Mr. Allison or Mr. Fanning were available. She went to check and returned to say that Mr. Fanning would be out shortly. She seated them in a reception area with red chairs, black tables and a tall black vase filled with bare branches. The modern building had enormous glass panel windows and a view of the downtown Nashville skyline. This was expensive real estate.

Steven Fanning came briskly into the room with his hand outstretched. He was a slim, relatively short man with a buzz cut and an intense look. After shaking their hands, he showed them into a conference room with an enormous rosewood table and red chairs. There was a sideboard with coffee, tea, hot water and china cups. Steven poured three cups of coffee and invited them to be seated.

Detective Nichols said, "Mr. Fanning, we're here regarding the death of Ruby Mead-Allison, your partner's wife. We'd like to talk to you about the evening of March fifteenth."

"Certainly. I'm happy to help out. I don't see what I could tell you that would be pertinent. I need to check my calendar. I'll get my secretary." He pushed a button on the clear glass panel on his side of the conference table, and a tall, brown-haired woman came into the room.

"Linda, could you tell these men about my schedule for March fifteenth?"

She opened the planner in her hand. "March fifteenth was the day you were meeting with the representatives from Dymond Development Corporation all afternoon. You took Mr. John Rogers and Miss Stephanie Wilson to dinner at Café Margot."

"Thank you." Steven Fanning rose and ushered her out.

"What did you do after dinner?"

"We left the restaurant about nine o'clock and I escorted Miss Wilson to the Hyatt. John Rogers lives in Nashville but Stephanie is the corporate representative from Memphis. When we got to the hotel, she asked me to join her at the bar for a nightcap and I did. I left the bar around ten thirty and went straight home. I was at home the rest of the evening with my wife, Robin."

"When you drove home, did you come from the north or the south end of Little Chapel Road?"

"I always drive in from the south end."

"So, you must have driven past Ruby Mead-Allison's house on your way home?"

"Yes." Steven's glib demeanor was rapidly being replaced with caution.

"It would have taken you half an hour to drive home from the Hyatt, meaning you drove past Mrs. Mead-Allison's home around eleven?"

"Yes, that's about right."

"When you drove past her home, did you notice your partner's car in her driveway?"

"It was dark but I think I saw David's car. They have separated but I know they saw each other from time to time. My wife hoped they were getting back together."

"You weren't surprised to see your partner's car there?"

"No. Although David was originally planning to have dinner with us, Ruby called at the last minute and David decided to have dinner with her. I was pretty pissed, actually. He's the chief architect for the buildings Dymond Development is planning to construct. David said Ruby wanted to talk about their divorce. He was trying to work out something that they could both agree to, in terms of a property settlement."

"I'd like to point out a contradiction in your story, if I might," Wayne Nichols said quietly.

Steven swallowed audibly and then nodded.

"First, you told me your wife thought David and Ruby were getting back together, but Mr. Allison told you he couldn't go to dinner because he wanted to work out a property settlement with Ruby."

"Yes, well, you know how women are."

"Actually I don't. Suppose you tell me."

"Well, David and Ruby were our neighbors. Since their separation, David has been staying at our house. We have three small children and David is taking up one of the bedrooms. Obviously, Robin hoped for their reconciliation or a divorce. She wanted David out of the house. She was starting to press him about how long he'd be staying. My daughter doesn't like bunking with the boys."

"David told you he needed to skip an important business meeting to work out a property settlement? That shouldn't have required a late night visit to Ruby's house. So, what did you think when you saw his car in Ruby's driveway?"

"I was already irritated with him and when I saw his car, I was furious." Steven's fair skin flushed an angry red.

"You drove up your street and saw David's car in Ruby's driveway. What happened then? Mr. Fanning, I want to caution you—this is a murder inquiry and the night you saw Allison's car in the driveway was the night she died."

Steven was taken aback and seemed to choose his words carefully. "What did I do? What could I do? I drove past, cussing like a sailor."

"You didn't drive into the driveway? Why don't you take a moment to gather your thoughts, Mr. Fanning, and tell me what really happened?"

There was a pause. "You're right. I did drive in. I sat there in the driveway in my car thinking about what I should do. I was going to go in and talk to him, to both of them. However, I'd told Robin I'd be home by ten, and I knew she'd be none too pleased with me anyway. In the end, I drove home. Robin can tell you I was with her all night."

"Earlier you said you thought it was David's car in the driveway. Couldn't you immediately recognize David's car?"

"I'm sorry, Detective. Yes, I knew it was David's car."

"I'm going to ask you again what you did when you drove into the driveway. Did you go up to the house?" The detective paused and watched Steven Fanning closely. "Remember, I'm going to be talking to your wife about the time you arrived home and I'm very good at knowing when people are lying to me."

Steven took a deep breath. His voice was steady. "I watched the house until David came out and got into his car at almost eleven thirty. By then, I'd moved my car out of the driveway and parked it on the street in front of Ruby's place. When David drove down the driveway and headed toward my house, I followed him. I pulled into my driveway right behind him. When he got out of the car, we had an argument. David was very upset about his encounter with Ruby. Then Robin came outside and said we needed to come into the house. She told us to quiet down. We both came in. She got us drinks and left us in the living room. I didn't leave the house again all night."

"Was Mr. Allison in the house the remainder of the night?"

"I think so, but I can't say for sure. My wife and I have a

bedroom fan, and unless one of the kids opens the bedroom door, we don't hear much. I guess he could have left, but I don't think he did. He was more depressed than angry. He changed clothes, I know. Got into jeans and a t-shirt. When I went up to bed, he was sitting in the living room, downing shots of Johnnie Walker Black. When we woke up the next morning, our daughter, Tiffany, told us that when she got up Mr. Allison was still asleep on the couch."

"When you went to bed, leaving Mr. Allison drinking in the living room, did you notice the time?"

"Yes, it was right around one."

"When you got up the next morning, did you notice whether he was wearing the same clothes he had changed into the previous night or not?"

"I didn't actually see him. By the time I came into the kitchen, David was in the shower. You'll have to ask my wife."

"Okay. That's enough for now. We'll be speaking with Mr. Allison, and we may be back to ask you some more questions. I want to remind you to hold everything you told us in confidence. Do not discuss this matter with anyone, not your wife, your partner, nobody. Do you understand?" His tone was gentle, but very firm.

"Yes." Steven looked Wayne Nichols in the eye. "I understand clearly. You have my word, Detective. I won't talk to anyone else about this."

As THE OFFICERS walked down the hall toward Allison's Office, Deputy Fuller turned to Wayne Nichols. "Man, I don't know how you do it. Mr. Fanning was hostile and defensive. He didn't want to tell you anything. Then by the end of the conversation, you got him to open up and give you a lot of information. How do you do it?"

"We can talk about this when we get back into the car." Wayne knocked on Mr. Allison's office door.

David Allison needed no introduction to Detective Nichols

or Deputy Fuller. He said hello without shaking hands and waved them into his office.

The two officers sat in dark gray chairs facing David's teakwood desk. The office was decorated in gray striped wallpaper with an entire wall of windows. A framed photograph of Ruby sat on the console behind Allison. Her red hair was the only spot of color in the room. The pale gray carpeting made the office feel as it were floating off into the cityscape beyond.

Detective Nichols looked at David across the desk. "We've already talked to you about Ruby's death. I want to ask you again to describe your movements on the night she died."

"I already told you and I see no reason to do so again." His tone of voice was cool. David was plainly irritated by their visit.

"Mr. Allison, the first time we talked you didn't tell us the truth about your whereabouts." Wayne Nichol's voice was soft but pitched perfectly to raise David's fears. "We know you took Ruby to dinner at the Bistro at six forty-five. You left the restaurant around nine. We also know you drove to her house, arriving around nine thirty. You stayed at her house until at least eleven thirty. Ruby died that night."

David took a deep breath. He gripped the arms of his chair. Nichols noticed sweat on his temples.

"Do you deny that this accurately summarizes your actions on the night of March fifteenth?" Wayne kept his voice soft and almost kindly.

"No, you're right." David again took in a breath and exhaled. He seemed to relax a bit.

"You originally told us that you attended a dinner meeting. However, we now have positive identification from the wait staff at the Bistro, identifying you as Ruby's escort. We have your credit card slip showing that you paid for dinner. We also spoke with your partner, Steven Fanning. He said he drove by Ruby's house around eleven and saw your vehicle there. Do you have anything you'd like to add?"

"Only one thing. Ruby was alive and well when I left her house that night."

"Why didn't you tell us all of this earlier?"

"I knew I'd be a suspect, especially if I admitted that I was with her until almost midnight. I was scared." He scrutinized his desk.

"I understand, but now you have a bigger problem. Because you didn't tell us what really happened that night, we're more interested in you than ever." There was a pause, and then he leaned forward. "Mr. Allison, look at me. Tell me what really happened between you and Ruby the night of March fifteenth. This is going to be worse for you if you don't tell me everything."

David was pale now, but his voice seemed to strengthen as he spoke. He met the detective's eyes. "At the restaurant, Ruby told me she was pregnant. I was stunned. We had tried to have a child for about four years. After a couple of minutes, I was thrilled and hoped this would perhaps get her to consider reconciliation. Detective, I wouldn't have killed my pregnant wife. I regret lying to you, but I'm not a killer."

Wayne leaned back in his chair and nodded. "Go on."

"The chef stood right by our table when Ruby told me she was pregnant. He overheard and offered me a congratulatory after-dinner drink. I was on cloud nine when we left the restaurant.

"About an hour later, when Ruby poured us wine at her house, I asked her if she should be drinking, since she was pregnant. She got angry and said it was none of my business. I told her I thought it was, since she was carrying my child. She told me then that I wasn't the baby's father." His last words were almost inaudible.

"Did she tell you who the father was?"

"This is how pathetic the whole thing was. I never even asked. I told her I still wanted her, wanted us to get back together. I even said I was glad about the baby."

David's face was full of pain as he looked into the detective's eyes. Wayne nodded at him as if he understood. "What happened then?"

"Ruby wasn't interested. She didn't intend to get back together. After I saw that she couldn't care less about my offer, I was so humiliated I decided to leave. I drove to the Fannings' house. Steven had parked his car right where Ruby's driveway exits onto Little Chapel Road. When I got to Steven's house, he pulled in behind me and jumped out of his car. We got into a big argument."

"What was the argument about?"

"Steven practically attacked me. He was furious. I was emotionally spent from finding out about Ruby being pregnant. Steven kept asking me why I couldn't make dinner with the visiting VIPs and why I took Ruby to dinner instead. I finally broke down and told him that Ruby was pregnant and that I wasn't the father."

"What happened after that?"

"Robin came out and said we were waking the neighbors and told us to quiet down. I don't know if she heard what I said about Ruby or not, but I think she probably did. She told us to come into the house and we went inside."

"David, I want to believe you, but we have no one who can vouch for your movements after you got back to the Fanning residence. You could easily have walked back down the road to Ruby's house and killed her later that night."

There was a long silence while Wayne waited for David to say something else. "Learning his wife was pregnant by someone else could make a man angry enough to kill," Wayne said.

David's breathing was ragged. "Well, I didn't kill her. I was angry, yes, but I think I was more hurt than anything. Discovering Ruby had had an affair with someone else while I was hoping she might come back to me made me feel like a fool. The worst was what I learned about myself that night—even pregnant with another man's child—I was still in love with Ruby."

He stood up at his desk and glanced back at Ruby's framed photograph. "I'm sorry, Detective. I have a meeting now. I really need to go."

"All right. We're done for now. We may have to bring you in for further questioning, though. I need you to stay available."

Walking out to the car Deputy Fuller said, "Sir, I was surprised you got either of those guys to open up. Mr. Fanning was pretty slick, and Mr. Allison was very defensive at first. You really do have a knack."

Wayne shook his head, smiling. "I went to a conference once where we interviewed actors pretending to be murder suspects. Our task was to get the suspect to share information with us, even information that would portray them in a bad light.

"We worked with biofeedback machines. They taught us how to synchronize our breathing and how to get our heart rates down. Sometimes making eye contact and breathing at the same rate as the suspect makes them open up. They showed my interview to the rest of the conference as a good example of how to do the nonverbal stuff. I was proud of that."

"Do you think you do this instinctively or did you learn how at the conference?"

"I think it's a combination. Growing up in foster care, tough as it was, gave me the skill to read people. I never wanted to call attention to myself. I learned how to get other people to talk in order to take attention away from me. I can usually tell when someone is lying. It's helpful in my work."

Wayne looked at Robert Fuller, who listened intently. The young man seemed to be soaking up every word.

"I use the breathing technique when I need to get information that a suspect doesn't want to share. In some cases where I'm only getting background information, like when I talked to Lucy Ingram or Jack Ryan, people I don't necessarily suspect of a crime, I don't need to use the nonverbal stuff. Then it's more of a normal conversation."

"Could you teach me how to do it? Then sometime when we

have a suspect at the office, could I try to interrogate them?"

"If you want to practice, you should probably interview me first. Then you could interrogate a suspect, as long as the sheriff is okay with it."

"Um, all right then." Deputy Fuller gave him a sideways glance. "You said you grew up in foster care. Where were you living then?"

"In the Upper Peninsula of Michigan."

"Way up there. So, how did you end up in law enforcement in Tennessee?"

Wayne got behind the wheel of the car and tried to compose himself while Deputy Fuller walked around to the passenger side and climbed in. He looked at Wayne expectantly.

"With me, parallel questioning would probably work better." Wayne started the car and pulled out of the lot. "A lot of people are uncomfortable when you stare directly at them. Those people will reveal more when you're facing in the same direction."

"Got it." The young deputy faced forward and let some quiet build in the car.

Wayne nodded approvingly. "It's often a good idea to wait someone out. Then you can start your questioning."

Robert Fuller kept his gaze on the windshield. "How did you come to be a detective in Tennessee and what sparked your interest in law enforcement?"

Wayne had to be careful; the kid was actually pretty good. "After I left my last foster home, I worked on a wheat farm. Once the crop was in, the farmer told me to move on. I hitched a ride across the Mackinaw bridge and ended up in Traverse City at the beginning of fall. I was only seventeen, but I was big and strong. I got a job working for the hospital as an orderly, doing patient transport."

"Did you live alone?"

"Yeah, in a rented room." The detective allowed himself to get lost in memories. "I heard all kinds of stories. All day long patients talked to me. One old man told me that he had killed somebody in a fight over a woman. I didn't believe him then, but now I do. I went back to my room every night alone and thought about the things I heard." His voice drifted into silence.

"So you were interested in people's life stories, and that's why you wanted to be a detective?"

Wayne gave his head a quick shake. "Not merely the stories. I wanted to know the truth about those people. To me, being a detective is all about finding out the truth. One of the men I transported to dialysis died. I went to his autopsy. Several police officers also attended. I was impressed by how serious they were about it. Then I started going to mass, and one of the priests took an interest in me. I think he thought I'd go to seminary, possibly join the priesthood."

Robert stifled a laugh at this, and Wayne gave him a stern look.

"I know it sounds funny to you, but if this were a real interview, you would have just lost my trust."

"Well, you're kind of the ladies' man of the department. I can't picture you as a priest." Robert was carefully not meeting his eyes. "Let me try again. That sounds like a difficult time for you, Wayne. Is it all right if I call you Wayne?"

"Very good; build rapport, show sympathy. I think we should stop now. We're almost back at the office."

He drove into the office parking lot.

"Thank you, sir. I appreciate your help. Maybe I'll buy you a beer sometime and you can tell me your whole story."

"Sure." Wayne knew he'd never have that beer with Robert. He was an intensely private person. He had never told anyone how deeply his past affected him, how the things that happened long ago still determined his life. In fact, he had surprised himself by telling the young deputy as much as he did. Most of his stories stayed buried deep.

Chapter Twenty-Three

—

March 25
Detective Wayne Nichols

Connolly's refusal to give them a saliva sample piqued Wayne's interest, and he investigated the lawyer in detail. Ruby and her attorney had certainly been busy in the months leading up to her death. Wayne had discovered a wealth of information that pointed to an affair between Connolly and Ruby. They needed that court order for the saliva sample.

"Dory, which judge was going to sign the court order for Connolly?" He yelled out the door of his office.

"Judge Cochran."

"Could you get him on the phone for me, please?"

"Well, I could get her on the phone."

There was a short pause. "Yes, please, Dory."

About fifteen minutes later, Dory buzzed his office to tell him that Judge Cochran was on the line.

"Hello, Judge Cochran?"

"Yes, this is she." Wayne could tell from her tone that she was, in Southern parlance, "all bidness."

"This is Detective Wayne Nichols with the Rose County

Sheriff's office. We requested a court order to obtain a cheek swab from attorney James Connolly. Has it been signed yet?"

"Detective, I'm not in the habit of jumping to sign court orders requesting a cheek swab from attorneys of the court. I need full justification for this."

"Do you want to discuss this on the phone, ma'am, or do you need me to come to your office?"

"Neither. I need a written report with evidence that justifies such an order. This better not be a fishing expedition."

"May I fax it over this afternoon?"

"Yes, you may. I'll put you back on with my secretary. She'll give you the fax number. Oh, and, Detective, make that report comprehensive."

"Yes, ma'am." Sighing, he hung up the phone and began typing a report. After he was finished, he took it out to Dory.

"Dory, could you please make sure this report is perfect and fax it to the Judge?

Dory rolled her eyes, but checked his draft and faxed it over to Judge Cochran's office.

Report for Judge Cornelia Cochran
March 25
1:30 p.m.
Sheriff Bradley's office
Report prepared by: Wayne Nichols, Detective

Re: Obtaining a court order for a cheek swab from Attorney James G. Connolly

This office is investigating the death of Ruby Mead-Allison, D.O.D. March 15, 2013. Ms. Mead Allison was pregnant at the time of the post-mortem examination (M.E.'s Office March 19). There is reason to suspect James G. Connolly, attorney for the late Ms. Allison, of having carnal relations with the decedent.

Interviews with Mr. Connolly's staff and careful perusal of his calendar indicates over twenty-five late evening meetings with Mrs. Allison, including dinner and alcoholic beverages on multiple occasions over a one-year period.

Mr. Connolly maintains an apartment in the city for late-night meetings. The apartment is cleaned only at the request of Mr. Connolly. On six separate occasions, on the day following his evening meeting with Mrs. Allison, Connolly instructed his staff to order cleaning services for the apartment. This included washing sheets and remaking the bed.

Sheriff's department personnel interviewed Ms. Judy Grover on March 21. Ms. Grover is the cleaning person for the building at 406 Robert Street in which Mr. Connolly has his apartment. Ms. Grover admitted seeing used condoms in the wastebasket when she cleaned. In addition, on one occasion, she found a thong (black undergarment) from Victoria's Secret, size small.

Upon arrival at the M.E.'s Office for post-mortem examination, the victim was wearing a thong undergarment purchased from Victoria's Secret, size small. Another pair of underwear was found tangled in the sheets when they were changed. The lab ran a DNA analysis on the secretions on the undergarment found in Connolly's apartment. The DNA found on the underwear matched the DNA from the victim's body.

The above-mentioned evidence constitutes probable cause for a court order for a cheek swab from attorney James Connolly. He is a material suspect in the killing of Ms. Allison, who may have posed a serious risk for Mr. Connolly, given his marital status (married). He is the father of two children. If Mr. Connolly was having carnal relations with one of his clients (to wit Mrs. Mead-Allison), he could be brought before the ethics board. This could be career-damaging to a family attorney's practice.

Signed,
Wayne Nichols
Chief Detective
County of Rose

While waiting for the Judge's reply, Wayne walked down the hall to see if his young boss was in.

"Sheriff?"

Ben frowned, then looked up from his computer and asked Wayne to come in and sit down. "Where are we right now on the investigation?"

"I faxed the court order request to Judge Cochran for Connolly's cheek swab. She's insisting on a full report since Connolly is an attorney and an officer of the court."

"Did you already speak with her?"

"Yes. She was firm about needing the paperwork." Wayne scowled.

"I could call and ask her to hurry up." Ben grinned. "I am her favorite nephew."

"Well, that would have been good to know. I might not have needed to write the damn report."

"You still would have needed to do the paperwork. Aunt Cornelia is a stickler. Let me know when she signs it. If we don't get her approval today, I'll call her. We're running out of time."

"I know we are." Wayne stood up, nodded at Ben and walked out.

AN HOUR LATER, Dory entered Wayne's office. "Here's the fax from the judge."

"Thank you, Miss Dory."

Dory winked at him. "Detective Nichols, do you have a girlfriend?"

"Why do you want to know? Miss Dory, are you auditioning?"

"Could be, Detective, could be. Or, maybe I'm asking on behalf of someone else. You're so smart. I bet you'll figure it out. Do you want me to tell the boss his auntie came through for us?"

All he could do was nod. She sashayed out of the room. Wayne shook his head, got up from his desk and collected Lab Tech Emma Peters to go to Connolly's office with him. Dory loved to tease him. She was very attractive for a woman her age, but he'd never gotten a single vibe from her indicating that she might be interested. She was probably just messing with him.

When he first started working for the sheriff's office, he overheard her sharing a piece of very confidential information. He was infuriated. He called her into his office and read her the riot act. Dory was undaunted. Her response startled him.

"You men always want complete confidentiality. Usually, I need to give a little information to get a more important piece of information in return."

Over the next few weeks, he had realized how often Dory knew things that turned out to be enormously helpful.

"Life's a web, Detective. We're all inter-connected. If you disclose something about yourself, or ask for someone's help with something, the other person feels safe in sharing something with you. Over time, there are no secrets."

Wayne Nichols had many secrets. If he ever got closer to Dory, she'd probably find a way to uncover them all.

Wayne Nichols and Emma Peters arrived at Connolly's office shortly before five. His secretary showed them in.

"Mr. Connolly, we have a court order for a cheek swab to determine if you're the father of Ruby Mead-Allison's child."

"I'll need to see the order." Connolly's face was flushed, and his light brown hair was rumpled. The smell of whiskey floated in the stale office air.

Wayne reached across the imposing rosewood desk and handed him the paperwork. He scanned it and nodded with a resigned expression.

"Please open your mouth." He did and Emma deftly got a cheek swab from the inside of his cheek with a Q-tip. She put the Q-tip into a glass tube.

"Thank you, Mr. Connolly." She snapped the top closed.

"We should have the results tomorrow. With all the effort the sheriff is putting into solving this case, the lab is running our stats immediately. If the swab establishes paternity, we'll bring you in for more questioning,"

"Damn it, I didn't murder the woman. If you try to bring me in for questioning, I warn you, I will have counsel present."

"I assumed you would." Wayne was calm.

They left the office and took the cheek swab immediately to the lab. Emma agreed to do the test right away and call the detective with the results as soon as possible.

"Thanks for bringing me along." Emma smiled at Wayne as she gracefully exited the car.

"My pleasure." There was a bit of extra sway in her walk. Nichols wondered if she knew he was paying attention.

Chapter Twenty-Four

———

March 25
Mae December

THE LITTLE CHAPEL Road neighborhood meeting was scheduled for seven that evening. Mae called Beth Jensen around six and asked if she should bring some wine.

"We don't usually drink at the meetings, but everyone needs to relax," Mae said.

Beth agreed.

Ben called again, saying he couldn't pick her up after all, but that he'd meet her at the Jensens' house.

Mae got to Beth's house early and helped her put out the snacks and drinks. They heard muffled thumping and music coming from the closed door of the den, where Beth's three kids had holed up for the duration of the meeting.

"They're doing homework," Beth grinned after a particularly loud thump. "Or so they tell me."

"My sister and I did homework that way, too." Mae laughed.

They talked about Ruby's funeral. Beth admitted to feeling some relief after the service, even though everyone wanted the killer caught and hoped that the sheriff would make an arrest soon.

"Now we can finally get this road widened. According to the plans the road commission approved on Friday night, we'll have a real bus stop. I never want to have anyone go through what we did with my son."

Mae remembered the day the school bus drove past Billy Jensen, leaving him standing in the tall weeds.

Beth asked Mae to answer the door, welcome everyone, and take coats. Mae stationed herself in the front entry with a glass of wine as people began to arrive. The Ryans were first and Mae was glad to see Jack's ankle was much improved. Eveline still wasn't looking very well.

Lucy Ingram came in looking tired, still dressed in scrubs and not wearing lipstick. Tammy would not approve.

"Hi Lucy." Mae gave her a hug.

"How are you doing?" Lucy asked. "This has been a rough week for you, hasn't it?"

"You could definitely say that." Mae shook her head, remembering everything that had happened since the day she reported Ruby missing.

"How are you sleeping?"

"Not well, but I know it's because of this situation."

"Well, don't hesitate to go and see your doctor if you feel you need something to get you through a few nights."

Lucy was such a warm empathetic person. Her patients must appreciate her calm kindness in the midst of their traumatic situations. Next, Robin Fanning came in without her husband.

"Hi Robin. Where's Steven?"

"He got caught up in something for the new project. I thought he was going to be home by seven to stay with our kids but he called and said he needed to work late. Getting a babysitter at this late hour was a pain." Robin was blessed with striking black Irish looks—fair skin, dark brown curls and blue eyes. When she was in a good mood, her smile was radiant, but tonight she seemed very tired.

"Are you okay?"

"Yes, but having David stay with us is getting old. My daughter doesn't appreciate having to share her brothers' bedroom. It's tough getting all three of them settled down and David often ends up sleeping on the couch, anyway." She gave a sharp exasperated sigh. "We also have Elvis to deal with now, and the extra laundry is a pain. David says he's looking for a condo. I hope he finds one soon."

"How's your sister?" Robin's sister, Laura, was married to James Connolly. Mae knew her life would have been turned upside down by this situation as well.

"My poor sister. All of this is awful for her and when Laura's in bad shape, I always get the call." She shrugged, but her face was tight. She went to join the rest of the group.

Joe and Neesy Dennis came up the walkway holding hands. Mae was surprised that they had come but then remembered Joe saying his mother was moving into an assisted living situation. MaryLou had fallen earlier this spring and broken her hip. She was about to be released from the rehab center, but her doctor didn't think she could live on her own any more. Joe and Neesy were moving into her house and selling theirs. They would all be neighbors soon, as well as friends.

"Hey there you two, glad you could make it."

Neesy gave her a smile. "With four kids, I count this as a date. At least I'm out of the house."

The Van Attas came in right behind them. Both looked cheerful.

"Hi Annie, Jason."

"Hi yourself. It's almost planting season." Annie smiled. "We need to get together to do our Garden Walk planning."

"I know and I'm looking forward to it." Annie and Mae organized the neighborhood Garden Walk each year and one family hosted it. Ever since they had started, the neighborhood held a fall bulb and perennial exchange. There was a long tradition of "pass along plants" in the middle South, and all those donations contributed to beautifying Little Chapel Road.

"Once we get this road widened, there will be lots of landscaping to do along the new shoulders."

"We can try out some new shrubs and flowering perennials."

Jason gave Mae a quick hug and walked into the living room. She suddenly remembered the issue between Ruby and the Van Attas. It had been about the song Jason wrote; the one Ruby had stolen. Mae wondered briefly if Ruby making money from Jason's song would be a sufficient motive for murder.

At bit later, Mae peered down the driveway, wondering when Ben was going to show up. Moments later, he came in with a gust of spring wind and gave her a hug. He smelled like the fresh outdoor air. She smiled and asked him how he was doing.

"I'm fine." He looked at her for longer than strictly necessary. "You look very nice tonight."

"So do you." He wore jeans and a dark blue shirt. His eyes were almost navy in the dim light of the entryway. "Let me show you in."

Beth introduced Ben to the group and said since he was so involved in the neighborhood, she thought she should invite him to the meeting.

There was polite laughter.

"Thanks for having me. I don't have much information for you, except to say we're making good progress on the investigation and hope to have this whole thing buttoned up soon. I think I can guarantee that by the next neighborhood meeting, the killer will be in jail."

There were a few raised eyebrows and a short silence. The front door opened and Mae hurried to greet the late arrival. Silas stood there in the entryway. She glanced quickly behind him, but he was alone.

"Hi Silas." Mae didn't meet his eyes. She was still upset and conflicted over the incident with his partner, Terry.

"Hi Mae. I thought I'd come to represent the Mead family. Bill Jenson asked me to do so at the funeral. I hope this isn't going to be awkward. I'm sorry about Terry. He isn't usually like this. The stress of this whole thing has been awful for all of us."

"Everyone," Mae announced, "Silas is here representing the Mead family."

There was silence for a moment, and then Eveline Ryan, who'd known the Meads for decades, rose slowly from her chair. "Silas, it's nice to see you. Won't you come and sit by me?"

He smiled and joined her. After a few awkward moments, the conversation resumed and Beth called the meeting to order. The chairperson rotated yearly, and this year Beth was chairing the meetings. She announced that they needed to do a road clean-up and remove some dead trees.

"We can have the county do it, but they'll charge us, and it always strengthens our sense of family here on Little Chapel Road when we do these things together."

After that, the group seemed to relax and the murmur of conversation continued. Mae took the bottles of red and white wine around the room and refilled glasses.

The meeting moved forward, establishing a day for road clean-up, dead tree removal, the Garden Walk and the Spring Fling. Mae offered to host Spring Fling.

It was close to ten when the meeting ended. Mae walked to the door with Ben and Robin Fanning. Robin's demeanor seemed cool. She practically snatched her coat when Ben handed it to her. How could she be comfortable with David, who might have murdered his wife, living with her children? Did Robin know more about Ruby's death than she let on?

"Do you want to stop by my house?" Mae asked Ben as they walked out to his car in the spring evening.

"Yes, I want to, but I can't. Mae, please be patient with me. A sheriff's life is awfully demanding, especially during a murder investigation."

"I understand. Goodnight."

Mae went home alone, wondering if she and Ben would ever have a real date.

Chapter Twenty-Five

March 26
Mae December

IT WAS MAE'S morning to volunteer at the elementary school. Once a month she took a dog or two up to the school library for reading time. A creative English teacher had started the program. She believed that children who struggled with reading aloud in front of their classmates would improve by reading to dogs. Dogs gave everyone unconditional positive regard, and when children felt accepted, their skills improved.

At first, the program used only registered therapy dogs, but since Tallulah, Titan, and Thoreau had completed their Canine Good Citizen training, the school was happy to have them. She decided she'd bring both Tallulah and Titan today. Thoreau, Noah's old Rottweiler, had hip joints which gave him trouble in damp weather, and getting him in and out of the car was hard on him.

Mae got dressed in jeans and a special sweatshirt she had made for this program. On the front of the sweatshirt was a picture of all three dogs. Tallulah was wearing glasses. Beneath the picture the wording read, "What! Dogs Can't Read?" When the kids saw the sweatshirt, they usually giggled.

She loaded Tallulah and Titan into the car and drove to the school. The bright sunny morning with a light breeze made her spirits rise as she drove down Little Chapel Road and turned onto River Road. The trees were leafing out and the smell of honeysuckle floated through her open window.

Walking into the beautiful library, Mae was greeted with smiles and waves from the kids and a quick hug from Cecilia Llewellyn, the English teacher. The library was quite large for an elementary school, with bookshelves four feet high on all the exterior walls. The architect had installed clerestory windows above the bookshelves, and natural light poured into the space. There were a half dozen low tables with six chairs around each one. Mae always got a kick out of the miniature furniture. It was just the right size for first graders.

Only five children were waiting to read to the dogs. She knew them all by now and said hello to each. Cecelia had provided nametags in the beginning, to help Mae learn their names. Two other women came in with their dogs. The children clustered around each dog.

Each child had selected a book to read to the dogs ahead of time. She saw some Dr. Seuss books and remembered the fun of reading those books to her nephews and niece.

Mae sat at the table with her two students, Jackson and Will. Jackson had selected a book about recess and the Seuss children's classic, *The Foot Book*. Will had picked one that was all about dirt. She looked at her furry children to be sure that they were sitting quietly before asking Jackson to begin.

"One foot, two foot, red foot, blue foot …" Jackson's little voice was serious. He focused on the words and then shifted his gaze up towards Titan, as if he wanted the corgi's approval. He was adorable.

Will started reading his book, which also rhymed. Rhyming books were easier for the kids to read aloud. They seemed to get into a rhythm that made the words flow more smoothly.

When Mae started with the program, she had met with the reading teachers and asked if she should correct pronunciation. They said no. Instead, she was encouraged to become invisible once they started reading. Sitting there, hearing their small voices gain in confidence and volume and looking at the napes of their necks as they bent over their books, Mae wondered if she'd ever be lucky enough to have a child of her own.

After they read their books, Mae showed the boys the newest trick the dogs had learned. "Sit dogs. Now wave." The dogs lifted their right front paws. The kids giggled.

After all the children were finished reading and had assembled by the checkout table, Mae told them about Tallulah's five puppies.

"They're too little to come to school today, but I'll bring them up after they have their first shots."

"What kind of puppies are they?" a little girl asked.

"They're called Porgis. They're a combination of their mother Tallulah, the black pug and their father Titan who is a Welsh corgi."

"Can they eat puppy food yet?"

"No, they're still nursing and Tallulah needs to get back to them soon. So, I have to go."

"Children, time to go back to class now," Cecelia told them. "Say goodbye and thank you to Miss Mae, Mrs. West and Miss Worthington."

"Thank you, Miss Mae. Goodbye, goodbye."

As they trooped out, she turned to Cecelia. "I should really be the one thanking them. It's a pleasure to work with them in this program."

The teacher smiled, nodded her head in agreement and helped Mae get the dogs back into the car. Mae drove out of the school parking lot feeling calm and peaceful. A few blocks later, her cellphone rang. Caller ID showed "Don December."

"Hi, Honey. It's Dad. I found a few more pictures of our mystery man in my digital files. Funny thing. In almost all of the shots, he's staring at you. You're still sure you don't know him?"

"I'm pretty sure, Daddy. I do think there's something creepy about him, though. "

"Well, baby, don't worry. He was probably an aspiring songwriter, and Noah beat him to it. I don't want to leave anyone important out of the book. I'm going to go through my old police photos, too, just in case."

They said goodbye and Mae looked left to check oncoming traffic before her turn. When she faced forward again, she saw a man hurrying down the sidewalk to her right. He quickly turned his head away from her, almost as if he didn't want her to see him. He was a big man wearing a long winter coat. A little bit of blond hair stuck out from under his hat. Mae drove home with images of the man in Daddy's pictures running through her brain.

Chapter Twenty-Six

March 26
Sheriff Ben Bradley

B EN ASKED DORY to let him know as soon as Wayne Nichols arrived. He planned to check with Tech Johns about the results he had gotten from the lab studies. Hopefully, there would be something pertinent to gather from the tests on the clothing. Hadley Johns was waiting for him in the conference room.

"We struck out with both David Allison and James Connolly. There was no blood on either set of clothing. All the fluids we found belonged to them. The paternity test came back early, though, and we have our daddy. It's Mr. Connolly. Emma ran the test last night."

"Is she sure?"

"Yes, sir. I even re-ran the test. He's the father. It's a match."

"Thanks for the rush on the results." Dory buzzed Ben saying Detective Nichols was there. "Okay, Hadley, you can get back to work now. Detective Nichols and I need to have a meeting."

As soon as the skinny tech left the room, Wayne Nichols walked in.

"Good morning, Wayne. Hadley just gave me the news. James Connolly is the father. That's a big break for us. So, let's review where we are."

Wayne nodded.

"We're concentrating on two major suspects, David Allison and James Connolly. Let's go over what we have on the attorney first."

"We already knew that Connolly was having an affair with Ruby, but we now know he was the father of her child. Mr. Connolly kept an apartment in downtown Nashville that he used for late-night meetings, or for early morning court appearances. The affair took place there. We found two interesting things in the bedside stands when we searched the apartment—a fake gun and a pair of restraints."

"What do you mean by 'restraints'?" Ben asked.

"Like handcuffs but not as heavy. They're loose when a person puts them on but tighten up if the person struggles. They're lightweight and look sort of like bracelets. They're used sometimes for S and M sex."

"This must be my week to learn things I don't want to know. How do you know about S and M sex?"

"Hey, I'm a man of the world, Boss." Wayne grinned. "Did I tell you that Ruby met with James Connolly when she got back from vacation and gave him an expensive cigar? My guess is she told him she was pregnant and that he was the father. That couldn't have been good news. The man is married and has two kids. So, unless he was deeply in love with Ruby, he must have felt his back was to the wall."

"What else?"

"There's the business aspect of their relationship. He was trying to finalize a deal with Dymond Development that would have made Ruby and him very rich. They probably initiated the lawsuits about the road widening to delay the construction long enough to get the county to up their offer for the property. Lucy told me that Ruby wanted to buy the vacant lot next door to her and that she got angry when Lucy wouldn't sell."

"Sounds like Ruby and her attorney were trying to do a land grab. I wonder who Henriette Mead plans to give her property to after she dies?" Ben rubbed the spot between his eyebrows where a headache was starting.

"Yes, we can't dismiss Silas yet. But I think James Connolly is our most likely perp. He had the means, motive, opportunity and Ruby's power of attorney. Once she was dead, he'd be the one to deal with Silas on the property. Then Ruby turned up pregnant. That gave her power over him which could have ruined his marriage and his practice as a family attorney."

Ben nodded. "James also drives a pickup truck. He could have gone to Ruby's house and killed her after David left. His wife told you that he took the babysitter home. If we could get Lucy or Mrs. Ryan to identify the truck and its driver, we might be able to focus on James Connolly."

"I also think Mrs. Connolly knows something." Wayne narrowed his eyes. "Her behavior was a little strange when I was at her house."

"I'm not completely ready to dismiss David Allison either," Ben said. "He was with Ruby the night she died. She taunted him with the fact that he wasn't the father of her child. It must have been devastating news. He also had the means, motive and opportunity. On the other hand, he didn't stand to inherit her property—although I'm not sure he knew about the specifics of her will. He doesn't strike me as the type that would resort to violence easily. He has no record, in fact quite the opposite. He's mild mannered and has nothing more than a few parking tickets."

"What did the lab find on his clothing from that night?"

"There was nothing there. Bottom line, who do you like best for this, Wayne, Ruby's husband or her attorney?"

"Attorney. David Allison seems like a gentle guy who was deeply hurt about the way Ruby treated him. While anyone can be driven to murder, I doubt a guy like David could kill a pregnant woman."

"I agree. Does having the murder weapon show up in Mae's barn change anything? She has no motive as far as we can discover. It's much more likely that someone else put the shovel there in order to frame her."

"Well," the detective gave the sheriff an appraising look, "I think the pretty lady is pretty interested in you. Possibly, she's trying to distract you from thinking she's involved in the crime. You have to admit, finding both the body and the murder weapon is suspicious."

Wayne sounded like he was kidding, but his face was dead serious.

"Knock it off," Ben said. "You know she isn't a suspect. She had no reason to want Ruby dead." They locked eyes for a minute until Wayne dropped his gaze and cleared his throat.

"I investigated Lucy Ingram's background, by the way," Ben said. "Did you know she changed her name right after she entered medical school?"

Wayne seemed surprised but stayed quiet.

"Yeah, her last name was Sherman. Do you remember the Sherman case in Memphis?"

"Of course I do."

"Lucy is Dr. Marcus Sherman's daughter. She found her mom dead in the bathtub. The case was never solved, but everyone in Memphis thought Sherman killed his wife. It's easy for anesthesiologists to get away with murder, I guess."

Wayne took a deep breath. "Poor kid. What's your point? It certainly wasn't Lucy's fault her mother was killed."

"Of course not. I wasn't implying that it was. She obviously lived through some horrible times. There were some other entries about the Shermans in the police files over the years, neighbors calling in with child abuse allegations. Both those girls were in the E.R. a lot."

"Lucy has a sister? She never told me."

"Yeah. She has an older sister, a junkie. Her name is Colleen. She's been in and out of rehabs most of her life. You brought up Mae as a suspect; so I want you to think carefully about Lucy. With a background like that, being sued by Ruby and pressured to sell her property, do you think she might have felt threatened enough to try to stop her?"

Wayne shook his head vehemently. "It wasn't Lucy. There's no way in hell. I've watched her in the E.R. She wouldn't hurt someone deliberately."

Ben shrugged. "You're the one who says everyone is capable of murder."

"I didn't say she wasn't capable of murder. If there was ever a mercy killing, I might suspect her, but braining her neighbor with a shovel? Not Lucy."

Ben tapped his pencil on the desk. He glanced down at the handwritten list of suspects on his desk. "What about Terry Lerner? He admitted to Criminal Trespass. He was inside Mae's barn and he leads us straight back to Silas. However, having seen and heard Silas at the funeral—his grief appeared real. He seems to be a good-natured person who loved his sister. I think we can eliminate Silas as well as Lucy and Mae." Ben looked at Wayne, who took a sip of his cold coffee, nodded and then dumped it into the wastebasket.

"I think we can only dismiss Silas," Wayne said, "if you're sure the Mead property isn't a factor." He put the tips of his fingers together.

"Good point. Given the enormous value of Ruby's land, I want to talk to Silas one more time before we let him go. The only thing Terry did was tie red ribbons on Mae's kennels and door. I don't like the creep, but I doubt he's the perp." Ben rubbed his nose.

"I agree. I don't think he's violent enough to do this, although he doesn't seem to have any respect for private property. If Terry was at Ruby's and found the shovel, he might have taken it to Mae's place to increase interest in Mae as a suspect. I'll get him in here and you can try to rattle him."

Ben was confident in his ability to narrow down the suspects, but he had serious doubts about being able to rattle them the way his Chief Detective did. He'd seen him in action. When questioning suspects, he appeared to be barely keeping his violent nature under control. The suspects felt it. Often that was all it took. He would stand up and walk around behind someone he was questioning. Then he would lean down and crack his hands down on the table loudly and tell them exactly how the crime was committed. Now that was rattling a suspect.

"I think rattling suspects is more your thing, Wayne. How about I call David Allison and get the scoop on the Mead property from him. Unless I learn something new, I'll probably go ahead and tell David he's not being considered a suspect anymore. Let's bring in James Connolly, Silas, and Terry Lerner." Ben stood up, downed the last of his cold coffee and called Dory. When she came into the conference room, Ben told her they were bringing in three suspects.

"Where're you puttin' all those men?"

"I don't know, but I need this room cleaned up. I may need an empty cell in the jail, too. Don't just stand there, young lady."

Dory and Wayne exchanged a meaningful look, but they both got busy. Satisfied that he'd made some impact, Ben went back to his office to make some calls.

HE GOT RUBY's ex-husband, David, on the phone first. "I have a problem, Mr. Allison. I hope you can help me out. I have several suspects in this case, but you seem to be one of the few who's actually depressed about Ruby's death. The rest of them aren't acting that way."

"I am depressed about her death and the death of her unborn baby. I wanted the child to be mine. Ruby felt she needed a baby to carry on the family line. Her dad messed her up, you know. He made her feel like she'd be worthless if she didn't give him a grandchild. She thought if she had a child, she'd get her hands on the entire estate."

"What do you mean? I thought she got the whole thing."

David Allison gave a humorless chuckle. "No. She didn't get the acreage at the back of her property that adjoins Henriette's."

"Isn't that over on Mead Road?"

"Yes. It's a five hundred acre tract altogether. As the crow flies, it's actually not that far. You go down to River Road, turn right and then right again when you get to Mead. You know why it's called Mead Road, don't you, Sheriff? It used to be their driveway."

"Why didn't Ruby get the adjoining parcel?"

"It wasn't her dad's property to leave. Henriette owns that piece. She always planned on leaving her property to Silas. The entire parcel would be worth millions."

"Thank you for telling me all this. You've been a big help. I'd like you to know that we have no plans to arrest you. Please contact us if you think of anything else we should know."

"I will. Thanks, Sheriff. Ruby and I had our problems, but I'd do anything to help you find her killer. I don't want her murder to be an unsolved case."

"Don't worry. It won't be."

BEN PLACED A call to Terry and Silas. Terry Lerner answered the phone at the carriage house.

"Mr. Lerner, this is Sheriff Bradley. We've uncovered some new evidence about Ruby Mead-Allison's death we'd like to discuss with you and Mr. Mead. I need you to come to the office."

"Both of us? Why?"

"The evidence links you to the murder." It was an empty threat, but he wanted to unsettle the sneak. Since Nichols thought he could, he'd try. The bluff had worked with the trespassing incident.

"That's impossible!" Terry exclaimed. "I didn't kill Ruby, and neither did Silas."

"Be that as it may, Mr. Lerner, I need you both to come in. If you do so voluntarily, within the hour, we can be civil about this. Otherwise, I'm signing a warrant for your arrest." With a sense of satisfaction, Ben hung up the phone. He set the timer on his wristwatch for fifty-nine minutes.

AN HOUR LATER Wayne called from his car to let Ben know that James Connolly had been Mirandized and was exercising his right to remain silent.

"Has he lawyered up yet?"

"Of course he has. You know we aren't getting anything out of him until his attorney shows up."

"You're right. Attorneys are the worst people to question. Find an empty cell for him until then and get here as soon as you can. I'm going to talk to Terry and Silas. I'd like you to be with me for James Connolly's interrogation."

"Things are starting to shake loose, aren't they?"

"It's about time." Ben walked out of his office and up to Dory's desk to ask her a question. At that moment, Terry and Silas walked in with Deputy Fuller.

"Should we tell the Rent-a-Cop he can stop following us now?" asked Terry.

Ben had had more than enough of his attitude. "That's a Rose County deputy fulfilling his assigned duty. Don't push me." He turned to Dory. "Miss Dory, would you please show Mr. Mead into the conference room? Lerner, come with me."

He led Terry Lerner to a small separate interview room and ushered him inside. He decided to let him sweat it out alone for a while.

"Wait here. I'll be back to talk with you shortly."

SILAS MEAD WAS sitting in the conference room. He was leaning back in his chair with his eyes closed. When Ben entered the room, he shut the door with a bang and Silas leaned forward with a start.

"Mr. Mead, I'm trying to figure something out. Can you tell me, prior to Ruby's death, what Henriette's plan was for who would inherit her estate?"

"My grandmother promised, since Ruby got our parents' property, that I would inherit hers. I think Gram wanted to make it up to me for my dad cutting me off."

"Interesting. So you didn't need to kill Ruby to get your family estate. Although Ruby's pregnancy would have allowed her to cut you out."

"She was pregnant?" Silas' voice shook at the revelation. "Oh, God no."

Silas' eyes were moist and then, as if he'd held it all back for a long time, he started to cry. His harsh sobs filled the room. Ben sat there patiently, waiting him out. When the outburst was over and Silas was quiet, Ben handed him a box of tissues.

"Why is the information about her pregnancy this devastating for you?" Ben's voice was full of concern.

Silas' eyes filled once more. "I'm already dealing with the fact that my sister was murdered. To find out I could have had a niece or nephew, a member of the Mead family who'll never be born, is terrible. My whole family is gone."

Ben remembered Silas at the funeral, his moving tribute to Ruby and his palpable suffering.

"Please wait here." Ben rose and left the room.

Chapter Twenty-Seven

March 26
Sheriff Ben Bradley

T HE SOLUTION TO Ruby's murder was coming closer. Ben could feel it.

"Is Wayne back with James Connolly yet?" he asked Dory.

Dory shook her head. "No. He's in the interview room with the sassy one."

Ben walked back to the interview room and knocked. Wayne opened the door.

"Where's Deputy Fuller?" Ben kept his voice low so Terry couldn't overhear.

"He's waiting over at the jail. As soon as Mr. Connolly's attorney shows up, he's to call me."

"Mind if I join you?"

"Come on in."

Ben entered the room and sat down. "Terry, I have a few questions for you. My guess is that you thought you were protecting Silas' inheritance."

He shrank away and narrowed his eyes. "What are you talking about?"

"When you killed Ruby. You must have found out she was pregnant and planning to disinherit Silas, so you killed her. The irony is that if you hadn't threatened Mae and hidden the murder weapon, the shovel, at her house, we might not have figured this out."

His eyes opened wide. "Ruby was pregnant? I didn't know that. I didn't hide anything at the December house and I did not kill Silas' bitch of a sister. Why was there a murder weapon? Everyone knows she was strangled."

"That may have been the rumor you heard, but there was a murder weapon. Miss December found it in her barn after you trespassed there."

"Then I'd think you'd be questioning her, not me. I'm calling my attorney. I'm done talking without one." Terry clenched his fists on the table.

"Read him his rights, Detective Nichols. Then he can call his attorney, and we'll find a cell for him."

Terry Lerner's voice got squeaky. "Sheriff, I swear I didn't leave a thing at Miss December's house except the note and ribbons. I'll take a lie detector test if you want."

"Excuse us for a moment, Mr. Lerner," Wayne said. "I need to speak with the sheriff."

They walked out into the hall. Wayne waved Ben into his office and closed the door behind them.

"No offense, Boss. I'm partly to blame since I told you to rattle him, but it crashed and burned."

Ben nodded. He felt his face warming. Damn it, Wayne was right. He got nothing out of Terry with his accusations.

"Plus, you told him about the shovel and that information wasn't known outside of our department before this. But we did learn something. The murder weapon information was a total shock to Mr. Lerner. He isn't our killer. I think someone else took the shovel over to Mae's house."

"Yeah, I think so, too," Ben tried to hide his chagrin. "We can let him go, but let's warn him that we may run a polygraph on him later. Both of us know it won't be allowed as evidence in a trial, but he might not. I'm going to dismiss Silas also; he completely checked out. Bring James Connolly back here when his attorney shows up, will you?"

AFTER DISMISSING DAVID Allison, Silas and Terry, Ben paced around Dory's work area. She sighed, got up from her desk and gave him an oversized cookie from the stash she kept in her desk drawer.

"Sheriff, you aren't going to get anywhere with that slick lawyer and his attorney unless you're real, real calm."

"Good advice. Thanks." Ben took the cookie back to his office. It was the first food he'd had in hours. He ate the whole thing in two bites and put his head down on his desk.

A sudden knock on the door startled him awake.

"They're ready for you now in the conference room, Sheriff," Dory said.

"I'll be right there." He went to the sink in the small restroom adjoining his office and splashed his face with cool water. "It's game-time. Tighten up your jock strap. Let's go," he said to his reflection.

When the sheriff walked into the conference room, Wayne Nichols introduced him to Ms. Emerson, James Connolly's attorney. The sheriff and his detective sat on one side of the large wooden table. Mr. Connolly and his young, leggy attorney sat facing them. Her jacket exposed a discreet amount of cleavage. Ben smiled at her and was rewarded with a scornful smirk. Dory came in with a fresh pot of decaf coffee, cups, sugar, and cream. She turned on the audiotape equipment and left the room.

At first no one spoke.

Detective Nichols cleared his throat. He looked directly at the built in microphone saying, "Wayne Nichols and Ben Bradley interviewing James Connolly represented by his attorney, Counselor Emerson. Mr. Connolly, as you know, you're suspected of murdering Ruby Mead-Allison on the night of March fifteenth. You were read your rights and you have counsel present—Ms. Paula Emerson. As you're aware, Tennessee is a capital punishment state and in this case, we're prepared to go for the death penalty. We're on the record and I ask you to re-state your movements on the evening of March fifteenth."

James Connolly spoke in a loud and somewhat pompous voice. "I came home from the office on March fifteenth around five thirty p.m. Laura and I got ready to join our friends the Mitchells for an evening out. Laura drove over and picked up the babysitter—her name is Nora Takichi—and we left for dinner around six fifteen. We dined at Solo Mio and then went to the symphony. The performance started at eight and there was an intermission at nine. The performance resumed at nine fifteen, and we left the Schermerhorn Symphony Hall at ten thirty. We stopped for drinks afterward and got home by midnight."

"Go on."

"When we got home, we talked with Nora about our daughter, Marie. She's only three and has been having nightmares. As usual, Marie had tried to talk Nora into letting her stay up later than her bedtime, but Nora put her in our bed and she was sound asleep when we got home. Laura took the babysitter home. I went into the guest room to sleep."

"I thought you drove the babysitter home."

"No, Detective, Laura thought I'd had too much to drink. She took Nora home."

"Which car did she drive?"

"I assume she drove her Mercedes. She doesn't like to drive my truck."

Wayne stood up and walked around the table until he was right behind Connolly. Then he leaned forward, close to Connolly's ear and almost whispered, "I think what happened was, after your wife got back from taking the babysitter home, you went to Ruby Mead-Allison's house, called her out to the back step and killed her." He shot a covert glance at Ben. "Or, you were the one who took Nora home and you killed Ruby after you dropped her off."

"No, I didn't." James' eyes narrowed. "Laura is adamant that I don't take babysitters home when I've been drinking. I'm a lawyer, I know the law. I'd been drinking that night. Laura doesn't drink. She can't because of her meds, so she's always the designated driver. I didn't kill Ruby. I would never do something like that!"

"What was to prevent you from taking the other car and going to Ruby's once Laura left?"

"Leaving my three-year-old daughter and seven-year-old son alone in the house? Jesus, I'm in family law. Leave my kids alone in a house after midnight? I'd lose my license. No way."

Wayne caught Ben's eye, wanting him to step in. The sheriff took a deep breath. He'd screwed up badly with Terry Lerner. That had turned out not to matter, but it was best not to take any chances this time.

"We have evidence to support our contention that you killed Ruby, and since Tennessee is a double murder state, we plan to charge you with double murder."

"What are you talking about?" James Connolly glared at him.

"Just a moment, Sheriff, I'd like a word with James." Paula Emerson and her client went to a corner of the room and conferred quietly. Wayne Nichols shut off the recorder and turned the machine on again when they returned to their seats.

"Sheriff, I'd like you to clarify how you plan to charge my client with double murder," Paula Emerson said.

"Ruby was pregnant with Mr. Connolly's child. In killing her, he killed both of them."

At this, the last of the color drained from James Connolly's face and he looked helplessly at his attorney.

"The two of you may wish to consider the seriousness of this matter. Excuse us for a minute."

Wayne and Ben walked out of the room and to the water cooler for drinks. For a minute or two, neither of them spoke.

Finally Wayne said, "Since we seem to be getting two different stories about who took the babysitter home, I'll check with Mrs. Takichi about which of the Connollys brought her daughter home the night of the fifteenth. We should have done this before. I'll go call her now."

He was back in a few minutes with the information that Mrs. Takichi was almost certain Laura Connolly had brought her daughter home the night of Ruby's death. Although she said she couldn't swear to it.

"If Laura Connolly took the babysitter home, her husband may be off the hook. Damn it! I need to check with the M.E. again to get his estimate of Ruby's exact time of death. Possibly, there was time after Laura Connolly got back for James to have left and killed Ruby. We need to get Laura in here, too."

"Why would Mrs. Connolly say that her husband had taken the babysitter home? What was the point? Do you think she was trying to lead us away from her? Or that they were in on the crime together? Maybe you should call the D.A.'s office and see if they want to indict them as co-conspirators."

"We don't have enough yet to involve the D.A. Since Mrs. Takichi wasn't ready to swear that Laura Connolly brought her daughter home, we need to ask Nora. Damn it, we should have double-checked this earlier."

Wayne nodded and put his cell to his ear. "Hello, Mrs. Takichi, this is Detective Nichols again. I'm sorry to bother you. Is Nora home? Could I have your permission to ask her who brought her home that night?"

There was a pause. "Nora, who drove you home when you sat for the Connolly's on March fifteenth?" He looked at Ben and nodded. "She did. Okay, do you remember what car she drove? The pickup? What time did she drop you off? Twelve thirty? Thanks."

After Detective Nichols hung up the phone, Ben said, "Laura drove her home, I take it. We have to get her in here ASAP. We could keep James here until then without charging him. I want to ask him if he knows what time his wife got back that night."

After a pause, Wayne nodded. "The key to figuring this out is knowing the latest possible time of death. I am going to ask Doc again about the time. I'll text you as soon as I know, okay?"

"Go," said the sheriff. "I'll talk to the suspect and his good-looking attorney." Ben went back into the room where he met with a hostile stare from James Connolly and an inquiring look from Ms. Emerson.

"What is my client's status right now?" she asked.

"I have a few more questions for him." Ben took the chair opposite James. "Do you know what time your wife got back from taking the babysitter home that night?"

Connolly gave him a disdainful glance. "Yes, it just so happens I do. I was in the guest bedroom asleep. I woke up when I heard the water running in the shower. The head of that bed shares a wall with our master bath. I went downstairs to get a drink. The clock on the stove read one-oh-five. Laura didn't leave until twelve fifteen and it's a good twenty minutes over there and then twenty back. She must have driven like a bat out of hell."

Ben's cellphone vibrated in his pocket and he took it out. The text from Wayne read, "Doc says 12:30 earliest—1:30 latest. He consulted with an entomologist. Insect evidence on Ruby's body is irrefutable."

Ben thought for a minute. Then he turned back to James. "I'm going to release you for now, Mr. Connolly, with our apologies. Your story checks out."

Paula Emerson raised her eyebrows and turned to look at her client. He shook his head and exhaled sharply, puffing out his cheeks.

"You damned well better apologize. C'mon, Paula, let's go. We've wasted enough time here." He surged to his feet and stalked out with his attorney close behind.

"Tell your client he has to stay in town."

Paula gave him a quick nod over her shoulder and disappeared around the corner. Ben went back to his office and sat down at the desk with a thump.

Not a single solid suspect left. Joe Dennis, David Allison, Terry Lerner, Silas Mead and James Connolly—all of them dismissed.

He thought through the timeline again. Ruby was alive when David left her house around 11:30. Laura Connolly dropped the babysitter off at 12:30, possibly 12:40. If Laura went over to Little Chapel Road after that (which would have taken her about fifteen minutes) killed Ruby and dragged her body into the grove (which would have taken another half hour). It would have been at least 1:30 by then and she had a good half hour drive back to her house. No way could she have gotten into the shower until at least 2:00 a.m. If James Connolly was telling the truth, both he and his wife had been at their house at 1:00.

Ben wondered if it was even worthwhile to bring Laura in. If they indicted both of them, they couldn't be compelled to testify against each other and he didn't have a single piece of physical evidence linking them to the crime. They needed to find someone else who had a motive strong enough to kill.

Chapter Twenty-Eight

——

March 26
Mae December

THE PHONE RANG as Mae walked into the house after volunteering at the elementary school.

"Have you sold all your puppies yet?" Mae's sister, July, asked.

"I have deposits on two of them, so one female and two males are left."

"Perfect. Fred and I have decided to let the boys have a dog. They each need their own so they won't fight over it."

"They're at a good age for the responsibility. I'm guessing you want the puppies for their birthday?"

"Yes, that's what we were thinking. I know the puppies aren't ready yet. Could the twins come and see their puppies next week? Then you can let us know when they are ready to leave their mother."

"I can't believe the twins will be nine already. Do you want me to hold the two males for them?"

"Yes, that's perfect. Nathan and Parker will be thrilled. Olivia already knows, but we want to surprise the boys. Don't say anything to them, okay?"

"I won't, but isn't Olivia going to want a pet of her own?" July's daughter usually got what she wanted, but she was such a charming little girl, no one really minded.

"Six is too young for a puppy. We'll probably get her a lovebird for her birthday in June."

"You better plan on a pair of them. Love is pretty hard to come by alone, even for a bird," Mae laughed. A familiar yap came from her front step. "I have to go, Jules. I think Elvis is here."

"Who?"

"Elvis. Ruby's dog. Robin must have let him out. I'll call you later."

The yapping continued as Mae walked over and opened the door. The nervous little dog jumped when he saw her but kept on barking.

"Quiet down, Elvis." She picked him up and grabbed a leash.

She clipped the leash on Elvis' collar and started to walk him back to the Fannings' house. Deputy Phelps' car was still parked in her driveway. Mae stopped to tell him where she was going. He got out of the car and stretched.

"Should I go with you?" he asked eagerly.

"No, I'm just taking Elvis home. I don't need an escort. Thanks, though."

Mae walked Elvis down the driveway and turned toward the Fannings' house. She wondered when David Allison would get around to finding his own place. It must be quite a strain for Robin to host a house guest for so long, Mae thought. She picked Elvis up, carried him to the front door and tapped on it. No one answered. Mae waited a few minutes and then took Elvis around to the back, thinking Robin might be in the kitchen.

The back screen door stood open a few inches. Mae pushed the door open a little, thinking she'd just put Elvis inside. The back entry was empty except for hooks holding sweatshirts and hoodies. Mae unhooked the leash from Elvis' red collar and was about to release him into the house and leave when she heard Robin's laugh from the other room.

"Laura, you crack me up sometimes. Mother got her driver's license pulled? What in the world was she doing? She wasn't drinking, was she?"

"No. Apparently, she was driving along Hart Road. God knows why she was out past ten at night. She told me she was sleepy, probably dropped off for a second and when she came to, she was driving in a cornfield. Then she saw a large piece of farm equipment right in front of her and collided with it. The farmer ran out, collared Mother and brought her into the house. He called the sheriff's office and they sent a deputy out."

"I can just see Mother looking furtive and embarrassed." Robin's laugh rang out again. "Did they take her license right then?"

"Well, they might have let her get away with it, since she was sober, but when the deputy said he was considering taking her license, she called off-road driving a 'trivial infraction' and said something to the effect that traffic laws were 'guidelines, not laws.' I don't think that went over very well. Now she has to go to court to have her license re-instated. She is super pissed off."

Both women giggled as Mae put Elvis down on the kitchen floor. Then Laura spoke very softly. "Robin, the other one, where did you put it?"

"I put hers in the shed. Don't worry. Nobody's ever going to look there."

Mae backed out of the house, shutting the door as softly as she could. Her mind raced as she cut across the Van Attas' front yard and ran back toward her house. She was sure Robin and Laura were talking about her shovel. She waved at Deputy Phelps, who was back in the car, and then went inside. Mae sat down in the kitchen to think. She needed to talk to Ben to see if he'd order a search of the Fannings' shed.

When Mae called his office, Dory said Ben and Wayne Nichols were both questioning suspects, so she left a message asking Ben to call her cell immediately when he finished. Like always, there was work to be done in the kennels. Taking her phone with her, she went out to the barn and got to work.

Annie Van Atta called later. "I meant to ask you at the meeting. Jason and I want one of your puppies. I ran into your mother at Kroger yesterday. She told me I better call you right away, because they go fast."

"She's right. They do go quickly. If you want a female puppy, you're in luck."

"That's fine. We've waited over a year now since Jasper died. I think a little girl dog is exactly what we need."

The Van Attas were a childless couple. Jasper, their red poodle, had been their "baby." He died of old age last year. Mae had wondered if they'd ever want a new dog.

"I'll hold this puppy for you then. She won't be ready to leave for several weeks, but if you and Jason want to meet her, you can come anytime."

"Thank you. I'll call and set up a time."

"I know you'll give her a wonderful home. I don't mean to change the subject, Annie, but can I ask you something?"

"Sure."

"Did you and Ruby ever resolve your disagreement last fall? It was about Jason's song, wasn't it?"

Annie's voice sounded very different when she answered. "Yes." She gave a short laugh, devoid of humor. "If by 'resolve' you mean let her have her way, we did. It's the only way anything was ever resolved with that woman. I don't want to speak ill of the dead, but I can't find much to say about Ruby that's positive."

"Thanks Annie. Call me whenever you have time to meet her."

"Thanks. I'll call you soon."

IDEAS WERE COALESCING in Mae's mind. She needed to tell Ben about the shovel and that Annie was still angry at Ruby.

She seriously doubted that Annie would hurt anyone, but she wanted Ben to know. She felt a sudden qualm about the puppy. If Annie was involved in Ruby's murder, should she have agreed to let the pup go to them? She sighed, realizing she'd already made the commitment.

Despite her momentary hesitation, Mae was happy to have found good homes for all five puppies. She dismissed her suspicions about Annie. She had known the Van Attas for years. They were good people. The puppy money would come in handy, of course, but she'd be glad just to have the pups in their new homes and away from hers. Ever since she had found Ruby's body and seen the red ribbons in the kennel, Mae had felt a little less safe on Little Chapel Road. She was unsettled and would continue to be until Ruby's killer was apprehended. She hoped it would be soon. She checked her cellphone to see if Ben had called. No luck.

After she updated her website, putting "sold" signs on all the puppy pictures, Mae straightened up the house a bit. While she was cleaning her bathroom mirror, she noticed that her hair was even wilder than usual. She appraised it with a critical eye. Sometimes she wondered why anyone would find her attractive with this mop. She thought briefly about driving to the sheriff's office and trying to talk to him or Nichols about the shovel. However, her out of control hair said she was clearly overdue for a trim. She called Kim, her stylist, to see if there were any openings. Kim said she could squeeze her in while her client's highlights processed. Mae put on a hat and some lipstick and went out to her car.

"I think the sheriff wants me to stay here," Deputy Phelps said glumly when she told him she was leaving.

"I'm sure he does. I'm only going to get a quick haircut. You can go in the house if you need something to drink or to use the bathroom. Anytime," Mae told him with a smile.

HAVING LIVED IN Rosedale her whole life, Mae sometimes

forgot to appreciate the beauty of her surroundings. Pansies and snapdragons filled the window boxes and planters along Main Street. All the old storefronts were freshly painted. If a person blocked out clothing or cars, this could have been a scene from a hundred years ago. Birdy's Salon appeared quite retro, at least from the outside. Tammy's mother, Grace, had updated the interior recently.

Grace had inherited the business from her mother, Birdy. Tammy had worked here until she started her dating service. Grace ran the salon. She was still a very pretty woman. Mae often wondered why she never remarried after being widowed so young. Grace looked up from the appointment book and smiled.

"Hello, Mae, I didn't realize you were coming in today."

"Hi, Ms. Grace." Mae gave her a hug. "I called Kim on her cell with a hair emergency. She said she could work me in."

"I'll let her know you're here, Mae. Do you want anything to drink?"

"I do if you have any sweet tea made. I wish you'd tell me how you make yours. It's delicious."

"Oh, child, you'd be horrified if you knew how much sugar I put in." Grace laughed. "I'll get you some."

She returned with a tall glass of tea, garnished with a mint sprig.

Mae took a long swallow. "Absolutely delicious. Should I go put on a smock?"

"Yes, Kim will be with you soon. Have a seat after you get your smock on. Mae, would you turn your cellphone off, please? I'm trying to achieve a spa-like atmosphere."

Mae suppressed a smile. A spa atmosphere was a bit of a stretch. She quickly checked to see if Ben had called. There were no messages. She set her phone on vibrate. As soon as she was done at Birdy's, she would drive to the station. Changing into a smock, Mae found a seat near Kim's station and said hello to her.

Kim was the cutest thing. She had a big pregnant belly, which on her little frame was adorable. After she greeted Mae, Kim put the last few foils on her client and took her over to sit under the dryer. When the woman stood up, Mae saw her face. It was Laura Connolly, Robin's sister. She must have left for her hair appointment directly from Robin's house.

Laura talked and laughed with everyone in the shop. It's hard to look your best with pieces of tinfoil all over your head, but she seemed to be in such a good mood, everyone smiled. Her body was as wonderful as ever. She went to the same Pilates class as July did and always looked extremely fit, even in an unflattering smock. Laura wasn't as pretty as her sister, but she was very attractive in her own way.

Mae greeted Laura, who raised a hand on her way to the dryer. She was flushed and her eyes gleamed. Kim came back and asked Mae to take off her hat. She ran her experienced fingers through Mae's hair.

"Are you sure you only want a trim? I could put some layers in and maybe do a deep conditioning treatment."

"Would conditioning calm the wildness? The spring humidity is already kicking in and I feel like it's getting bigger every day."

"It should help. Don't worry. I won't take much length off."

They went back to the shampoo bowl. Kim washed Mae's hair, massaged her scalp and applied a conditioner that smelled like apples. Then Kim put a plastic cap over her hair and seated her under the dryer for fifteen minutes. What a nice change it was to have someone pamper her a little. She was lucky to have such a sweet friend.

While Mae sat under the dryer, she thought about what she had overheard at Robin's house. If Robin had put the murder weapon in her barn, Mae couldn't imagine why. Or when. If her shovel was in the Fannings' shed, she had to know how it got there. She didn't think Robin had any reason to want Ruby dead. She wanted Ruby and David to get back together so she could have her house back. On the other hand, she didn't seem worried about David being the killer, or having him in the house with her kids. That meant Robin probably knew who the killer was.

Kim flipped the dryer up and took Mae back to the shampoo bowl for a cool rinse. She told Mae to have a seat in her chair and went to check Laura's highlights.

"A little longer, Mrs. Connolly." Kim came back, cut Mae's hair and smoothed some pomade through it.

"Are you all right with air drying? I want to get back to Laura. She's telling us a funny story about her mother losing her driver's license."

"That's fine." Mae handed her thirty dollars. "Thanks for squeezing me in. Does this cover my bill and your tip?"

"Plenty." Kim smiled at her. "See you next time."

Mae waved goodbye to Ms. Grace. She walked around the corner and stuck her head in the door of Local Love. Tammy, who was on the phone, held up a finger.

"Is this going to be a long call?" Mae asked in a whisper.

Tammy nodded yes. Mae mouthed, "Call me later" and went out to her car. She turned her phone back on and listened to a message from Ben telling her to call. Having repaired her hair, she decided she looked presentable enough to stop by his office and see if he was free.

Miss Dory was at her desk, looking stylish as usual. The office was quiet when Mae walked in.

"Hey, Miss Dory. How are you today?"

"I'm fine, unlike some people. The sheriff is ill as a hornet. Did you want to see him?"

"I guess so. I have some news for him. Maybe it'll perk him up."

Dory buzzed Ben. When Mae started to walk past the desk, she glanced at Dory's computer. There were little colored icons on certain days and Mae noticed Friday was marked with a small red heart.

"Have something special planned for Friday?"

"I sure do. Elmer's back in town, playing a gig in Nashville. He called and asked me to come hear him play. It's been ages, and I surprised myself by wanting to go." When Dory smiled, she looked like a thirty-year-old.

"Would you ever want to get back together with him?" As soon as she asked, Mae was embarrassed about putting Dory on the spot. "It's none of my business. Sorry, Dory."

"Sometimes I think about it." Dory's voice was pensive. "We'll probably always love each other. He wasn't always the most faithful husband in the world. But most of the time I think that train has left the station. I'm going to get myself a new dress for the event, though. I want the man to know what he's been missing." She nodded her head decisively as the intercom buzzed.

"You can go on back, Mae."

The wall outside Ben's office was mirrored and Mae stopped to look at her reflection. She checked her hair and took the lip-gloss out of her purse, carefully painting her mouth with the little brush and puckering her lips at her reflection. Tammy was right, as usual. A little color and shine made a big difference.

There was laughter and Ben opened his door, looking embarrassed. "Hi Mae."

Detective Nichols came out of the office and gave her his typical cocky grin. "Nice lip gloss."

Mae gave him a confused look.

"That's not a mirror on the wall. It's a one-way view window. The sheriff was, let's just say, too distracted watching you apply your lipstick to finish his sentence." He sauntered down the hall, laughing.

Mae's face was hot.

"Come in." Ben was flushed and awkward. "Sorry, Mae, I'm a little out-of-sorts right now."

"About Ruby's case?" She was relieved to change the subject. "I overheard something Robin Fanning said that might be helpful. Do I still need to have someone guarding my house, by the way?"

"Until we solve this, you do. There are way too many connections with people on your street."

"I never got to tell you about my shovel, did I?"

"No. What about it?"

"It's missing, and I think I know who took it."

"Has it been missing long?" Ben raised his eyebrows. "Should I write up a Missing Shovel report?"

"Ben, be serious. I think the person who put the murder weapon in my barn must have taken mine so I wouldn't notice anything out of place. I think I know who took my shovel and where they hid it."

Ben gave Mae a long speculative look. "Have you been meddling, I mean investigating, again?"

"No, not at all. I was on the phone with my sister and heard barking on my front porch. I got off the phone and opened the door. Elvis was there."

"Hang on. Should I be writing this down?"

She knew he was teasing. "I think you should. When I took Elvis back to the Fannings' house, I overheard Robin talking to her sister, Laura. Robin told her not to worry, that she'd hidden 'hers' in her shed. I think she was talking about my shovel."

"Does she know you heard them talking?" Ben sounded worried.

"No, the kitchen door was open a little and I put Elvis inside. Robin didn't see me. I'm sure of it."

"When do you think she might have put the other shovel— the murder weapon—in your barn?"

"The only time I can think of is after I found Ruby's boot and came to your office on the eighteenth. Robin was out walking that morning. Maybe she saw me stopping at Ruby's and hid the weapon while I was in town. I probably would have noticed the shovel earlier, but I didn't need it for anything. I have a hard time believing that Robin killed Ruby, but how else would she have known to hide the shovel?"

"She may have helped David Allison commit the crime. I think that's the only suspect she has a connection to. Is there anyone else?"

"Is James Connolly a suspect? She definitely has a connection to him."

"I shouldn't tell you this, but we questioned him earlier today. What's the connection between Robin Fanning and James Connolly?"

"She's his sister-in-law. Robin and Laura are sisters. They don't favor each other very much because their coloring is so different."

"Could you identify your shovel if you saw it? Is there anything unique about it?"

"It's really old and cruddy, and it's got a smear of bright blue paint on the handle."

"I'm writing this up right now." Ben was clearly excited. "I'm getting a warrant to search the Fannings' shed. Mae, this could be the breakthrough we've been waiting for."

Ben's eyes crinkled in the corners and he grabbed Mae and hugged her.

Chapter Twenty-Nine

—

March 26
Sheriff Ben Bradley

IT WAS AFTER five when Ben finally got his search warrant. It had been a grueling day already with the interrogations and then dismissals of all the other suspects. He drove to the Fanning residence with Emma Peters. Robin answered the door. She seemed wary.

"Mrs. Fanning, I have a warrant to search your garden shed."

"My shed?" Her eyebrows lifted.

"Yes, ma'am. Is that a problem?"

She crossed her arms. "Well, I guess not. I need to see the warrant. My husband's going to ask me about this."

The sheriff handed Robin the warrant.

She read it over carefully.

"Shall we go out to the shed?" Ben asked.

She didn't reply but shrugged and grabbed a jacket. Followed by the ubiquitous Elvis, all three of them walked through the immaculately landscaped yard to the Fannings' shed. The door opened easily. It was quite dark inside. Ben pulled out a flashlight and shone it all around the space. Finally, the light landed on a shovel.

"Is this your shovel?"

"One shovel looks pretty much like another, but since it's in my shed, I guess so."

"Just a minute. I see you have two shovels."

"For all I know, we have a dozen shovels." Robin shook her head. "Steven is the gardener, not me."

"I see only two. I'm going to take both of them."

"Okay." Robin looked calm, but he thought fear lay beneath her confident facade.

Emma Peters quickly put on her gloves, took the shovels to the car and loaded them into the trunk.

"Thank you, Mrs. Fanning." Ben got behind the wheel.

EMMA TURNED TO the sheriff once they were back in the car. "You told me we were going to get a shovel and I just put two and two together. We already processed one shovel—the murder weapon—so one of those two shovels in the trunk must be the shovel from Miss December's barn. Maybe Mrs. Fanning took the shovel in order to prevent Miss December from noticing the murder weapon right away. Have I got that right?"

"You're a very smart woman." Ben smiled. She was cute, too. Of course, he'd never say that. His deputies all had crushes on her. Like the rest of the women in the office, Emma only had eyes for Wayne. Ben found the whole thing baffling. If Wayne was that good with women, why wasn't he married or in a long-term relationship? It was a mystery, like so many things about his Chief Detective.

"Yes. We believe the perp took the murder weapon—let's call it shovel number one—from Ruby's house and put it in Mae's barn. Then someone, maybe the murderer or an accomplice, took Mae's shovel and put it in the Fannings' shed."

"Do you think Robin might be an accomplice, or even the killer?"

"I don't think she's the killer. She doesn't seem to have any reason to want Ruby dead. I think it's more likely that she's covering for somebody."

Ben called Wayne on his cell. They commiserated for a few minutes about having dismissed all their suspects. Ben smiled inwardly. "Actually, we have a new lead, maybe even a new suspect, and it's a woman. Mae overheard a conversation between Laura Connolly and her sister, Robin Fanning. That led us to search the Fannings' shed. Tech Peters and I are on our way back to the lab right now with shovels number two and three we found there. Mae thinks one of these might be her shovel. She's on her way to the lab to see if she can identify it."

"Too bad it's not a dog," Wayne said laconically.

"What do you mean?"

"If the shovel was a dog, you wouldn't be wondering, you'd know she could identify it." He laughed. "I'll meet you there. If one of the two shovels belongs to Mae, are we going to interview Mrs. Fanning?"

"You betcha." Ben felt more upbeat than he had been in days.

BEN AND EMMA were waiting inside the lab when Mae walked in with Wayne Nichols right behind her. The space had metal lab benches on all four sides. Windows above the benches let in the last of the afternoon sunlight. She went directly over to Ben and put her hand on his arm. Ben smiled down at her. Wayne and Emma exchanged a sidelong look, which Ben caught but decided to ignore, and they all looked at the shovels.

"Yes!" Mae's voice was excited. "It's my shovel. I was worried I wouldn't be able to identify it, but that's the blue paint I told you about. It's from the day I painted the upstairs bathroom. I didn't even have time to clean up from the paint job. I ran down to the kennel to take care of some 'poo' in the dog run before a client arrived." She grinned. "Just the hazards of my job, I guess."

"Do you have any idea why your shovel was in the Fannings' shed?" Wayne asked.

"If Robin took the murder weapon from Ruby's house and put it in my barn, then she must have taken my shovel to her house. What I don't understand is why she would take the murder weapon from Ruby's in the first place."

"I don't know, either," Ben spoke up, "but I think Robin Fanning is in this case right up to her beautiful white shoulders."

Mae jerked her head back. "Her beautiful white shoulders? When have you seen Robin's shoulders? I personally don't think they're that beautiful and I've seen them several times."

Ben opened his mouth and closed it again while she glared at him. Wayne and Emma burst out laughing.

THE SHERIFF CALLED Robin Fanning and asked her to come down to the station. It was getting dark when she arrived; she was dressed in jeans and a black sweater with a blue scarf tied at her neck. She was very accommodating about coming late in the day and didn't object to having her fingerprints taken. She was doing a great job of acting like someone with nothing to hide, he thought.

After she was fingerprinted, Ben led her to the sink where she could clean her hands. She dried them on a paper towel, seemingly relaxed. He cleared his throat and Robin focused on him with wide, light blue eyes.

"Sheriff, I'm not denying my fingerprints could be on a shovel you found in my shed." Her voice was whispery and sensual. He fought the impulse to lean in closer.

"Can you tell me how that shovel ended up in your shed, Mrs. Fanning?"

"Is the possession of a shovel a crime in Rose County these days?"

Oh spare me. "Only if you hurt someone with it. Come with me, please."

Without another word, she followed him down the hall and into the interview room.

Ben stuck his head into Wayne's office to tell him they were ready to interrogate Robin Fanning. "Do you have Laura Connolly set up to come in yet? I'd really like her to be here tonight."

"I tracked her down, but tonight isn't going to work. Once a month Laura is part of a research study on mood disorders and sleep. She has to sleep at their lab tonight. I called and she's already wired. Plus, they give them something to knock them out. She couldn't talk to us if we did get her out. She'd be practically comatose. It would be 'AMA, against medical advice.' I even talked to the supervising physician. It's a no go. At least we know she's not going anywhere and nobody can talk to her or text her. No cellphones allowed."

"Damn. Let's go talk to Robin Fanning."

They walked into the conference room together.

"Mrs. Fanning, I know you met Detective Wayne Nichols earlier in the investigation and this is Deputy Fuller." Ben gestured toward his deputy who was already sitting at the table. "Do you prefer to be called Robin or Mrs. Fanning?"

Deputy Fuller unobtrusively started the tape recording equipment.

"Robin." She smiled. "Mrs. Fanning is my mother-in-law."

"Okay, Robin, then." Wayne smiled right back at her. "Let me provide a little history here. After Ruby Mead-Allison's death, we found her shovel in Mae December's barn. As you know, we later found two shovels in your garden shed. One of those shovels turned out to belong to Miss December." He looked relaxed and casual, as if discussing a high school football game, or plans to go fishing.

"Please tell me why Miss December's shovel was in your barn and the other shovel was in hers?"

"I'm not sure, Detective. We do a fall and spring cleanup on our road and often people's shovels get mixed up. That's probably what happened."

"Tell me about spring clean-up. Did it already happen this year?"

"No, we set the date, but it hasn't been done yet." She gave Wayne another pretty smile, showing her dimples. Robert Fuller was staring at her, so captivated that one would think he'd never seen a pretty woman before.

"You're saying your shovel has probably been in Miss December's barn since last year then?" His tone indicated he was immune to that smile. "That seems like a long time, doesn't it? Miss December remembers having seen her shovel recently, in the last couple of weeks, in fact."

"I simply have no explanation, Detective." She down looked at her hands. Her nails were very short and it looked like she bit them. Wayne glanced at the sheriff, his signal for Ben to ask the next question.

"Robin, we already know you're involved in this case. You can help yourself by telling us everything. You need to tell us how Mae's shovel ended up in your shed." The room was very quiet. The deputy's stomach gurgled.

Robin continued to study her hands. Then she looked up. "The night of the eighteenth I got a text message."

"A text message …" Ben prompted her to continue.

"Yes, it read, 'Come to Ruby's now.' "

"What time was this?" Wayne asked.

The sheriff leaned back in his seat. He had broken the dam and now Wayne would get the details. They were starting to be a team.

"Around midnight, I think."

"Who sent the text?"

"My little sister, Laura. When she gets depressed, she calls me."

"Your sister is Laura Connolly, right?"

"Yes, that's right."

"Then what happened?"

"I got up, grabbed my jacket and boots and left right away. When I got there, Laura was standing by Ruby's garage. She handed me a shovel."

"I'm trying to envision the scene. It's very late at night, your sister is standing by your neighbor Ruby's garage and she hands you a shovel? I guess if my sister asked me to come to her neighbor's house, especially in the middle of the night, and handed me a shovel, I'd think that was pretty bizarre behavior."

Robin lifted her head and took a deep breath. "You just don't understand."

"So, help me understand. Where did you think Ruby was?"

"I assumed Ruby was asleep in the house."

"What was going through your head at that point? Why did you think Laura had called you to come over there?"

"I thought Laura was having another bad episode." Robin's eyes were fixed on Wayne. The muscles of her jaw stood out against her pale skin.

"Do you have your cellphone with you, Robin?" Ben asked.

"No, I left it at home."

A wave of discouragement went through Ben. They weren't going to be able to confirm the time or content of the text from that evening. "Does your sister have mental issues?"

"She was diagnosed with emotional problems as a teenager. They call it an impulse-control disorder. It's characterized by an inability to control urges that might be harmful to her or to others. But that's just their term for it. It's only a diagnosis, a label. Laura is much more than her diagnosis. She isn't very badly affected. Really, she isn't." Robin's voice was pleading. She rubbed her hands together.

"So you took the shovel from Laura and left it in Mae December's barn."

"Yes, and then I took Mae's shovel to my shed. Now you know all I know about this. At that point, I didn't know Ruby was dead. Laura didn't kill her. She has called me before to come and take things away that bother her. Once she was terrified by a carton of milk! I'm sorry I didn't tell you this before. I should have."

"I think I understand. You always protect your little sister, don't you?" Wayne's voice was soft.

"I try to." Robin's face crumpled and then the tears came down. "She tries so hard and it's so awful for her."

"Actually, it sounds pretty awful for you, too."

"Excuse us for a moment." Ben signaled Wayne to follow him. They stepped out of the room, into the dim hallway.

"Robin seems to be covering for her sister, but the timeline doesn't work for Laura to be the killer," Ben said.

"You realize that it could have been Robin who committed the murder, right? I'm not sure how much of her story to believe. That woman is damn good at manipulating men. Her sister could be a scapegoat."

"I'll give all this some more thought, but I don't see it. What motive did Robin have?"

"Maybe she was protecting her sister. She knew about James and Ruby's affair. Maybe she didn't want Laura to know her husband was cheating on her. Too bad she doesn't have her cellphone with her; we could check on the text right now."

"I agree. However, in terms of Robin being the killer, I think it's a stretch, Wayne. I don't think her motive is strong enough. I want to let her go and have Robert follow her, see what she does. Normally, I'd be worried about her calling her sister, but that's not going to be a problem tonight. It's critical that we get Laura as soon as she's discharged tomorrow morning. I can't see how the timeline works for Laura to have done it, but we need to talk to her."

Wayne nodded.

Ben looked at his watch, it was 9:30. "It's late, but we need both Robin and Laura's phone records. Can you get that started? And tell Robin she can leave, just make sure Robert follows her."

Ben went back to his office to think. Would a woman kill another woman just to conceal information from her sister? It didn't add up. He just couldn't see Robin Fanning as the killer.

Chapter Thirty

———

March 26
Mae December

WHEN SHE GOT home from the lab, Mae invited her sister July over for an after-dinner glass of wine. Robin and July had been in high school together, and July and Laura took some of the same fitness classes. July would know their history.

Mae checked on all the dogs and fixed herself a plate of fruit and cottage cheese for dinner. July rolled in about two hours later and brought some of the lasagna left over from their meal.

"Thanks, Jules," Mae mumbled between bites. "This is a lot better than my dinner."

"You're welcome. Didn't you mention wine?"

"Indeed I did. Would you rather have red or white?"

"Whatever you think is the best. You always have such good wine. How did you learn what to pick?"

"I get whatever Boyt tells me to buy." Mae walked into the kitchen. She took a nice Riesling out of the wine chiller, opened the bottle, and poured each of them a generous glass.

"What's Boyt? Is it an online wine guide or something?"

"Boyt is not a what, he's a person. Boyt Mill. He owns World of Wines. It's in Nashville. Try this." She handed the glass to her sister. "It's a Riesling."

July took a sip and smiled. "That's delicious. I can't believe you drive all the way to Nashville to buy wine. This tastes expensive."

"It's very reasonable. I give Boyt a budget and he puts a case together for me. I go in every six weeks or so and see what he has for me. I didn't invite you over to talk about wine, though. I wanted to ask you about Robin Fanning and Laura Connolly, the Kelley sisters. Let me tell you what's been happening."

July listened intently as Mae filled her in on what she had overheard at the Fannings' house, about her shovel turning up in Robin's shed and its identification at the lab and reminded July not to tell anyone about this newest development in the case.

"I don't understand why Robin would hide the murder weapon at your place, unless she was the killer. Or maybe she was protecting someone." July's forehead wrinkled.

Mae didn't say anything, but an idea was growing stronger in her mind. The December sisters were sitting on the porch and Mae was getting chilly.

"I'm going to grab a blanket. Do you want one?"

"Yes, please."

When Mae came back with two blankets, July smiled at her. "This is nice, isn't it? I feel like I never see you anymore. I guess our lives are very different now. I think Robin and Laura have stayed close their whole lives. I know Robin always watched out for Laura."

"Wasn't Robin in your class?"

"No, she was a year ahead of me. I always liked her, but she mostly kept to herself, or did things with Laura. I don't know that Laura got any better, but when Mr. and Mrs. Kelley sent Laura away, Robin actually got a life."

Mae hugged her knees to her chest. "Sent her away where? When was that?"

"It was my sophomore year in high school. Robin was a junior. Laura would have been a freshman. You were in the eighth grade—still in middle school. You probably didn't hear all the gossip."

"I don't remember hearing much about Laura back then. One of the girls in my class had an older brother who called her Crazy Laura. I didn't know why. I thought it was a nickname or something."

"Was it Dean Aiken?"

"Yes, Carol Anne's big brother."

"He had good reason to call her that." July shook her head. "He was in my class, but he always flirted with the freshman girls. Laura apparently thought he was her boyfriend. When she saw him kissing Ginny Baker in the parking lot, she attacked her."

"Laura? She seems incredibly uptight. I can't imagine her losing control like that."

"Laura started screaming at Ginny and calling her a boyfriend stealer. Ginny started to fight back. Dean got in the middle and tried to hold the two girls apart. I'll never forget it. Robin came running from the other side of the parking lot. She put her arms around Laura and led her away. The minute Robin showed up, Laura stopped fighting with Ginny, as if someone had thrown a switch. She followed Robin like a little lamb or something. Laura appeared completely calm, almost in a trance, but Ginny's face was bleeding and a big chunk of her hair was on the ground."

"Laura pulled Ginny's hair out? Over Dean Aiken?"

July laughed. "Believe it or not. The administration questioned all of us about it, and the principal suspended Laura. There were rumors that she tried to kill herself later." July's dark eyes looked huge in the dim light of the porch as she recounted that day. "Robin was the one who found Laura after the suicide attempt."

"Found her where?"

"In the bathtub, with her wrists cut."

"Oh my God! That's horrible. Poor Laura and Robin. How do you ever get over something like that? They seem to be all right now, don't they? I mean Robin seems fine. What about Laura? Is she stable?"

July didn't answer right away. "I don't know how well controlled she is. One of my friends who knows her pretty well told me Laura has an impulse control disorder. She overreacts to things most of us would shrug off. Apparently she can become easily enraged."

"Is she being treated for it?"

"She's on some medications, but there's no magic pill for whatever demons pursue Laura Connolly."

"Do you think Robin hid the shovel for her sister?" Mae asked.

July's voice was serious. "Robin would do just about anything for Laura."

Mae was quiet for a moment. "Thanks, Jules. On a lighter note, I can't deny I'm enjoying getting to know Sheriff Ben Bradley during this process." Mae smiled.

"I can tell." July grinned. "You have feelings for him, don't you?"

"I do. It's going so well I'm almost afraid to talk about him to anyone. Mama, of course, didn't even need to be told. Jules, can I ask you something else? Are you happy? Being married to Fred?"

July nodded. "He's a good man and he's crazy about the kids."

"You're both crazy about your kids, but that's not what I asked. Are you happy being married to Fred? I know he's a good father and a good provider. I remember Tommy Ferris, though, and the two of you when you were young and deeply in love." They were both quiet then.

"Tell me what you remember, will you?" July's voice held a plaintive note. "I've worked very hard to forget those times. I think I've blocked a lot out. Maybe by now I've finally gotten enough distance to look back at my crazy young self with some humor. I can't believe almost fifteen years have gone by."

Mae thought for a minute, trying to put herself into her young mind-state again. "Well, it was blindingly obvious you and Tommy were crazy about each other. I remember thinking you two would probably get engaged in college and I'd be a junior bridesmaid at your wedding. I even imagined myself catching the bouquet! I'd be gorgeous, of course, and everyone would tell me I was lovelier than the bride and how glamorous I looked." Mae shook her head, remembering her silliness.

"Really? You thought we'd get married?"

"Duh… July! Mama and Daddy drove themselves crazy trying to keep you two from ever being alone in the house together. I overheard a conversation between them once. Mama said she needed to think of a way to file her column without leaving the house. She was absolutely not going to leave you two alone. She was laughing about carrier pigeons, but I think she hired a neighbor boy to courier a few times. This was before she could send things electronically. Once I overheard Daddy ask her if she'd given you the talk. About the pill, I guess. Oh and Tommy wasn't allowed on the second floor. Kind of like dorm rules. If there was a boy in a girl's room, three feet had to be on the floor. Actually, I think the rules only encouraged sexual creativity."

July appeared very far away and sad.

"I'm sorry, sweetie. Here I've been babbling on. Are you okay?"

July stood up without answering and said she needed to get going. She got her things together, found her car keys and looked at Mae. "I still wonder what happened to make Tommy disappear from Rosedale for fifteen years." The pain in her voice was wrenching. July was almost in tears. Mae couldn't remember the last time she'd seen her sister cry.

"July December," Mae reached out and took her sister's hands in hers, "when we were talking about Laura and Robin, you told me Robin would do anything for her sister, remember? Well, I'd do just about anything for you, too. You know that, don't you?"

July ruffled her hair as if she was ten and left. The screen door clicked into place.

After July's taillights faded away, Mae called Ben's cell. His voice was rough when he answered the phone.

"I know it's late," Mae said. "I hope I'm not disturbing you. I was wondering if you'd like to come over for a while. My sister left and we didn't finish this wine."

"I would. I'm just sitting here obsessing over the case. I'll be right there."

Ben's headlights shone in the driveway about ten minutes later and Mae walked out to meet him. He leaned on the door of the sheriff's department car, talking to the deputy. He straightened up when he saw her and the deputy started his car and drove away.

"I guess I'm unguarded tonight." She smiled. "Did you tell George he could go?"

"I told him I'd take the night shift," Ben replied in a husky voice. "I hope it's all right."

Mae walked over closer and touched him on his shoulder. His skin was hot and he smelled wonderful. Ben leaned down and Mae turned her face up to him. They shared a gentle kiss that lasted for several seconds.

"Let's go inside," he murmured in her ear.

Mae shivered as his breath fluttered across her cheek.

"I can keep an eye on you better in the house."

"Do you want to know what I found out about Laura Connolly?"

They sat on the couch, his arms wrapped around her. His hand rolled the edge of her collar and he stroked her neck.

"Could you tell me later?" He smiled. "I'm kind of busy right now."

"I can tell you in the morning," she whispered.

His blue eyes darkened. He bent his head down and touched his lips to hers. "Maybe you can tell me then, but I might still be busy. God, your skin feels good."

He ran his hand up her back.

She didn't want him to stop. Unfortunately, she smelled dog breath. The panting wasn't coming from Ben.

"I think Thoreau wants to say hello."

"Hello, Thoreau. I thought you liked me."

They both laughed and disentangled themselves.

"He does like you. Go to your bed, boy."

"Ladies first."

"I was talking to the dog. Sorry. You're on the couch tonight."

"Don't make me sleep on the couch, please, Mae. I've wanted you from the minute I first saw you." His voice was husky again. "You really get to me. I feel like a boy around you. I want to kiss you again."

She gave him a long, lingering kiss. "I'm sorry, Ben, but it's too soon. Let's get some wine and talk for a while. I want to tell you what I learned about Laura Connolly."

Mae had several glasses of wine while they talked. Ben had only one, reminding her he was on "guard" duty. It was nearly midnight when Ben stifled his third big yawn in a row. Mae found pillows and a blanket for him. He lay down on the couch.

"I'm going to say good night now," Mae said with a smile. Then she summoned up all of her willpower and walked upstairs alone.

THE NEXT MORNING she stayed in bed for a few minutes after she woke up. Would things be awkward? Would he think her a tease? Frigid? Not interested? She could hear clanking sounds issuing from downstairs. Mae dressed quickly and headed for the kitchen.

Ben looked up from the eggs he was frying and smiled. "You look exactly like I pictured you would in the morning."

"With my hair standing on end?"

"Perfect, except for the clothes."

"What's wrong with my clothes?"

Ben turned off the burner and walked over to her. "Your shirt is on inside-out. Of course, I'm only guessing now, but I think those clothes would look a lot better lying on your bedroom floor." He kissed her forehead. "Want some breakfast?"

He didn't seem too irritated about his night on the couch, and he sure looked good standing in her kitchen.

"Yes, please. I'm starving."

He turned back to the stove and dished up two plates. Carrying them to the table, he set them down and met her eyes.

"I almost forgot to tell you. Your dad emailed me a photo of this guy he's trying to identify for his new book. I found the man's name in the state database. It's Harper, Vince Harper."

"Okay. I'll tell him. Maybe the name means something to him. It doesn't ring any bells with me."

"Harper was charged once with stalking a woman. She dropped the charges, and the case never went to trial. Do you know why your father was asking about him?"

"The man's in several pictures he wants to use in his next book. Daddy says he's staring at me in most of them."

Ben frowned. "I'll dig into this a little more when I have a chance. That doesn't sound good."

As they sat at the table, Ben asked her several more questions about what she had told him the previous night about the Kelley sisters. When they finished eating, Ben took his dish over to the sink.

"Are you going to this fundraiser tonight?" He tapped the invitation on her fridge.

"Yes. Why?"

"Who's your guest?"

She wasn't about to make this too easy for him. "I noticed the invitation said 'bring a guest.' I guess I could take a friend." She gave him a little smile.

He smiled back. "A friend like me?"

"Would you like to go? I know how terribly busy you are. You're probably way too busy to spend time at some social event with me."

Ben lifted his eyes to the ceiling, then back down at her. "Could I be your date, please?"

"I guess I could use some security at the event."

He laughed. "You're bad. I've got to run. Deputy Phelps will be here soon to watch the house. I'll see you tonight."

"Oh, there was one other thing I've been meaning to tell you. It's about Annie Van Atta and her husband, Jason."

"What about them?"

"Ruby took credit for a song written by Jason Van Atta. She promised to show the work to one of her singer clients. She later told Annie her client wasn't interested, but the song ended up on the radio. Annie gave Ruby the song because Jason was too shy to ask her. Annie thought she was helping, but she couldn't prove it was Jason's. Ruby and her client got the money for it."

"I didn't know Jason was a songwriter."

"Well, he's trying to be. He works for his dad's company."

Ben shook his head. "Ruby certainly pissed off a lot of her neighbors, that's for sure. I'll send someone to talk to the Van Attas again. Got to run. See you later."

Ben got in his car and drove down the hill. After taking care of the dogs, Mae went upstairs to shower. Suddenly, she remembered a night almost five years earlier. She and Noah had walked into a club in Nashville. He stopped to talk to someone while Mae got in line for a table. When she looked back to see if Noah was coming, the man he was talking to was staring at her face and then her body. Could that have been Vince Harper?

Mae shook off her fears. Even if that man was Harper, and he was stalking her, as of tonight, she was officially dating the Sheriff of Rose County. She didn't have a thing to worry about.

Mae called Tammy after her shower. She sounded a little

grumpy at first but when Mae told her Ben stayed over the previous night, Tammy (aka Cupid) perked right up.

"You're not regretting this, right?"

"Not at all." Mae laughed.

"Well, how was everything? I want details."

"I'm not going into any details. It's private."

"Oh pooh! Well I'll probably get the story out of you sometime, anyway. So, did you even remember how to do it?"

"Tammy! We didn't do it. He slept on the couch. We definitely have chemistry, though. I was very tempted. It's been such a long time. Anyway, I have a favor to ask. Could you do my makeup tonight? Ben and I are going to a fundraiser."

"Is this your first real date?"

"Yes, he asked to join me when he saw the invitation on my fridge. It's for his nephew's school. The event is always at Jill Chapman's house, and its 'denim and pearls' attire."

"I can do your makeup at the salon at six. Right now I need to go get ready for work."

"One other thing. Could you take Ben out of the Local Love database?"

"I already did." Tammy stifled a giggle. "Ben told me to take him off the list a few days ago."

"Why didn't you tell me?"

"I thought you might freak out. I didn't want to mess anything up between you two. If you thought he was taking you for granted, you might not have been very happy."

Tammy really was a bit of a mind reader. It was scary how right she could be sometimes.

"You're probably right. I'm glad you didn't. You're such a good friend. Thanks."

"You're entirely welcome. I really have to go, though. Bye, Mae-Mae."

"Bye, Tammy."

Chapter Thirty-One

—

March 27
Sheriff Ben Bradley

Ben left Mae's house and went home to shower and charge his phone before heading to the office.

As soon as he walked through the office door, Dory caught him. "Your mother called."

"My mother called? That's unlike her. She never calls me at work."

"She said your cell was off." Dory gave him a reproving stare. He was supposed to be available twenty-four seven.

"My phone died. I didn't have my charger with me at, uh, where I was last night."

Dory tilted her head and gave him the once-over. "It's not like you to be tomcatting around. Unless you were having a sleepover with a certain young woman …" Her eyes narrowed. Ben bolted into his office and quickly closed the door. Dory would figure out where he was last night soon enough, without him standing in front of her with what he was sure was a transparent face.

Sitting at his desk, he dialed his parents' house. The phone rang five times, and he was about to give up when his mother answered.

"Good morning, Mom. You sound sleepy."

"It was a long night at the hospital and I crashed at home on the couch. Did the phone ring very long?"

"Quite a while. What did you want? I'm in the middle of a murder investigation. I don't have much time to talk."

"Yes, I know. Your father was a police officer for twenty-seven years. I remember. I wanted to let you know Katie Hudson's in town."

Ben took a deep breath. "Mom, I don't need this right now."

"She's not here for a visit, Son. She's divorced and wants to move here. She's staying with a friend of hers and looking for a job."

His morning was in free fall now. He had been engaged to Katie. She was probably in town visiting her sorority sister, Charlotte. He used to like Char—that is, before she introduced him to the woman who broke his heart.

"Is she staying with Char?"

"I think so. Katie was in the Peds ER last night with her little boy, Matthew. He had a broken wrist. I assisted on his surgery and the surgeon pinned his arm."

Ben took a deep breath, trying to achieve control of his rocketing emotions. "Thanks for letting me know, Mom. I have to get back to work."

"Just listen, will you? You need to talk to Katie."

"I'm not talking to that woman. She's out of my life. I've really got to go."

"Ben, you need to talk to her. I'm sorry, but I must insist."

"Okay, okay, but not until this murder is cleared up. Then I'll talk to her. I really have nothing to say, and I don't understand why this is important to you, but I will. Can we let it go now?"

"I love you, Ben."

"I know you do, Mom. I love you, too. Bye."

Not all women are loyal like you, though. He'd avoid Katie as long as possible.

IT WAS MID-MORNING and Ben was still reeling from his mother's news when Dory called on the intercom to let him know that Laura Connolly and her attorney were waiting for him. After hearing Robin's bizarre information about the midnight text message, He and Wayne were anxious to question Laura. He walked down the hall to get Wayne.

"I take it you had Laura picked up right when she was discharged? Is she okay to talk?"

"Guess so. I picked her up. She seemed sleepy but otherwise coherent," Wayne said.

Laura and her attorney, Paul Bennett, were in the conference room when Ben and Wayne walked in. Dory followed them and offered coffee. No one wanted any, so she left the room after starting the tape recorder.

"Good morning, Mrs. Connolly," Ben began. "We appreciate your coming down to the office. I wish to state for the record that you are represented by counsel. Thank you for coming, Mr. Bennett." The pale, gray-haired man nodded. "Laura, you're here to be questioned in connection with the death of Ruby Mead-Allison."

He paused, looking her over. Laura wore black slacks and a white sweater with a blouse underneath. He was no expert on women's fashion, but the clothes seemed baggy and ill fitting. Maybe she had lost some weight recently. There were two very bright spots of pink on her cheeks. Ben couldn't tell if they were makeup or not.

"I'd like to introduce Detective Wayne Nichols."

"Mrs. Connolly and I have already met." Wayne looked at her. "Is it all right if I call you Laura?"

"Yes." Her voice was soft, her eyes cast down.

Ben nodded at Wayne, giving him permission to proceed.

"All right, Laura, I'd like to ask you some questions about the night Ruby Mead-Allison was killed. Can you remember what you were doing on the night of March fifteenth?"

"Yes, my husband and I and our friends the Mitchells went to the symphony. We had dinner beforehand at Solo Mio and drinks afterwards."

"Good." He smiled at her encouragingly. "After you arrived home that evening, what happened?"

"I took the babysitter to her house. The Takichi girl sat for us that night. Then I returned home."

"Who stayed with the children while you did that?"

"My husband."

"What time was that?"

Laura locked eyes with her attorney at this point and he nodded. They had obviously discussed how she was going to provide this information.

"It was about midnight when I left the house with Nora, our babysitter, and about twelve-thirty when I got to her house and dropped her off."

"Then what happened?"

"I drove directly home. I got home about ..." she paused and glanced again at her attorney, "about one."

"When you and I talked earlier, you said your husband took the babysitter home."

"Did I? I don't remember."

Wayne gave her a withering look. "Okay, let's leave this for a moment. I'd like to ask you about the evening of the eighteenth, three days after you went to the symphony. You texted your sister, Robin Fanning, around midnight, correct?"

Laura gave her head a quick shake. "I don't remember that."

"You did. We know you texted her. You asked her to come over to Ruby Mead-Allison's house. Are you remembering this now?"

"No." She was almost whispering, the pink blotches fading from her cheeks.

"When your sister arrived at Ruby Mead-Allison's house, you gave her a shovel."

Laura didn't respond.

Wayne paused a moment. "Why did you give your sister a shovel at Ruby's house?"

"I didn't." Laura was on the defensive. The pink spots on her cheeks darkened again.

Wayne questioned Laura in detail. She continued to deny that she had sent her sister a text. Finally, he sat back and stared at her for a long time. He looked at Ben and tipped his head toward the door.

"Would you excuse us for a moment, Laura?" Ben asked.

He and Wayne walked out into the hall.

"Laura has me baffled, Boss. I think her disorder is throwing off my ability to tell if she's lying. She knows more than she's telling us, but I can't figure out whether she's protecting herself, Robin, or her husband."

"James said he checked the clock after Laura got home and it was one o'clock. According to James, she was in the shower by then. If that's true, she couldn't have done it. They've independently alibied each other. What do you want to do now?"

"Did we get the phone and text records?"

"No. It was after nine when we were finished with Robin last night. I tried early this morning and we were able to get the phone records, but texts are apparently another thing. Is there any way we can find out if Laura really did text her sister on the night of the eighteenth?"

"Well, there're a few ways we could do it. We obtain a subpoena and get the cell service provider to turn over the phone records, which would even include deleted text messages. I'm afraid that would take too much time, though."

"You're the boss. What do you want to do?"

"Let's go back in and get Laura's phone. Maybe we can see the text in the history."

Wayne and Ben entered the conference room, where they interrupted Laura and her attorney in what looked like a difficult interaction.

"Laura, I need to see your cellphone. Do you have it with you today?"

Laura seemed uneasy. "I got a new one. It's home charging."

"What happened to the old one?" Wayne asked.

"I took it to the company for recycling."

Had Laura decided to get a new phone because she knew perfectly well that she had texted Robin? Maybe ordering a new phone at this time was simply coincidental, but Ben tended to be wary of coincidences.

"What cellphone company do you use?"

"Freestyle Communications."

"I need your cellphone number."

Laura glanced at her attorney, but when he nodded, she quickly gave them the number.

"I need your password, too."

"It's two-one-one-two."

"When did you turn in the phone?"

"About four days ago."

"All right, we have to check out your story. I apologize, but I need you to stay here for another few hours. Dory will put you in the break room. It has a couch so you can sleep for a while, okay?"

Laura didn't answer at first. Finally, she nodded.

Ben and Wayne departed immediately for the cellphone provider's office.

"Dory, will you call us with the address of Freestyle Communications?" Ben asked on their way out.

"Yes, sir."

"I hate it when she calls me sir." Ben said as he and Wayne walked to the parking lot. "It always means she's mad at me about something."

"They were out of her special blueberry donuts this morning, weren't they?" Wayne got into the car with a grin.

"Yes. It's always my fault somehow."

BEN KNEW WHERE the general vicinity of the cellphone store was. He drove for about five minutes before breaking the silence.

"I meant to tell you, Mae's dad asked me to I.D. a photo that turned out to be a guy named Vince Harper. He has a stalking charge from five years ago. The gal who reported him dropped the charge before it came to trial. The case occurred before my time here. Do you remember him?"

"Yeah, I remember him. Big guy, used to play ball for UT. He was a nasty piece of work. The victim never pressed charges because she was terrified of him. Why is Mae's dad asking about him?"

"Harper was in some of the pictures he wants to use in his next book, but no one could identify him. He's apparently looking at Mae in most of the shots."

Wayne shook his head. "That's not good. We need to find out what ol' Vince is up to these days."

"Exactly what I was thinking. I'll tell the deputies to keep an eye out for him. Can you ask around, too? You seem to be the one with all the street informants."

Wayne cracked his knuckles. "Maybe I should pay him a visit myself. Can I try and obtain a little information in a slightly unorthodox way?"

"Please do." Ben gave a wink.

Just then, Ben's phone rang. Dory rattled off the address. Shortly afterwards, they arrived at the strip mall where the cellphone store was located.

The men walked in together and went back to the service counter. When they showed their badges to the clerk, he asked them to wait while he got his manager.

"Hello, gentlemen, what can I do for you today?" The

manager was young, with a mild case of acne. He looked like he should still be in college.

They showed their badges. "We're looking for a phone that was turned in recently. We need it for an important investigation we're conducting. We have the phone number. The customer's name is Laura Connolly. Or the account could be under the name of her husband, James Connolly."

"I need to talk to someone before I can release it. Do you have a warrant?"

"No, we don't. We can get one, but it would take a little time to get a subpoena. If we had the phone we could get the message from the history."

"Do you know when the customer turned the phone in?"

"Four days ago."

The manager excused himself and left the office. He returned almost immediately.

"I'm sorry, Sheriff and Detective Nichols, but the recycling contractor picked up our old phones at eight-thirty this morning. Unfortunately, the pickup included all phones from the last two weeks."

Frustrated, they thanked him and left the building. As they walked to the car, Ben noticed a trim woman with short brown hair reaching into the backseat of her car to release the belt on a child's car seat. She lifted a little boy out of the car and started to walk into the cellphone store. The child rested his arm on the back of her neck and gazed sleepily back toward Ben. He was a cute little boy with curly hair and bright blue eyes. His arm was in a cast.

Ben almost stopped breathing. It was Katie and her son. He ducked his head and turned away so she wouldn't see him.

"Let's go get Robin's cellphone. We might be able to retrieve the text messages from her phone's memory. Of course, we may have to get a ten-year-old to do it for us." Wayne laughed. "Or Dory."

Ben didn't answer. He couldn't believe he'd just seen Katie.

"Ben, are you with me? I said Dory could get the messages."

The sheriff tried to get control of his emotions. He cleared his throat. "I'm glad to know Dory can get data from phones. Getting information out of phones is not my forte. I can't even change my ringtone."

The sheriff's phone rang. When Ben saw the caller ID, he felt better immediately.

"Hello, gorgeous. What's up?" Looking over at Wayne, he mouthed "It's Mae."

His detective rolled his eyes. "No surprise."

Ben clipped the phone to the dashboard and hit the speaker button.

"Ben, I think I remember Vince Harper. I saw Noah talking to him in Nashville outside a club about five years ago. Noah went over to say hello, but while they were talking, Harper kept looking at me. I remember feeling uncomfortable."

"What were you wearing?" Wayne asked.

There was a brief silence. "Am I on speakerphone or something?"

"You sure are. I'm in the car with Detective Nichols. We were talking about Mr. Harper a few minutes before you called."

"Well, I don't remember what I was wearing that night. It was years ago."

"Listen to me, Mae," Wayne said. "I remember this weirdo. If you were dressed in anything revealing, or if you smiled at him, you could have triggered his interest. If you remember anything else, or see him, call one of us or nine-one-one right away."

"Um, all right. I will. Bye guys." She hung up.

They arrived at Little Chapel Road about twenty minutes later and drove to the Fannings' house. Nobody was home.

"Do you have Robin's cellphone number?"

"Yes, I'm dialing her now."

The cellphone rang but Robin didn't answer. Wayne left a

message asking her to stop by the sheriff's office immediately and to bring her cellphone. They drove back to the office in silence.

Chapter Thirty-Two

March 27
Detective Wayne Nichols

DORY WAS ON the phone when the men returned to the office. "Hi Mrs. Fanning, I'll put you through to him," she said and waved Wayne back to his office.

He picked up his desk phone. "Robin? Detective Nichols."

"Yes, Detective."

"We talked to Laura this morning and she denies sending you that text message. We need to have your cellphone in order to verify that she sent the message."

Robin hesitated. "I'm going to have to call my husband about this and maybe my lawyer, too."

"That's certainly your right. However, without proof that you ever received this text, the sheriff is thinking that you made this whole thing up. He thinks you're a lot more involved than you told us. He thinks you killed Ruby."

There was silence.

Nichols sighed. "Robin, I know how protective you are of Laura, but you can't withhold evidence from the police. The sheriff could charge you with obstruction. He wants to nail somebody for this murder and unless you give us the cellphone, you're handing yourself over on a silver platter. Did you do it, Robin?" His voice was soft and quiet. "Did you kill Ruby?"

There was another long silence; then the line went dead. Which sister had the strongest reason to kill Ruby? He had no doubt that either of them could have done it. He no longer believed in the inherent kindness and decency of women.

As Wayne began working on a report, his thoughts returned to the women in his life. He trusted none of them. Some women were what they seemed, but most were an enigma, like his battered foster mother, or Tiani—slippery as a fish rising out of the water on a summer evening.

Tiani had broken his heart, led him on. He had met her at the Tribal Council offices when he got to Traverse City after working for the Hagströms. She smiled when he came into the office. Her long, dark hair was like silk flowing across her shoulders. She was the prettiest girl he'd ever seen.

"Can I help you?" she asked.

He tore his eyes away from her low-cut shirt, recalling himself with a start.

"Um, yes. I just got here from the U.P. I think I might be Odawa—or part Odawa, anyway. I need a job."

"Do you have your tribal card?"

"No. I lost it." He couldn't remember ever having one. "How do I get a new one?"

She went through old records and tried to help him, but he had no idea who his real parents were, only a shadowy recollection of an old man by a fire. He had been in foster homes most of his life. His little brother wasn't even really related to him. Still, he had hated leaving him behind. Tiani found a room for him to rent and told him who to talk to in the personnel office at the city hospital. She said they were often looking for people to do patient transport.

He worked for a few weeks and then went back to see her. "I

want to thank you, Tiani." He felt shy. "I got paid yesterday. I'd like to take you to a movie."

She looked unsure. "I probably shouldn't. I have to work most days. I can take a walk with you tomorrow though, if you come back at the same time."

He tried to see her as often as he could. Sometimes she let him kiss her and touch her breasts in the coat closet of the old building where the council met. Sometimes she walked with him, but the northern Michigan winter was fast making their walks impossible. They talked about her family and his dreams for the future, but she wouldn't come to his room, no matter how he pleaded.

One frigid November day, he went to see her. A different girl sat behind the desk.

"Where's Tiani?" He stomped the snow from his boots.

The girl gave him a sour look. "Who wants to know?"

"I'm Wayne. Her boyfriend."

She laughed. "No you're not. She married her boyfriend yesterday. She's pregnant, going to have a baby in the spring."

His heart pounded and he turned to run, his cheeks burning. He slipped on the wet floor near the doorway and caught the doorframe. Straightening up, he left the tribal council office for the last time, the girl's mocking laughter ringing behind him.

Wayne shook his head to displace the memories, walked out of his office and down to Ben's. "Robin hung up on me. I'm going to look for her. Do you want to come?"

Ben nodded and hollered to Dory. Telling her to check on Laura, he grabbed his jacket and followed Wayne out to the car. They drove to the Fannings' and parked near the driveway. Before Wayne had time to cut the ignition, Robin's car pulled up to the driveway and came to a stop.

Wayne got out of the car and walked around to the driver's side of Robin's vehicle. Ben followed him.

Robin put her window down. "I need your cellphone, now," Wayne said.

She reached into her purse and handed him the phone.

"I need your password, too."

Robin closed her eyes and told him the password.

They got back into the car and watched as Robin turned into her driveway.

"Let's go." Wayne started the car. When they arrived back at the office, the sheriff asked Dory if she knew how to retrieve text messages on Robin's type of cellphone.

She looked at them and shook her head. "Just who do y'all think you're dealing with?"

"Dory, if you can find a text message from Laura Connolly on the eighteenth of March, at around midnight, I swear I'll get you flowers every week for the rest of the year. The password is one-four-nine-two."

She grabbed the phone. "Just leave me be."

They retreated.

Chapter Thirty-Three

—

March 27
Sheriff Ben Bradley

About ten minutes later, Dory strutted into Ben's office. She'd found it. He picked up his phone.

"That call better be to the florist."

He put the receiver back down. "Perhaps you might like to call the florist yourself and put in your weekly order?"

Dory beamed. "I'd be happy to, but I need your credit card. This isn't going on the office dime, you know."

"Of course not." He handed his card over and called down the hall to Wayne, "We got it." Dory frowned. "Let me rephrase that. Miss Dory, the Goddess of Information, the Queen of all Knowledge, has given us the smoking gun."

"You're the best." Wayne gave her shoulder a squeeze as he walked into the room.

Dory left looking pleased. "And next time, Bradley, I'm getting a personal trainer and he's going to be cute and buff."

"She'd do it, too," Ben told Wayne, who grinned. "I live in fear of that woman."

THE WIND WAS blowing hard and the small sycamore trees in front of the sheriff's office waved wildly, as if trying to escape from their cages. Ben and Wayne stood in the main lobby. They were waiting for Laura Connolly's attorney. Laura was already in the conference room.

When the four of them were seated in the conference room and the equipment was turned on, Ben began. "Laura, when we talked with you earlier, you told Detective Nichols that you didn't send your sister a text message on March eighteenth telling her to go to Ruby's. We were able to obtain the evidence today that your sister received that message shortly before midnight. The text said, 'Come to Ruby's house, now.' "

Laura's face crumpled, and her breathing became ragged and uneven. She seemed on the verge of tears or collapse.

"Why did you send Robin this text?" Wayne asked.

"I needed her help."

"With the shovel?"

Laura hung her head. Her voice was so soft they could barely hear her. "The shovel was scary."

"I'm sorry, Laura. I couldn't hear you. Did you say 'The shovel was scary'?"

"Yes." There was a long pause and then she said, softly, "It had a face." The room got intensely still. Ben held his breath.

"Whose face was it?" asked Wayne.

"It was my husband's face," Laura whispered and began to cry.

Mr. Bennett turned. "May I have a moment with my client?"

They left the room and stood in the corridor. Ben pulled the door closed behind him.

"Do you think we have grounds to arrest her?" Wayne asked.

"I think we do. We have the physical evidence of the shovel. We know that Laura called Robin and that Robin took the shovel to Mae's barn, but the timeline just doesn't work. It's possible Laura's trying to protect her husband. She may think, or know, that he killed Ruby—although the timeline doesn't work for him, either. Maybe he's lying. Perhaps that's why she saw her husband's face when she looked at the shovel."

"This case is a nightmare," Wayne said.

"I know it."

Paul Bennett stuck his head around the door. "Gentlemen, my client isn't feeling well. She needs her medications. She doesn't have them with her and they have to be taken on a very rigid time schedule."

"All right," the sheriff said. "However, I'm placing Mrs. Connolly under house arrest. She has to sign a form saying she won't leave her house for the rest of today and tomorrow. If she can't guarantee she'll stay at home, I'll arrest her and request remand."

Laura's attorney withdrew his head, clearly relieved. He closed the door.

Wayne looked at Ben for a moment in aggravated silence. "With all due respect, Sheriff, I think you're making a big mistake. We should hold her overnight at a minimum."

"I'd really like to, Wayne, but with her medical situation, that could get the case thrown out of court later. I'll have Deputy Phelps take her home and hang around there until tomorrow."

AN HOUR LATER Dory came into Ben's office with a strange look on her face.

"There's a woman here to see you. She won't say what it's about. I told her you were busy, but she insisted."

Maybe it's about the case. "Fine, Dory. Send her back. Did she give her name?"

"It's me, Ben." Katie pushed past a startled Dory. Ben stood up. She held out her hands and smiled. He heard a roaring in his ears. Dory backed quickly out of the room and shut the door.

Katie came closer and held out her arms. Ben turned aside. She brushed away the awkwardness saying, "I'm happy to see you."

Ben said nothing at all.

"I'm sure you're angry. I'm truly sorry. I regret everything I did, eloping, I mean. Greg, my ex-husband, is very charming. I fell for it. But after we got married, I saw that the love he had for his patients matched his love for every young female in the camp. When we weren't traveling together, he was always gone. Sometimes for legitimate reasons. Often not. Oh, this is coming out badly. I already regretted my hasty decision and my lack of self-control on the honeymoon. I can't tell you how much I've missed you."

"Katie, please stop. I'm not interested in hearing about your problems. I'm in the middle of a murder investigation. Just tell me why you're here."

"Ben," her voice was soft, "I've missed you, and..." She moved closer and he fought the pull of the familiar scent and her nearness.

"Damn it, Katie. What do you want?"

"I have a son. His name is Matthew and he's three and a half. He's a wonderful little boy. When he was born, right after our marriage, Greg said Matty wasn't his. Greg has two other sons with his first wife, and Matthew looks nothing like them. At first I didn't take any notice. I had a difficult pregnancy, a C-section. I lost a lot of blood. When the baby was only a few months old, and things were getting worse between us, Greg took him to the hospital for a paternity test."

Here it comes. She's going to try to get me for child support because the husband won't pay.

"Ben, Matthew is your son. The chances of his being Greg's are one in a million." The roaring in his ears grew louder.

"You can believe what you want," Ben said. "But I don't want to have anything to do with you, or him. I don't believe anything you say." He fought for control and took a deep breath. "We'll do another DNA test. If it proves he's my son..."

"Ben, please believe me. He can't be anyone's but yours. There was nobody else except you and Greg."

"Do you really think, after what you did, you can walk back into my life and we can just take up where we left off, only now with a little kid?"

"Yes." Her voice was very soft. "It's what I want. I still love you. I made a terrible mistake, but I want us to be a couple again. I want us to be a family for Matthew."

"That's not what I want." Ben closed his eyes, taking a deep breath. Mae's slender back came to mind for a minute, straight as a reed, walking up the stairs alone. Mae was the woman he wanted, not Katie.

"If a DNA test, done here, proves I'm the father, I'll assume responsibility for his child support. Let me be clear, Katie. I don't want you in my life again and I don't want a relationship with your son."

She closed her eyes and winced. "Ben, please don't close your heart to Matty. He's yours. He looks exactly like you. Your mother could tell right away when she saw him in the hospital. I saw it on her face. He's a strong, healthy little boy who deserves a family. I want him to have a father. He deserves to have a father. Please ..." her voice softened and her eyes pleaded with him.

Ben's head pounded like it might explode. In his public life, it would be impossible to shut the door completely on this boy. He'd be eviscerated in the press and risk his re-election. He shut his eyes and saw Mae's face. She will break up with me. I'll lose her over this. Before he could stop himself, he smashed his fist into the wall.

The pain was stunning. Ben shook his fist, pressed it into his other hand and glared at Katie. "I'll get the DNA test done. If the test establishes my paternity, I'll speak to the Family Court judge. I'll explain the circumstances and present my case. She'll make the decision and I'll live with it, but I will not have you in my life, not ever again."

"Ben," her voice was small and shaken. "Please remember how we were together. We could be a couple again." She reached her hands out to him.

"No, we couldn't. Not ever." Ben turned away from her. He groaned in frustration as he nearly ran out of the building, leaving Katie crying in his office. A startled Dory peeked through the window.

Ben jumped into his truck, slammed the door and roared out of the parking lot. It was only five-thirty, and he wasn't seeing Mae until seven. Without really thinking, he headed to his parents' house. When he walked into the kitchen, his mother, Joyce, took one look at him and got out her first aid kit. She was short with a sturdy build and had recently cut her curly, salt-and-pepper hair to chin length. She wore jeans with a loose green sweater and dried her hands on a dishtowel. She wordlessly gave his hand a none-too-gentle exam, bandaged him and told him that his dad was in the study.

With a quick wave, she picked up her purse and walked out to the garage. "Bye, Ben."

His tall, thin father, blue-eyed with gray hair in a buzz cut, appeared in the kitchen. "Hello, Son."

"Did Mom leave because of me?"

"No. She was going shopping with a friend. What's up?"

"I need some advice."

"Okay then. I'll get us each a beer."

He went to the fridge and handed him a cold one. Ben leaned against the counter. His damn hand was really sore.

"Here's to you solving this crime." Dad raised his bottle.

They walked into the den and sat down in the old comfortable leather chairs. Dad had installed a new television, one of the large flat screens. He flicked it off with the remote and leaned back.

"How'd you hurt your hand?"

"Katie came to the office today. I suppose Mom told you about her being back in town. She has a son. Katie says he's mine. You don't look very surprised."

"Your mom said the boy looks just like you did at that age."

"I've agreed to DNA testing. That way I'll know for sure. I got so frustrated I punched the wall in my office. It's cinderblock."

"I guess you didn't break a bone, or your mom would be dragging you to the E.R. right now." He paused for a sip of beer. "Was that what you needed my advice about?"

"No, it's not that. You know I've been working on the Ruby Mead-Allison murder. I think we're getting close to solving it. I told you last week I suspected James Connolly. He was having an affair with Ruby and they were planning to sell her property to some developer. They were both going to be well-off after the sale."

"Sounds to me like he needed her alive then."

"Well, he also had her power of attorney. He could have gotten his hands on the land if her brother gave up claim to it. If he wasn't implicated in her murder, he might have been able to get the whole Mead parcel. Ruby was pregnant with his child, so his marriage was at risk."

"Okay, I get the motive. What about method and opportunity?"

"Well, I'm a little shaky on opportunity. His wife, Laura, had method, motive, and might have had opportunity. The times don't quite work out, but she took the babysitter home at around the time Ruby was killed. Three days after the killing she texted her sister, Robin, at midnight, to come and take a shovel away from the property. That shovel turned out to be the murder weapon. Nichols says I'm missing the boat by not pursuing her over her husband."

"They both sound like scum. What's your gut tell you?"

"I still like James Connolly for it, but Laura's hard to read. She has some kind of impulse control disorder."

"It's a tough one. Since you're asking, I'd pursue the woman. Actually, I'd look very carefully at both women."

"Robin isn't the type. She's only being a protective older sister."

"Well, she might be protective in a motherly way, but you

definitely need to look into her alibi for the time of the murder. The maternal instinct tends to supersede anything else. As for Laura, can you find out whether or not she was taking her meds at the time Ruby was killed? Would her doctor tell you whether her episodes of rage are periodic?"

"It's hard to get doctors to tell us anything, but I'll try. Thanks, Dad. Very helpful. We'll definitely look into all of this. How did you get so smart, old man?"

"Probably from hanging around your mother. When are you going to the cabin again?"

"As soon as we wrap up this case, I'm outta here."

"Good. That's a healthier way to relieve stress than punching cinderblocks."

Ben finished his beer, thanked his dad and aimed his truck for home. He dreaded telling Mae about Katie and the boy, but now he had a better feel for Ruby's case.

His hand throbbed all the way home. *Better take some aspirin, moron.*

Chapter Thirty- Four

―

March 27
Mae December

M AE CALLED BEN to let him know she'd be getting ready
at Birdy's, and he asked her to meet him at his house.
She could leave her car at his house and they could ride to the
fundraiser together. He sounded a bit rushed.

"I know you're busy. I'll let you go. See you at seven," Mae
said.

"Hold on. I think I know what denim and pearls attire
means, but I wanted to double-check."

She laughed. "I think it's open to interpretation. For you,
it means nice jeans, a button-down shirt and a blazer. With
cowboy boots if you have any."

"Thanks, Mae. That's what I thought. I'll see you tonight."

Tammy had once been a makeup artist as well as a hairstylist.
She'd helped Mae get ready for countless events in her life, so
Mae knew the drill. Tammy always wanted her to shower, have
her nails done and arrive at Birdy's with wet hair and at least
two outfits. She would then style her hair, do her makeup and
tell Mae which outfit was best. Mae was always amazed at how

glamorous Tammy made her look. She thought Ben might be pleasantly surprised, having seen her mostly in sweats or jeans.

When Tammy finished working her magic, Mae left the salon, drove to Ben's house and parked on the street. Ben lived in Neely's Grove, one of the oldest sections of town. Most of the houses were shotgun style, with picket fences and front porches that sat close to the street. Ben's place was no exception. The house was charming and the exterior paint colors were striking with tobacco brown siding, barn-red trim and dark gold accents. Ben stepped out onto the porch and waved.

"Do we have time for a tour?" Mae walked up the steps.

Ben stared at her. "You look amazing."

"I have Tammy to thank." She smiled. "I can't achieve this look on my own."

Taking Mae's hand, Ben pulled her in close. "It's probably a good thing. You're distracting enough on a normal day. Tonight you look good enough to eat." He brushed his lips against the side of her neck and she shivered. He took her arm and they walked inside.

"I'd love to see your house. Would you give me that tour now?"

"Would you like a glass of wine first?"

"I would." Mae smiled and kissed him. "I like your roper boots. I'd love a glass of whatever you're having."

They walked through the front room, a living room/study combination and then into the kitchen. "Did you see my Malone painting?" He pointed to a small canvas, a wintry landscape that hung next to his pantry door.

"That's a nice one." Mae smiled.

Ben poured two glasses of Pinot noir and handed one to Mae.

"Mae, we need to talk." The whole house seemed too quiet. Something was wrong. Ben looked tired, and there was a large dressing on his right hand.

"Sure. We can talk, but show me the house first, will you?"

She was stalling. She didn't want to know what Ben wanted to talk about.

"The bedroom and bath are down the hall, and there's a sleeping porch over there." He gestured toward the back of the house. "There were two bedrooms, but I combined them. That way there was space for a bigger bathroom and a closet."

They walked through the bedroom and down the short hallway. The bath and closet were opposite each other. Beyond them was the screened-in sleeping porch with an inviting looking daybed. Ben sat down and patted the cushion beside him.

"This looks like the best place in the world to take a nap." Mae sat down next to him. "I love this porch."

"Me, too. I sleep out here every night in the spring and fall." He smiled at her, but his voice was flat, and the smile didn't reach his eyes.

She raised her glass to him. "To a man with style. This house is great." They sat together quietly for a while, sipping their wine. Finally, Mae took a deep breath. "What did you want to talk about?"

"Mae." He stopped, as if trying hard to find the words. "You know that I used to be engaged to a woman named Katie Hudson?"

"Yes. I've heard that."

"My mother called me yesterday morning to tell me she's in town. She's divorced. The marriage didn't work out. She has a son now, named Matthew."

Mae swallowed hard. "Have you seen her?"

"Yes." Her heart plummeted. "I didn't want to, Mae. She came by the office this afternoon. She wanted to tell me about her son."

"How old is he?" Mae tried hard not to cry. She knew where this was going. "Is he yours?"

"I don't know." He paused. "He might be."

"How did this happen? I thought she married a doctor."

"She did, but the baby was born about nine months later. It's possible she was already pregnant when she left on the trip to Guatemala." Ben looked at her. Mae's eyes stung.

She stood up, intending to walk out of the house, but he stopped her.

"Mae, I have no feelings left for Katie. She betrayed me. Please don't go. I've really been looking forward to this evening. Can we try to go and have a good time?"

She felt empty and lost. Ben might say he didn't have feelings for the woman, but she knew this wasn't over for him. *I'm all dressed up with no place to go.* Mae was unsteady and sat back down on the daybed.

They sipped their wine quietly for a minute. All Mae wanted to do was to go home, crawl under her quilt and cry.

"Please, Mae?" Miserable as she felt, she nodded.

Ben and Mae went inside to the kitchen and put their glasses in the sink. Ben put his arm around her waist and ushered her out the front door. He locked up and they walked out to his truck. He opened her door and she climbed in.

"Do you know where the Chapmans live?" Mae struggled to regain some vestige of her upbeat party mood.

"Yes, a burglary was called in there last year and I did the investigation. It's a really nice place."

"Jill's kids went to the school they're raising the funds for when they were younger, and she always throws a big party for the event. Her husband opens up their wonderful barn and she and her band perform after dinner."

"What's so great about the barn?"

"It's the ultimate Man Cave. Kind of like your F-150. You'll love it." The interior of his truck had been done in beautifully appointed leather.

"What, my two thousand thirteen King Ranch F-150?" He glanced at her shyly. "This old thing? I've owned it for oh, I don't know, two weeks?"

He grinned like a little boy. Mae smiled back. Ben reached across the seat with his bandaged hand and she let him hold her hand all the way to the fundraiser.

Chapter Thirty-Five

———

March 27
Tammy Rogers

AFTER MAE LEFT Birdy's Salon, Tammy cleaned up the makeup area and gathered together her brushes and Mae's clothes. Stuffing everything into a tote bag and grabbing her purse, she paused and checked herself in the mirror. She had spent the last hour beautifying her friend and now she had an important errand to run. She needed to look good, but not so incredibly fabulous that he'd wonder what she was up to. She smiled at her reflection. Tammy was a believer in rigorous maintenance. At times like this, her philosophy paid off. She'd gotten a brow wax, manicure, and pedicure last week. Yesterday, she had touched up her roots and her hair was a uniform silver blonde. Having put in a full day at Local Love, she knew her makeup was slightly smudged. Her hair was a little flat. Perfect. She was ready.

She walked outside, locking the salon door behind her. It was a beautiful spring evening. After the warm, perfumed air of the salon, the light breeze cooled her face. She took a deep appreciative sniff—honeysuckle, definitely. Better make sure he's home. She sent him a quick "Call me" text. The phone buzzed, and Patrick's picture came up on the screen.

"Hello."

"Hey there, where're you at?"

"Just leaving the salon." Tammy smiled. "What about you?"

"I'm on my way home. Do you want to get a bite to eat?"

Perfect. Tammy smiled again. "I'd love to. I'm starving. Can you meet me at C.C.'s?"

"The wine bar? Do they have any food?"

"They have lots of appetizers and small plates. Sandwiches, too."

"I'll see you there in about ten minutes."

"Good. I'll grab a table for us. Bye, Patrick."

C.C.'s was only a few blocks away from the salon so she decided to walk. The alley was dark. *I'll have to call the City Administrator's office again tomorrow and get them out here to look at the streetlight.* She hurried around the corner and down to the wine bar. Like many of the businesses in this section of Rosedale, the wine bar was in a re-purposed old house. Painted a soft plum with gray and cream accents, the Victorian building was now a gathering place for single people who'd outgrown the nightclub scene. Tammy was glad to see an empty table on the veranda. She walked up the wide front steps and through the open door.

"Hey, C.C.," she greeted the owner at the hostess stand. "Are you serving outside tonight?"

"Hi there." With sleek dark hair falling to her waist and a trendy wardrobe, the California transplant looked years younger than her actual age of fifty-three. She smiled at Tammy. "Grab any table you like. Are you flying solo tonight?"

Tammy shook her head. "I'm meeting someone."

"I'll send a server out in a few minutes then."

Settling herself at her favorite table, Tammy took a deep breath. Patrick would arrive soon. She wasn't sure how to handle this, but she needed to clear the air. She gazed at the metal tabletop, lost in thought.

"Earth to Tammy."

She looked up with a start, right into his clear blue eyes. He had managed to slide into his seat without her even noticing. "I like you, Patrick and I don't know what to do about it," she blurted out.

He frowned. "What're you talking about?"

She felt the heat in her face. "I sound like a second-grader. Maybe I should've punched your arm and run away. That'd be more mature."

He chewed his lip. *Oh God, was he trying not to laugh?*

"Do you mean you like me like me?"

"Yes, that's exactly what I mean." Tammy bit her words off. Her cheeks flamed with the humiliation.

Patrick laughed.

Tammy kicked his shin as hard as she could under the table. "It's not funny!"

He reached across the table and grabbed her hands. "Look at me, you crazy girl. It is funny. Do you want to know why?"

She looked at him without answering.

"I'll take that as a yes. I 'like' you, too, Tammy. I've wanted to ask you out for almost two years."

"Why didn't you?"

"I thought you'd say no."

Tammy looked at her hands.

Patrick squeezed them tightly.

TAMMY STOOD UP, walked around the table and sat down in his lap. "You're right," she whispered in his ear. "I would've said no then, but if you ask me tonight, I'm going to say yes." She kissed his ear. "I'm only worried about telling Mae we're …"

Patrick wrapped his arms around her. Turning his face so their lips almost touched, he looked directly into her eyes.

"Together? Are we going to be a couple? I won't just be a fling for you."

Tammy nodded. "I want us to be a couple, Patrick, but it might upset Mae. I don't want to break up the Three Musketeers."

He kissed her lightly. "Where is Mae tonight?"

Tammy laughed. "On a date with Ben. Getting on with her life."

The server set two wineglasses in front of them. "Should I bring menus?"

"Sure." Patrick's eyes never left Tammy's face. The door banged shut behind the server. Patrick kissed her again, a little more intensely.

She enthusiastically kissed him back.

He sighed deeply and pulled his lips away. "We should probably get on with our lives, too. If you don't want to tell her right away, I'm okay with that. As long as you and I know, I don't care who else does."

"That's a good idea." Tammy nodded her head in approval. "We'll have to figure out the right way to tell her. I'll know when the time is right." She stood up. "Are you still hungry?"

"Not really."

Tammy took his hands and pulled. "C'mon, let's go."

He jumped up, throwing a ten dollar bill on the table. They left the verandah, going down the side stairs, and out to Patrick's car. Tammy laughed when she heard the server say, "Where'd they go?"

"Sorry," Tammy yelled. "Something came up."

Chapter Thirty-Six

March 27
Mae December

THERE WAS A huge white tent set up behind the Chapmans' house, with round tables scattered throughout. White linen tablecloths covered the tables, each one topped off with a cowhide throw. Silver candelabra served as centerpieces. There were more tables along the far wall displaying silent auction items. An ornate, iron chandelier hung from the top of the tent and swags of white flowers draped the backs of the chairs.

Mae and Ben split up for a short while. Ben wandered through the silent auction area and Mae went to find the closest bathroom. She needed to repair her makeup and have a moment to herself. She caught up with him twenty minutes later, exploring the barn.

"C'mon," he said. "They're announcing the winner of the door prize in a minute. Did you save our ticket stub?"

They hurried to find their seats as Mae handed him the stub. Jill took the stage with her husband behind her. He held a punch bowl filled with raffle tickets. Jill reached in, pulled out the winning stub and handed the ticket to her husband, Randy.

He looked at the number, and started patting his pockets.

"Give me that. You can't read without your glasses, can you? The winner is ticket number forty-two."

Ben jumped up with the winning stub in his hand and made his way to the stage.

"Howdy, Sheriff." She grinned and quite obviously looked him over, drawing a laugh from the crowd. "I guess you and your pretty friend won the prize." She gestured at a huge brown and white cowhide hanging from the back wall of the barn. "Be sure to take it home with you."

Ben came back and sat down. "I've never won anything before. What are we going to do with this thing?"

"I'll ask July for ideas. She's a designer. I'm sure she'll think of something."

Ben gave her a quizzical look. "I've been meaning to ask you something. Your dad is a photographer, your mother a writer, and your sister a designer. How did you end up doing something so … well, practical?"

"Did you start to say non-creative?"

He laughed. "I was going to try to be a little bit more tactful, but yeah."

She took a deep breath. "This is hard for me to talk about. But since you've been honest with me about Katie, I'll tell you."

He nodded encouragingly and leaned in closer.

"After high school, I went to O'Meara College in Rosedale to study painting and art history. When I graduated, I got a job at a gallery in Nashville. That's where I met Noah. He and Patrick came in looking for a gift for their mother. He took my card and called me that night."

For a minute, Mae was lost in the memory of that time in her life.

"Anyway, I lived in a tiny little apartment. I'd go home and paint at night. I was starting to sell some paintings, and then, well …"

"Noah died." Ben's voice was quiet.

"No, that was later. I was going to say Hurricane Katrina hit. Noah and I were engaged by then and getting ready to buy the farmhouse. Noah had some musician friends in New Orleans and we went down to volunteer. We were there for quite a while and I got involved in doing pet rescue. Rescue is actually how I acquired Titan and Tallulah. We ended up bringing them back with us. Tallulah was pregnant and gave birth to a litter of puppies shortly after we moved into the house. She and Titan were a love-match." Mae smiled, remembering her first litter of puppies.

"The flooding in Rosedale must have brought back a lot of memories."

"It definitely did. I'll never forget that flood smell as long as I live. The stench was worse in New Orleans, but after the flood here, it smelled almost as bad."

"I know. At the office, we put Vick's VapoRub under our noses and wore masks but the air still reeked."

Mae nodded. "Anyway, I was planning to find homes for the puppies and to have Tallulah spayed and Titan neutered when Tammy came up with the idea to call the puppies Porgis and sell them. She convinced me there was a good market for designer mutts. I made quite a bit of money and my dog-breeding career was born. I quit my gallery job, although they agreed to continue handling my paintings. I was doing well, too, but after Noah died, I stopped painting."

Ben put his hand on Mae's arm and gave it a gentle pat.

"I converted the barn and started boarding and breeding. Noah insisted on a pre-nup when we became engaged. He said that if anything happened to him, the money would make it possible for me to keep the house. That's how I ended up in a non-creative career. I've gone on too long."

"No, you haven't. I have one more question. Why did you sign your paintings with the name Malone?"

Clearly, he was onto her little deception.

"How did you know it was mine?"

"I just guessed."

Mae cleared her throat. "You know how I feel about my name. I wanted a brush name, an artist's name, one that wouldn't change when I got married, so I used my middle name. It's from my mother's side of the family. Do you like the painting in my kitchen?"

"I don't like it …" He shook his head. "I love it. It's probably none of my business, but I think Malone needs to pick up her paintbrush again."

Mae didn't answer, and the waiters began serving food. There was an announcement made, telling everyone that the silent auction was closed. Ben had bid on one of the vacations, but someone had outbid him right before the cutoff.

After dinner, Jill and her husband announced that they had just received information about a large donation. She wanted to acknowledge the donor personally. She called Laura Connolly up to the microphone.

"What the hell is that woman doing here?" Ben muttered under his breath. He pulled out his cell and dialed. He gestured to Mae that he had to step away to make this call.

Mae had noticed Laura before the announcement. Laura's gaze locked on hers for an uncomfortably long moment.

"Everyone, I'd like to introduce Laura Connolly. Laura, please come on up. Mrs. Connolly is representing her husband's law firm. The Connolly, White, Putney and Swift firm has donated ten thousand dollars to the school. Let's hear it for the Connollys!" Jill stood by Laura and raised Laura's right arm in the air. Mae noticed that Laura's hands were clenched into tight fists. The applause was enthusiastic and prolonged.

"Laura's husband, James, was busy tonight, but she graciously offered to bring the donation to us. Thank you so much, Laura." Jill smiled as Laura exited the stage.

Jill and her band played a short set. Her voice was appealing, a combination of rough and smooth. Her band, called Tough Act to Follow, was composed of all old-school musicians;

people who sounded the best live. Ben returned to the table and touched her arm.

"Mae, we have to go right now. Laura wasn't supposed to leave her house. I hate to go during the set, but I have to find out how she managed to get out of the house. "

"We can sneak out after this song," Mae whispered. "I'm pretty tired anyway."

The song ended and they ducked out. Mae looked back at Laura Connolly. Her fixed gaze was extremely uncomfortable. Mae waved at Jill and Jill winked with a thumbs-up. Ben must have passed inspection. They said goodbye to Jill's husband and stuffed their giant door prize in the back of the truck.

Ben made several phone calls on the drive back to his house.

Mae wasn't really listening. She was still thinking about Katie Hudson, Katie's son, who also might be Ben's son and whether the woman still wanted a relationship with Ben. They sat in the truck for a minute after he parked.

Ben called the office again and left messages for Nichols, Dory, and Phelps.

Mae turned to him. "Did you see how Laura stared at me at the fundraiser? I think she knows I told you about the shovel. I have a terrible feeling that Laura had something to do with the murder. I've been feeling like this ever since I heard her ask Robin where the shovel was."

"I think she's protecting her husband. Don't worry. We're keeping an eye on both of the Connollys. Mae ..." he hesitated, "would you come in?" He leaned over to kiss her.

She turned her head away. "I don't think so. I'm sorry, but I need time to adjust to all this." He pulled back with a hurt expression. He got out of the truck and walked around the back to open her door. Mae stepped down on the running board and he took her arm to help her down.

"I'll call you soon," he said in a quiet voice. "I'm going to check on some things at the station now."

Mae let go of his arm and gently kissed him on the cheek.

He walked over to his patrol car, started it up and drove out of the neighborhood. Mae turned and walked toward her car. She wondered if he'd really call her. He might not. His ex-fiancée was back and he had probably just found out that she was the mother of his son. He'd be under immense pressure to reconcile with her.

Tears started to fill her eyes. Their relationship would be over before it really began. She'd be alone again.

As MAE UNLOCKED her car, a woman in a long trench coat walked toward the car parked in front of Mae's. The night was very dark and her face was lost in the shadow of her hood, but there was something familiar about her. Mae got into the driver's seat, turned the key in the ignition and lowered her window to let in the cool night air.

The woman in the long hooded coat was standing right beside her. "Excuse me. Can I ask you a question?"

"Sure."

The woman pulled out a gun. "Turn off the car. Get out."

Mae was frozen. Was this really happening? Mae shut the car off, opened her door and got out. The gun was pressed against her back.

"Get in my car."

"What are you doing?"

"Get into the driver's seat in that car ahead of you. The keys are in it. Don't make a sound. This gun is loaded."

Mae thought she recognized the woman's voice. Her abductor hardly looked at her; her face was still concealed by dark shadows. Mae got in and started the car. The woman walked around to get into the passenger seat, all the while keeping the gun pointed at Mae through the front windshield. When she reached the rider's side door, the window was down. She kept the gun pointed at Mae through the open window as she got in the car.

"You're going to drive us to downtown Nashville. Take the

first exit after the Science Museum."

The entire drive, Mae talked quietly. She was desperate to get through to her kidnapper. She kept her voice low.

"Where are we going? Please, put the gun down. What do you want from me? Let me help you. You must think I can do something for you. What is it?"

"This is your fault," the woman said.

"What are you talking about? What did I do?"

The woman didn't answer. Instead she said, "We're going to the apartment building at four-oh-six Robert Street. Turn left at the next light."

They pulled up in front of an apartment building and at a wave of the woman's gun, Mae drove beneath the portico and down a side driveway. They were going into underground parking. Mae started to shake.

"If you make a sound, I'll shoot you. If you didn't have such a big mouth, I wouldn't have to do this."

Mae pulled into a parking place and shut the car off. Her abductor opened the door and stepped out. Holding the gun steady, she told Mae to crawl across the seat and get out of the car on her side. She held a pair of silvery bracelets. As soon as Mae stood up, there was a click on her left wrist. She was handcuffed to her kidnapper. She struggled, but the handcuffs didn't give.

Linked together, the two women walked to the elevator. The underground parking garage was dark and deserted. There was no one to help her. They got into the elevator and rode to the sixth floor. When the elevator doors opened, the woman motioned to Mae to stay back while she peered around the corner and down the hall.

"Remember, I have a loaded gun in my pocket," she whispered. "Don't make a sound."

She opened the door to Apartment 610 with a key and pulled Mae inside with her.

"For God's sake, what are you doing? Let me go. You'll never get away with this. The sheriff will come looking for me first thing in the morning."

"Do you really think he can save you?" Her tone of voice was completely unemotional. She sounded like a machine.

When Mae finally caught a glimpse of the woman's eyes, she had the strangest feeling. Handcuffs linked them together, but her captor simply wasn't there. She was somewhere far away. Her pupils were huge and her eyes glittered blankly. Mae peered into the face of madness.

The woman walked down the hall to the bedroom; Mae stumbled along behind her. She opened the door to the bathroom and pulled Mae inside.

"Get into the bathtub." She unlocked the handcuffs from her own wrist and pulled both Mae's arms behind her back. The handcuffs snapped together.

Teetering on her heels, Mae stepped into the tub. The bottom of the tub was slippery, and she started to fall. The gun came crashing down on her. There was a flare of light and then total darkness.

Chapter Thirty-Seven

March 28
Sheriff Ben Bradley

THE PHONE RANG and Ben sat up. It was very dark. After leaving Mae by her car, he drove to the station to see if he could find Phelps or anyone who knew how Laura had gotten out of her house. The station was empty except for the night dispatcher. He finally reached George and told him that Laura had escaped. Phelps was still in his car outside the Connolly's house. He was chagrinned, admitting he'd left his post, but only for about fifteen minutes earlier in the evening.

"I had to take a leak, Boss," he said. "I was hungry. I got dinner from a drive through but came right back."

Ben was too angry to discuss it. He sent the deputy back to Mae's house to watch for her return. Ben drove to the Connollys' house, but there was no one home. He checked with the Fannings and called every number he had for the Connollys, to no avail. After trying to track down Laura and failing, he returned home and fell into bed.

The bedside clock showed two thirty a.m. Caller ID read "George Phelps."

He growled. "Phelps, this had better be good."

"Sorry sir." He sounded very upset. "Miss December never came home."

"Oh my God." His mind raced. Mae wouldn't be driving around this late at night. Where in the hell was she?

He took a deep breath. "Go down to Ruby's house right now and look around. See if anyone's there. If you don't find Mae, go to the Fannings' house and search the whole property. I don't care if you have to get everyone out of bed and standing on the lawn. Go through the house from top to bottom. Don't forget to look in that shed! Call me if you find her at either place. Call Robert and have him check the Van Attas' house, too." Not waiting for a response, Ben hit the off button, pulled on jeans and a t-shirt and ran outside, quickly checking for Mae's car. Her car was still there and her purse was on the front seat. Mae was nowhere to be seen. He'd been so tired when he drove home that he hadn't even noticed her car. Damn.

Ben called Wayne on his cell. He answered, sounding very tired. "Ben, what is it?"

"Mae's missing. She was with me until around one. Her car's still parked outside my place, her keys are in the ignition and her purse is on the seat, but she isn't in the car. Phelps is checking Ruby's house, the Fannings' house and Fuller is checking the Van Attas. This is connected to the murder. I know it! You better go check the Connollys' house."

"I'm on my way." Wayne hung up.

Where is she? Where is she? Where is she? He started his car and turned out into the empty street. Ben turned right to go to the office when something clicked. *It has to be James. He has Mae. I know he does.* He was as desperate as he'd ever been in his life.

Where would he take her? Where? Ben slammed his fist on the steering wheel. The pain in his hand flared up.

I'm a damn fool. Why the hell didn't I see her safely into her car? Where has that son of a bitch taken Mae?

Images from the case came to him in a cascade—Ruby's house, Robin's house, Mae's house and then Connollys' downtown apartment. He swung the car around, put on his siren and drove to the Nashville apartment where Connolly had his affair with Ruby. The trip normally took thirty minutes. He was there in twelve minutes flat.

Ben drove under the portico of the building, left the car running and ran into the lobby. He pounded his fist on the desk, hitting the bell repeatedly. A frightened-looking young woman came out.

He showed his badge. "What number apartment is James Connolly's?"

"Six ten."

He sprinted to the bank of elevators.

"There's been a kidnapping. Can you open the door?" Ben called back to her.

"I'm coming."

They got into the elevator. As soon as it opened onto the sixth floor, he raced down the hall. His phone rang and Ben stopped for a second. George again.

"What did you find?"

"Nothing, sir. Mae wasn't in any of those places. Nobody knows where she is."

"Damn it! Search the barn, the fields." Ben clicked the phone off. It rang again, almost immediately.

"Wayne here. I'm at the Connollys'—no sign of James. Laura's here and she's saying that the kids are at her parents' house and she doesn't know where her husband is."

"That bastard has Mae. I'm sure of it."

The key worked smoothly and they entered the apartment. The sound of running water came from the bathroom. Ben raced down the hall into the master bedroom.

Water was everywhere. Ben threw open the bathroom door. The tub was overflowing. He shoved the shower curtain aside. Mae lay in the water. Only her eyes and forehead showed above the waterline. She was so white she was almost blue.

"Mae! Mae!" He lifted her head from the cold water. Shutting off the faucet with his other hand, he opened the drain and the water level began gradually going down. The girl from the front desk stood staring at Mae, transfixed.

Gently, Ben lifted Mae's water-soaked body and carried her to the bed. She wasn't breathing. He started CPR but then raised his face from her mouth, "Call nine-one-one and get a bolt cutter," he yelled.

The receptionist reached for the intercom on her belt and called security. "Come to six ten. Bring a bolt cutter. Right away!"

Tense minutes went by as Ben breathed into Mae's mouth. He kept counting, desperately praying for her to breathe. Her lips were ice-cold.

When the security guards arrived, Ben rolled Mae onto her side so they could cut off the handcuffs. He never stopped CPR. One of the men pinched the bolt cutter on the side of the cuffs but couldn't cut through the thick, silvery plastic.

"Is she breathing?" he asked.

Ben shook his head, lowered his mouth over Mae's and blew again. The whole time he kept pushing on her chest.

The security guard continued trying to cut the handcuffs off. Finally, they snapped. Mae's wrists were raw, chafed and bleeding.

Her eyes fluttered, and she retched violently. She coughed and heaved.

Pulling her to a seated position, Ben struck her on the back several times. Her head flopped forward onto his chest. He raised her face. Her pupils were hugely dilated. Euphoria sang through his veins like hard liquor. She was alive.

"Mae, it's all right. You're going to be fine," Ben whispered. "Who did this to you?"

She picked her head up and opened her eyes briefly. Looking over his shoulder, she mumbled something he couldn't understand and flopped forward again. Ben lay her down on the bed. She was so small and pale, with her thick hair plastered down, but she was breathing. Breathing! Nothing else in the whole world mattered.

Ben turned to the desk clerk. "What's your name?"

"It's Sandy."

"Sandy, I need your help, okay?" Her eyes seemed caught on Mae's wet, barely-breathing body, but at last she nodded. "We have to get all of her wet clothes off and get her wrapped up in blankets. We've got to raise her body temperature."

Chapter Thirty-Eight

———

March 31
Mae December

Mae was in the hospital for two days. The doctors were worried about brain damage from the few minutes her breathing had stopped. Daddy said she technically died, which was hard to accept or even think about. The last thing she remembered was stepping into the bathtub.

They kept her fully sedated for three days but everything checked out fine. The December family and several others, including Ben and Patrick, all wanted to be there when she was released. Mae whispered to her mother. She wanted Tammy to take her home. She couldn't face a big crowd of people. For once, Mama didn't argue.

When Mae saw her old farmhouse, she started to tear up. Once inside, she bent down to pet Titan, Thoreau, and Tallulah, who had come out from the laundry room to greet her. She lay down on the couch and turned on the news. The reporter said James Connolly had been arraigned on charges of murder and abduction. She ached all over. Her throat was sore and her wrists and head still pounded. She was a wreck emotionally and physically, but knew she had to call Ben.

"Hi, gorgeous."

She cleared her throat with a loud rasp. "Hi Ben."

"Oh Mae, I'm happy to hear your voice. How are you? Are you feeling better? Could I come by?"

"No. Not right now. I just wanted to tell you that I don't think James had anything to do with any of it. The murder, the kidnapping, the shovels; it was all Laura. You need to arrest her. He's innocent."

"You're calling about the case?"

"Well, I saw the news. Tammy brought me home a little while ago and she's in the kitchen fixing me some dinner. I turned on the TV and saw that you arrested James."

"We have Laura here, too. Don't worry. We were operating under the assumption that they were in on it together. I'll send someone to get your statement tomorrow, unless you want me to come?"

She thought for a minute. "I'm not physically or emotionally ready to see anybody right now. I gave a statement to a Nashville police officer when I woke up in the hospital, so they should have it."

He gave a deep sigh. "I'll contact them and read it. I'd like to see you, though. When you're ready, I mean."

"I know you came to the hospital—Mama told me you were there—but I don't remember. You saved my life. I can never thank you enough."

"You don't have to thank me. If I had walked you to your car, she wouldn't have gotten you in the first place. I was really angry about Laura showing up at the fundraiser and the complications with Katie and her son."

Complications? 'Her' son?

"Laura would have followed me and gotten me some other way. I know this whole thing has been really hard on you, Ben, and I'm sorry you're going through this, but I don't think a little boy deserves to be referred to as a complication, whoever his father is."

"You're probably right about that." He sighed again. "I'm just so sorry about everything Mae. You sound like you're recovering, though, and that's the main thing."

"I am. Why don't you call me when you get some things figured out?"

"I will. Feel better."

When Tammy came into the room with an omelet on a tray, she glanced at Mae with a little frown. Mae shook her head. She didn't want to talk about it. Tammy sighed, but asked no questions.

The omelet was delicious, and soft enough that it wasn't excruciating to swallow. After dinner, Mae wandered through the house and out to the barn. All her boarding dogs were gone, picked up by their owners. The kennel was silent. Patrick had taken care of Tallulah, Titan, and Thoreau while she was in the hospital. Everything was clean and quiet. Mae walked back into the kitchen. The puppies weren't even making any noise, snuggled up with their mother in the laundry room.

"Do you know where my bread starter is?" Mae gazed around.

"July has it. She told me she's looked after it before. She knows what to do."

"Good. I'm glad. I guess you and Patrick took care of everything." Mae started to choke up again. "I need to ask you for one more favor. Will you stay here tonight, Tammy? I don't think I can stay alone yet. If you can't stay, you know Mama will be here in a heartbeat, but I just can't take the drama tonight."

"Of course I'll stay." Tammy hugged her tightly.

Chapter Thirty-Nine

—

April 10
Mae December

IT WAS AFTER nine in the evening when the phone rang at Mae's house ten days after her release from the hospital. Silas Mead was on the line. He said he wanted to talk to Mae because spring clean-up day was tomorrow. Silas reminded her that since he and Terry had moved into Ruby's house, they'd be joining the work party.

Mae was quiet for a minute when Silas asked if they could stop by her house around seven thirty in the morning. He said he thought they should talk.

She took a deep breath. "I'll have the coffee ready."

"Thank you, Mae. Terry is hoping you've forgiven him. I hope so, too. He's normally a good person. The situation had us all doing things we'd never do in ordinary times."

They said goodbye and Mae walked up the stairs to bed, wondering whether she was going to be able to be as gracious in the morning as her mother had raised her to be. *I probably should forgive Terry and move on. We're neighbors now.*

SILAS AND TERRY drove up the driveway at seven thirty on the dot the next morning. The sun was out and the last wispy clouds were dissipating. The prediction was for a high of eighty. The walnut trees on either side of the driveway showed their sage-green leaves, fuzzy and small as the ears of a mouse. The entire world seemed to be welcoming spring. *I should try to be as welcoming.*

The doorbell rang. When she opened the door, she saw Silas and Terry standing on the stoop. Mae had never met Terry. He was younger than Silas and wore his straight dark hair short. His brown eyes were wary.

"Please come in." Mae opened the door all the way.

Silas came in and formally introduced Terry. Terry put his hand out to shake. After a little hesitation, Mae took it.

"Thank you for seeing us," Silas said.

"Would you like coffee?"

The next few minutes were taken up with Mae pouring coffee and offering cream and sugar. Mae invited the men to sit at the kitchen table, and they were all quiet for a few minutes. Mae waited, debating what to say next.

"Mae," Terry began, "I hope we're going to be the kind of neighbors y'all are famous for on this road."

People who weren't native Southerners could rarely get away with saying "y'all." Terry was no exception.

"I hope so, too, Terry."

"I appreciate you deciding not to press charges."

She shrugged, ruefully. "I actually forgot all about it with everything else going on. But I know we're going to be neighbors, and life is short." She looked at Silas. "Do you remember that Todd Snider song Ruby used to love?"

He shook his head.

"Something about life being short," she said.

"Oh yeah," Silas broke in, humming a few bars. "Can't remember the exact words, but they were all about loving and not wasting your time on hate."

Terry was looking at both of them with the beginning of a smile. "I've never heard that song before, but those sound like good words to live by, and I really appreciate your attitude. Silas and I have moved into Ruby's place. We're excited to be a part of the neighborhood. He's happy to be back in his childhood home and close to his grandmother. We wanted you to know we're hoping to be dog owners, too, sometime in the future."

Mae was quiet, remembering the red ribbons and vicious little drawing, wondering what kind of dog owners they would make.

"I don't know what to say," Mae finally said to Silas. "Do you think you'd be able to be good dog parents? It's a big responsibility."

"The Meads have always had dogs, mostly pointers and hounds. Since Terry and I are going to have enough space, we've been talking about getting one. I've missed having a dog."

"What kinds of dogs are you considering?"

"I've always wanted a Borzoi." Terry looked at her. "You seem surprised."

"A Russian Wolfhound? I don't know. Borzois are quite difficult to train and they need lots of exercise. They're not good with children, either. Why do you want a Borzoi?"

"I'm of Russian descent and I learned about them from my grandmother. Apparently, up until the Russian revolution in nineteen seventeen, they were the exclusive property of the Tsar. The dogs couldn't legally be bought or sold; only received as gifts from the monarchy. After the revolution, the peasants slaughtered all of the dogs. They thought of them as symbols of the decadence and ruthlessness of the Tsars. The breed survived only because a handful were exported to this country."

"Interesting. I wasn't aware of their history. I only know about them as pets. Did you know Borzois rarely bark? That can be a wonderful attribute in a dog. They're respectful of humans and have good manners, if trained properly. However, since they were used to hunt wolves originally, their natural tendencies need to be curbed."

Mae had always found Borzois spooky. They could sneak up on you so silently, you wouldn't even know they were there.

"What do you mean 'natural tendencies'?" Silas asked.

"If another animal, or even a child, runs by, the Borzoi is hardwired to attack and bring down their prey."

"Well, maybe I can get back into hunting."

"Silas, this is no pointer who will work the fields for you. Borzois can kill. It's a big decision."

"It's obvious we'll be needing Mae's expertise. We probably should get down to Beth's house. We don't want to be late."

The three of them walked out to the driveway and drove separately over to the Jensens' house. Everyone was arriving and saying hello. Coffee and pastries were ready. The Ryans brought fruit. People trooped in, windblown and cheerful.

When Beth asked everyone to divide into teams of two or three people, Mae looked directly at the man who had threatened her dogs and took a deep breath.

"I'll work with Terry," she said. She'd forgiven him, but she'd never forget the horror that swept over her when she realized her dogs were in danger. She wasn't ready to trust him completely yet.

As everyone walked out of the house to get wheelbarrows, rakes, and shovels, Terry turned around. "Mae, will you help us pick out a puppy?"

"It would be my pleasure," she said and meant it.

SEVERAL DAYS LATER, Mae got her coffee and shooed Thoreau, Titan and Tallulah out the door. She set her mug on the step and went back in to carry the last two puppies outside. They were nice and fat, and of all the puppies, they were the liveliest. She put them down on the grass next to their mother, who gave her an irritated look. It was a beautiful morning and Mae realized once again how good it felt to have things back to normal on Little Chapel Road.

The irises were in bloom in the flowerbed in front of her house and their distinctive scent filled the air. The blossoms on the magnolia tree were huge goblets of waxy white. In the far distance, near the base of the hills, three deer picked their way across the field. Something startled them and they raised their white flag tails and vanished. Thoreau dozed in the grass. Titan stalked a squirrel and Tallulah evaded her puppies.

Silas and Terry's large fenced-in enclosure down the road was nearly an acre in size. The fence was for the puppy that would arrive soon. It made a perfect square in their yard and already Terry was building flowerbeds nearby. They were also planting trees for shade. She waved at Eveline Ryan, who was practicing a "long down" with Toast in her front yard. Robin Fanning was out for a run. The puppies were play fighting with each other in the grass. The last two, who would be going to her sister's sons, were wrestling together, growling fiercely.

Mama had asked Mae many times if she didn't find it hard to keep a neat house with all the dogs, but she knew she'd rather have doggie nose prints on the French doors and chew marks on the rugs than perfectly clean windows and flawless floor coverings. The devotion in their eyes when they looked at her made the extra work worthwhile, although admittedly she got tired of the constant vacuuming. Mae got a kick out of her mother telling her to put all the dogs in the kennels when her own were always in the house.

There was only one thing she still needed to do. She needed to talk with Robin Fanning and there was no time like the present. From her front porch she could see Robin coming out her front door to start running. She picked up the puppies and walked down the driveway.

"Robin."

Robin's expression was wary, until she saw the puppies.

"I thought you might like to see my last two." Mae knew that puppies brought a smile to almost everyone's faces.

"They're really cute." Robin wasn't meeting her eyes.

"Would you like to come up? I have the coffee on."

"Thank you."

The two women walked up the driveway together. Mae handed the puppy she called Eric the Red to Robin. She carried Soot.

They went into the house and Robin commented on how much the kitchen, dining room, and living room had changed.

"I took out all of the non-supporting walls. It opens up the space quite a bit."

"It's really beautiful." Her voice shook.

"I'm glad you like it."

"Mae, I need to say something. I want you to know, the night I went to Ruby's house and took that shovel, I didn't have the slightest suspicion that Laura had killed Ruby. I thought Ruby was sound asleep in her bed. When I got my sister's text, I didn't want to wake Steven by putting on clothes. I put my jacket and boots on over my PJs. I assumed Laura was having another one of her episodes and took the shovel away to calm her down. Then I walked down Little Chapel Road to my house. When Lucy Ingram's car came down the road, I didn't want her seeing me in the middle of the night dressed in pajamas and carrying a shovel. It would have been too hard to explain. I darted up your driveway and put the shovel in your barn. Then I saw your shovel hanging there. I took it and walked home the back way, through the woods.

"Looking back now, I realize I must have subconsciously suspected that Laura had done something awful. I've been in denial about her condition for years. We both wronged you. I can't forgive myself for what Laura tried to …" her voice broke as she looked down at her feet.

"Robin, it's okay. You need to let this go. What Laura did isn't your fault. I know your family has a long road ahead and that you may face a jail sentence for withholding evidence. I don't want to make things any worse for you than they already are. What's going to happen to Laura now?"

"You probably know she confessed to killing Ruby. She's in a mental hospital. I still wonder if the whole thing would even have happened if I hadn't told her that Ruby was pregnant and that David wasn't the father. She confronted James and he admitted to the affair. I have a lot of days when I feel Ruby's death and your kidnapping were both my fault." She seemed to be pleading for Mae's understanding. Robin's shoulders were slumped and she started to weep.

"Robin, it never occurred to me that you'd feel the murder and kidnapping were your fault. Ruby was pregnant. In itself, that might have motivated James or Laura to try to get rid of her. Laura's mental health issues started a long time ago. You practically gave up your life to help her get better, but you couldn't save her, not all by yourself. She needed far more than a big sister, even a wonderful big sister, could have done. I think it's good she's getting treatment."

Robin nodded. "Laura's in a good facility and maybe they can help her. I tried and tried, but I couldn't ever fix her. Mom's staying with James to take care of the kids, which is hard on her because she's so angry with James about the affair. Everyone in the family is still in shock."

"Will you have to pay a fine or do community service?"

Robin sniffled. "Nothing's settled yet, but I hope community service. I used to work with the Seeing-Eye dog program. I'd like to work with them again." Neither of them spoke for a bit and Robin took a deep breath. "Thank you for being so understanding. Your kindness means a lot to me, especially after what you've been through."

"After losing Noah, and then going through this ordeal, the last thing I would ever do is hold a grudge. Life is hard enough without us being unkind to each other."

They walked back out to the front porch and watched the sunlight spill over the hills and across the valley floor. The perfect morning was marred only by the sound of bulldozers tearing up the road. The construction crew had started widening the road down by the river. Mae looked at Robin after a particularly loud scraping noise. She shook her head with a half-smile.

"We wanted this, right?

Robin gave a tentative smile in return. "I guess change is always rough."

Chapter Forty

—

May 1
Mae December

Mae's first year of hosting Spring Fling was going well. The weather was perfect and everyone seemed to be having a great time. The Fannings hadn't come, but Robin told her they were staying away this year. She understood. Silas and Terry were there and they brought David Allison with them. After Laura's arrest, David had found a loft apartment in Nashville.

"Hi David." Mae smiled. "It's good to see you. How's Elvis adapting to city life?"

"Very well." He gave a half-smile. "You're looking good."

"Thank you. So are you." She meant it. He looked like a different person than he had six weeks ago.

"Having closure on the investigation helps. I'll always miss Ruby, but Silas and Terry treat me like family. We get together often and I love living in Nashville. I'm close to my office and the downtown area is a good place for a single man and his dog."

"So you don't miss us out here then?"

"This was always Ruby's home. I never felt like I belonged here, at least not the way she did."

Mae looked over at Joe, who was standing with Neesy. She held their baby and the other three were running around with the Jensen kids.

"I'm glad Joe wasn't involved in Ruby's death," David said.

"I am too, but then again, I never really thought he was."

"I don't see Connolly's aunt and uncle."

"No, they put their house on the market and moved to their beach house. It's on Sanibel Island. I'm hoping my uncle Phil and aunt Jean will buy their house here."

"I'm going to mingle a little." David gave her a hug. "Thank you for everything you did to help the investigation. I'm sorry you had such a rough time."

"You're welcome. If you ever need help with Elvis, please call me." She felt incredulous that those words actually came out of her mouth. *Mae December, have you lost your mind?* Elvis needed to come back to Mae's Place about as much as Mae needed another murder on Little Chapel Road. He was just one dog too many.

David squeezed her arm, nodded, and walked away. Mae stood alone for a minute, watching her friends and neighbors enjoying themselves. Titan and Tallulah tried vainly to avoid the attentions of some of the younger guests.

The party was almost at an end when Ben came across the grass toward her. A little boy walked beside him, holding his hand. She and Ben hadn't seen each other since her discharge from the hospital.

Mae took a deep breath, walked toward them and crouched down beside the child. "You must be Matthew."

He nodded. He was a solemn-looking little boy with brown curls, round cheeks, and bright blue eyes. His left wrist had a cast on it.

"Could I offer him a cupcake?" She looked at Ben.

"Yes." Ben's face broke into a smile. When she looked back at Matthew, he smiled too.

Ben held his other hand out to Mae. She took it and stood up.

"Do you have chocolate?" Matthew's little voice was husky and deep for such a young boy.

"Yes. We have chocolate and red velvet cupcakes."

His eyebrows went up. "Could I have both?"

"It's up to your…" she looked questioningly at Ben.

"Daddy. I'm his father." Ben let go of his son's hand and tousled Matthew's curly hair. "He ate his dinner, so he can have two cupcakes."

Thoreau ambled over and nosed at Ben's leg. Matthew and the big dog were at eye-level. Mae watched them with interest. She knew Thoreau was completely trustworthy with children, but he looked a little fierce. Thoreau licked the boy's chin and Matthew giggled.

"The cupcakes are on the table over there." Mae pointed out the desserts. "Miss Annie will help you." Annie gave Ben and Matthew a big smile and beckoned to the little boy.

He ran off with Thoreau right behind him. There was an awkward silence and then they both started to talk at the same time.

"You first." Ben laughed.

"I'm glad you didn't need to investigate the Van Attas," she said, watching Annie put two cupcakes on a plate for Matthew.

"I talked to them again recently. I'm going to see if David Allison and Silas Mead will compensate Jason for the song Ruby stole. I've been thinking a lot about this case since we wrapped it up. We know Laura isn't legally sane, but she fooled her husband, Detective Nichols, and me.

"The night Ruby died she drove the babysitter home in James' truck, killed Ruby and dragged her body into the grove. Then she went home, changed the time on the clock to show an hour earlier and got into the shower, knowing James would wake up from the sound. He went down to the kitchen and saw the time, which gave her an alibi. If I'd dug a little deeper, she might never have had a chance to kidnap you.'

"Just because she's crazy doesn't mean she isn't smart." Mae looked at Ben. "She really was fanatical when she took me, though. I'll never forget her eyes." Mae's lips trembled and she wet them with her tongue. She folded her arms over her body.

"Deputy Phelps was watching the Connollys' house. When he left to get some dinner, Laura drove out and closed her garage door. When he came back, he didn't realize that she was gone. Later on, when we were looking for you, Detective Nichols went to the Connollys'. Laura answered the door and said James was gone, but really she'd drugged him and he was asleep upstairs. So I assumed James took you. Anyway, it's sad to say this, but with all the shady things Ruby was up to, if Laura hadn't killed her, someone else would have. I'm just so sorry you got hurt by this too."

Mae sighed. "I'm glad it's over. I don't like feeling like the world is out of control."

"Well, there're all kinds of crazies in the world. Speaking of which, Wayne has been following up on Vince Harper. He didn't stay in Rosedale after the stalking charges were dropped. He went back to Alabama."

Mae smiled. She didn't know what to do with her hands and just let them drop at her sides. "That's a relief."

"After the last time we talked, I was pretty upset. I didn't know what to do about Matthew, or our relationship. After we wrapped up the case, I invited Wayne and my dad to go out to the cabin with me. Have I ever told you about that place?"

"No, where is it?"

"It's south of Rose County, in the middle of nowhere. I think you'd love the old place." He smiled briefly. "I took Katie there once and the visit was a complete disaster. She kept complaining about the bugs, the wind, and the minimal bathroom facilities.

Even the darkness scared her. I guess I should have known she wasn't right for me then.

"Anyway, Dad and Wayne worked me over pretty good. Wayne told me what it was like to grow up without a dad, or any parents really. My dad talked about how becoming a father, raising my brother and me, made him grow up. We stayed for a few days and when we got back, I forced myself to call Katie." He grimaced and Mae saw the toll all this had taken on him.

"After I talked to her, she still wanted to get back together with me. I told her I could never be in a relationship with someone I couldn't trust. We did the DNA test. I guess it's obvious when you see us together, but I wanted to be certain. I'm his father. We're still working out the arrangements for custody and child support and I'm getting to know him."

"He seems like a sweet little boy." Mae paused. She put her hand on Ben's arm and looked up at him. "So, why are you here?"

"I think you know why." He took a deep breath. "I'm here because I can't stop thinking about you, Mae. I feel terrible about what you went through. I don't feel like I deserve another chance, but I hope you'll give me one. Can we start over, please? " He took her other hand in his. "I'm crazy about you."

Mae nodded wordlessly.

"I saw Tammy earlier this week and she told me you were throwing this party. I wanted you to meet Matthew and I have something to say to your guests, if that's all right."

Her chest was tight. She nodded.

Ben climbed up on a picnic table, put two fingers in his mouth and gave a sharp whistle. Everyone looked at him. "Could I have your attention please?"

There were cries of "Speech! Speech!" He shook his head. "I'll keep it short. I just wanted to thank our hostess. I met Mae because of this case, and although I thought she was pretty cute, I found her to be a little annoying." There was general laughter. "She wouldn't stay away from the investigation, but as it turns out, we could never have solved the case without her. My only regret is what Mae went through."

Joe walked over and handed Ben a beer from the cooler.

"To Mae!" He took a swig of beer.

"To Mae," everyone chorused.

Ben reached his hand down. When Mae took it, he pulled her up onto the picnic table beside him. He was flushed and grinning. She looked at her neighbors, and at Matthew. His face was covered in frosting. So was the cast on his wrist. Ben put his arm around her waist and kissed her.

"I'm speechless," Mae said, after their lips parted.

"I don't believe it," Joe yelled. "You're never speechless." Neesy gave a quick stomp to his foot.

"Thanks for coming, everybody. All I can say is, I know I'm right where I'm supposed to be tonight, and so are all of you."

Lyn Farquhar

Lisa Fitzsimmons

Lia Farrell is actually two people: the mother and daughter writing team of Lyn Farquhar and Lisa Fitzsimmons.

Lyn Farquhar taught herself to read when she was four years old and honed her storytelling abilities by reading to her little sister, Susan. Ultimately, her mother ended the reading sessions because Susan decided she preferred being read to rather than learning to read herself.

Lyn fell in love with library books when a Bookmobile came to her one-room rural school. The day the Bookmobile came, Lyn decided she would rather live in the bookmobile than at home and was only ousted following sustained efforts by her teacher and the bookmobile driver.

She graduated from Okemos High school and earned her undergraduate and graduate degrees from Michigan State University. She has a master's degree in English literature and a PhD in Education, but has always maintained that she remained a student for such a long time only because it gave her an excuse to read.

Lyn is Professor of Medical Education at Michigan State University and has authored many journal articles, abstracts and research grants. Since her retirement from MSU to become a full-time writer, she has completed a young-adult fantasy trilogy called *Tales of the Skygrass Kingdom. Volumes I and II (Journey to Maidenstone and Songs of Skygrass)*, available on amazon.com. Lyn has two daughters and six step children, nine granddaughters and three grandsons. She also has two extremely spoiled Welsh corgis. Her hobby is interior design and she claims she has the equivalent of a master's degree in Interior Design from watching way too many decorating shows.

Lisa Fitzsimmons grew up in Michigan and was always encouraged to read, write, and express herself artistically. She was read to frequently. Throughout her childhood and teenage years, she was seldom seen without a book in hand. After becoming a mom at a young age, she attended Michigan State

University in a tri-emphasis program with concentrations in Fine Art, Art History and Interior Design.

Lisa, with her husband and their two children, moved to North Carolina for three exciting years and then on to Tennessee, which she now calls home. She has enjoyed an eighteen-year career as a Muralist and Interior Designer in middle Tennessee, but has always been interested in writing. Almost five years ago, Lisa and her mom, Lyn, began working on a writing project inspired by local events. The Mae December Mystery series was born.

Lisa, her husband and their three dogs currently divide their time between beautiful Northern Michigan in the summertime and middle Tennessee the rest of the year. She and her husband feel blessed that their "empty nest" in Tennessee is just a short distance from their oldest, who has a beautiful family of her own. Their youngest child has settled in Northern Michigan, close to their cabin there. Life is good.

You can find Lyn and Lisa online at www.liafarrell.net.

6984904R00171

Made in the USA
San Bernardino, CA
19 December 2013